Scone Island

Books by Frederick Ramsay

The Ike Schwartz Mysteries
Artscape
Secrets
Buffalo Mountain
Stranger Room
Choker
The Eye of the Virgin
Rogue
Scone Island

The Botswana Mysteries
Predators
Reapers

Other Novels
Impulse
Judas
The Eighth Veil

Scone Island

An Ike Schwartz Mystery

Frederick Ramsay

Poisoned Pen Press

First Edition 2012

10 9 8 7 6 5 4 3 2 1

Library of Congress Catalog Card Number: 2012936469

ISBN: 9781464200533 Hardcover
9781464200557 Trade Paperback

Poisoned Pen Press
6962 E. First Ave., Ste. 103
Scottsdale, AZ 85251
www.poisonedpenpress.com
info@poisonedpenpress.com

Printed in the United States of America

The original Neil Bernstein
Had we not shared office space for a few years,
there would have been a sheriff, but probably not Ike.
Thank you

Acknowledgments

It is usual to thank the people who helped in the writing of a book for all their efforts. In the past I have done so always fearful I'd left someone off the list. With that in mind I want to thank again all the staff at the Poisoned Pen Press (you know who you are) for their encouragement and help. It is not easy, I think, to deal with the sort of stuff authors shove at them and turn it into a marketable, much less a readable book. Luckily, it is a small press and, unlike its grander competitors with large and mercurial staffs, it is possible to know and thank them all.

Also, many thanks to my publisher, Robert Rosenwald and my editor, Barbara Peters, both for their patience in the process and their continued willingness to provide a home for Ike and his friends.

Finally, to my wife who thinks I am doing something worthwhile in my office instead of merely scribbling, a special thank you for pretending it is so.

Frederick Ramsay, 2012

Archer had tried to persuade May to spend the summer on a remote island off the coast of Maine (called appropriately enough Mount Desert) where a few hardy Bostonians and Philadelphians were camping in "native" cottages, and whence came reports of enchanting scenery and a wild, almost trapper-like existence amid woods and water.

Edith Wharton
The Age of Innocence

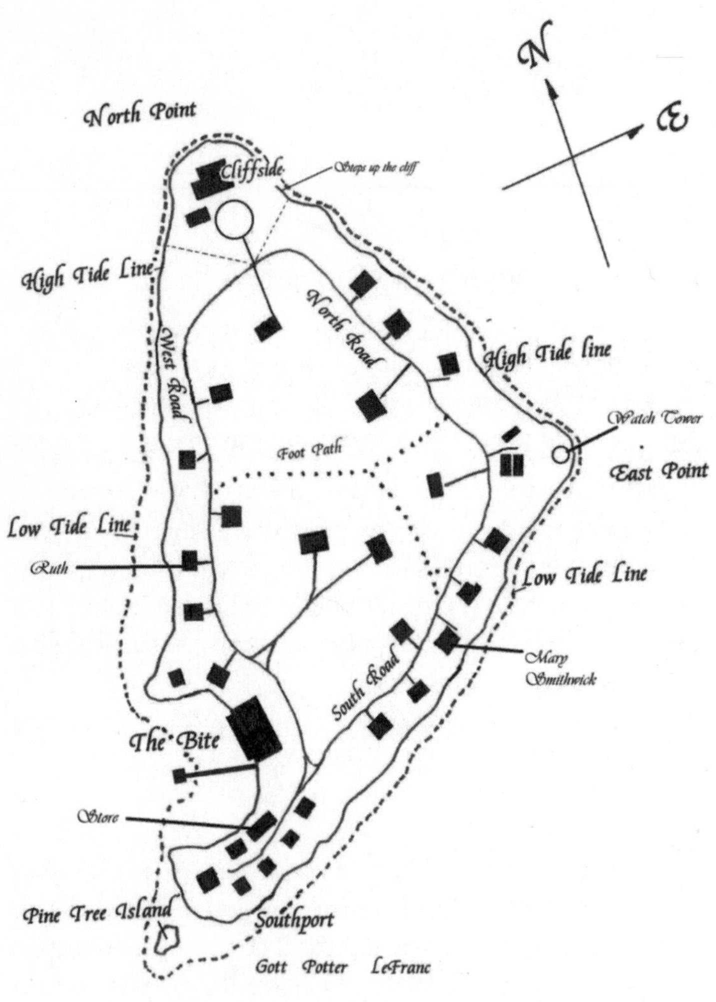

Scone Island, Maine

Chapter One

Harmon Staley would never be thought of as a patient man. Those who knew him well kept their distance unless business or necessity required them to do otherwise. Yet he'd listened to Barstow's offer several times. His response never changed. Would he sell Cliffside? No, he would not. Neither would he approach the Scone Island Owners Association about the project. Yes, he would support any plan within reason to develop the island into an upscale resort. He would not do so, however, if it meant investing in Barstow's company or a substantial dollar assessment on the other owners.

"Barstow, you do not strike me as Colin Tennant, and Scone Island is certainly no Mustique," he'd said at the time.

Barstow had replied, "Pardon?"

"Not important—some Scottish Lord who bought an island like you're trying to do, and after he had his fun with celebrities and their entourages, he lost his shirt. Are you prepared to lose your shirt, Barstow? There is no electrical power here, no certain supply of water, and no phone service. How do you plan to turn this rock in the middle of nowhere into a resort?"

But the man only smiled. "I suppose the same way you intend to turn that tumbledown monstrosity of yours into a bed-and-breakfast." And then he shrugged as if the two of them shared a secret, as if they alone knew what others did not, as if they coconspired in a complex scheme, an adventure. Harmon guessed that Barstow had no clue as to what either of them might or might not know, and the smug "I know something you don't know" expression infuriated him almost as much as the constant pestering. Only reluctantly had he agreed to meet Barstow for what he hoped would be a final and successful attempt to get rid of the developer. He couldn't possibly know the secret.

"A compromise," Barstow had said. "A sweetener."

In the days Harmon would refer to as his "previous life," he might have wondered at Barstow, would have had his antennae up, so to speak. Certainly he would have been more cautious. After all, he had not lived this long by being careless. But since he'd reinvented himself for this new stage in his life and since this was a piece of the Maine coast at the end of never, what were the chances something could go wrong?

Against his better judgment, he'd agreed to meet the man one last time. He paced the length of the big house's porch, oblivious to the structure's peeling paint and badly weathered and missing shakes, nothing that a small infusion of money could not fix. Where this money might come from remained a mystery to those who saw this latest member of the island's population as a somewhat seedy and down-at-the-heels opportunist. They could not have guessed that Harmon had assets. That he only had to sit tight for a few more months until no one would notice, or care, or dare object to the slow hemorrhage of funds from one or more of those ubiquitous off-budget, off-shore accounts into his personal account.

No need to stir up the suits in accounting or the IRS, not yet. Especially the IRS. Slow and steady would do the job. Hell, as far as Harmon was concerned, they owed him for all he'd done for them over the years, ungrateful bastards! They owed him big time. Instead, they'd chosen to dump him. Well then, they'd pay for that, simple. No way would he'd give it back either. To hell with the big shots and all the pussies who worked down there. He'd paid his life insurance premiums, and as far as they were concerned he was officially dead. So, okay fine, now he'd be his own beneficiary. He looked at his watch. What had happened to Barstow anyway?

Night rolled in from the west like the twelve foot tides that characterized this part of the Maine coast, accompanied by a salty mist that hung in the air and made Harmon uneasy. He couldn't say why. He walked to the center of the porch ignoring the squeak of loose boards, pivoted on his heel and started back the way he'd come. Soon he'd need to light a lamp. He stretched and searched his pockets for a match. What was keeping that smarmy wheeler-dealer anyway? He heard a scraping sound behind him. How had Barstow arrived at Cliffside without walking up the path? Harmon turned and squinted into the darkness.

"So, it's you," he said. And after a pause, "How'd you find me?"

"It was only a matter of time. I have friends in high places."

"How high would that be? Never mind. So, what happens now?"

"We walk. We talk."

Mary Smithwick had celebrated her seventy-fifth birthday the previous month, shortly before she left Chevy Chase to take up her annual summer residence on Scone Island. Her early arrival in late May meant it was her year to open her house before the rest of the family, if any, arrived in the third week of June.

She and her family, when she still had one, had spent the three summer months, June, July, and August, on the island every year as far back as she could remember. No, that wasn't correct. There were those years in the mid-forties during the war when it was not possible to travel from Utica, where she'd grown up, to the island. Her memories were sketchy as she'd been very young at the time. The government restricted travel back then and the Coast Guard had taken up a position on the island. They'd replaced the old light house on the eastern point of the island with a watch tower to surveil for German U-boats and to track convoys heading across the Atlantic to England or Murmansk. Also, they had established a Coast Guard Station in Southport in the Bite ostensibly to serve as a rescue point should one of the ships, Liberty Ships they were called, be torpedoed and sink.

The coast artillery arrived shortly afterwards and built gun emplacements on the point next to the tower as well. She couldn't remember if they'd ever fired at a German submarine—or was it aircraft? She never found out which, but in any case, she liked to think they had. During the war years, most of the cottages had been commandeered by the government to house their personnel. The few families who'd managed to get to the island then had stories to tell. Oh, my, yes. Well, that was a long time ago and the world had changed so much. Now she enjoyed her retirement after thirty years of government service, alternately living out the winter months in the snug condominium she owned in Maryland and summering on the island. Old friends from the past made sure there was always something for her to do so her mind stayed active and excited even if her body had lost some of its spring.

She walked steadily along the gravel path the residents insisted on calling West Road, to Cliffside, the largest house on the island. Harmon Staley, who'd bought Cliffside from the Willards back in the fall had said, "Yes, indeed, you're more than welcome to pick wild strawberries over on the fence line." Cliffside, for as long as she could remember, had had tiny wild berries ripening under the leaves that collected at the fence every spring—weeks before the cultivated ones were ready elsewhere. It had become a Scone Island tradition—or once was. Not many of the new owners or the descendents of the old ones cared for that sort of thing. Nobody picked wild berries anymore, much less put them up. If she gathered enough, she wanted to put up one jar of jam for Mr. Staley, poor thing.

Mary had a generous spirit and excused Harmon Staley's misanthropy where others might not. It must be, she thought, the result of burdens acquired in a previous, and by some accounts, very troubled life. She could only guess at what those troubles might have been. The sketchiest details surfaced when he arrived. Most folks on the island maintained it was none of their business what other folks did, and so made allowances for Harmon. Nevertheless, some of the newer families thought he was plain rude and said so. On the other hand Mary might admit, if pressed, that she found him rather dashing, in a superannuated Errol Flynn sort of way. The late actor had been a school-girl crush of hers, one she shared with her sister and at least half her high school class—Errol Flynn and also Billy Prescott, the captain of the football team and very dishy himself, but that was a long time ago and besides, no one called people dishy anymore.

As a courtesy, she knocked on the door of the guest house. Harmon Staley had been required to move from the big house to this smaller version when the former's leaky roof finally overwhelmed any of the local tradesmen's ability to repair it. The building was falling into disrepair, and Mary did not see any hope for its revival in spite of Harmon's insistence that he would get it into shape and open it as a Bed and Breakfast by next summer. The notion seemed unrealistic to her, there being neither electricity nor water available, not to mention the lack of telephone service. But who knew? Perhaps he was right. Very ambitious, this Mr. Staley.

No answer at the guest house. He must be out and about the place. No problem, she'd catch up with him eventually. She made her way to the fence and began picking, carefully raking the leaves aside with a gloved hand and plucking the dime-sized berries from their racines. The weather had been unseasonably mild, so berries were plentiful. In an hour, her peck basket nearly full, she reached the end of the east portion of the fence. She would, she hoped, fill a second or third on the longer section to the west. The fence came to an end at the point where it intersected the cliff face. Cliffside took its name because it had been built atop the sixty-foot granite cliffs that dropped sharply down to the ocean. Years had eroded some of the face away and in the last decade at least one section of fence on the western end and ten yards of back lawn had dropped onto the rocks below. Everyone knew that sooner or later the island would be swallowed up in the fury of the Atlantic storms. But granite was not limestone, and that time would be measured in centuries, perhaps millennia.

Mary had had a fear of heights since that day at age twelve when she'd slipped off the porch roof of the house in Utica. She'd gone there to play Amelia Earhart with her sister and discovered that a bed sheet made a poor parachute. Like others who suffer from acrophobia, she could not resist the temptation to peer over the cliff and into the abyss. She called it her "little death wish." She knew she would not fall, but she also knew she would have an adrenaline rush that would cause her heart to leap into her throat. "One day," she'd said to her sister, "I will have a heart attack doing that and then I might as well have thrown myself off the precipice after all."

She grasped the fence post, shook it to be sure it remained firmly anchored in the ground, leaned over the edge, and took a quick peek. Usually one look would have been enough. But today something down on the rocks, a splash of color, caught her eye. She took a deep breath, steeled herself, and risked a second look. No doubt about it. That was Harmon Staley down there looking more like an untidy pile of laundry than a man.

Chapter Two

Ike Schwartz awoke early, an unusual event for him. In fact, the sun would not clear the mountains to the east for another half hour. The advantage his A-frame, as a result of its location on the western slope of the Blue Ridge Mountains, lay in the countless sunsets he'd witnessed over the years. For someone who remained a determined "night person," this advantage was a godsend. However, his circadian rhythm seemed to reverse when he vacationed, and his normal night persona flipped to that of an early riser. So it happened that had he looked for it, he could have seen a sunrise. He didn't bother. The fact he almost never saw a sunrise meant little or nothing to him. Sunrise, sunset, the only difference he could detect between them was the sequence of events. Rising, setting, setting, rising—dark, gold, orange, light, or the reverse—same thing. Morning people disputed that, of course, but then morning people, as a class, believed that all night people were irresponsible slackers. In his darker moments, he suspected they were the same people who'd foisted Daylight Saving Time on an unsuspecting public. How is it possible to save daylight—or waste it either, for that matter? He had a friend in Arizona who assured him that since his state refused to follow the practice they had as yet not lost one hour of the stuff and, in fact, had a surplus, some of which they would gladly trade for Seattle's rain.

He stepped to the kitchen as quietly as his size fifteen hiking boots allowed and started the first of what would be several pots of coffee that he'd brew over the next twelve to fifteen hours. He'd decided to let Ruth sleep as long as she wished or needed. When she woke up he would help her in and out of the tiny tub/shower and reposition the cervical collar that for the last several months had made her look more like a vicar in an Anthony Trollope novel than president of a moderately prestigious mid-Atlantic university. That, of course, assumed that Trollope's nineteenth century clerics would have countenanced a woman among their number. Ike felt certain they would not.

It had been an extremely difficult year for her, but one that had finally come to an end, as T. S. Eliot would say, *not with a bang, but a whimper.* Thank God for small mercies. All the conflicts and the potential scandal that had spewed forth like so much hot lava after the murder of her vice president in the fall had finally settled and cooled. Not, however, without what passed in academe for land grabbing and looting. Faculty, Ike thought, more accurately tenured faculty in the rarified air of universities, were behaviorally more like supermodels with PMS than the academic super stars they were alleged to be. He'd said that to Ruth and she'd smiled then smacked him with a manila folder for "acting like a sexist pig." He'd said he'd take that as a compliment given what she used to think of him when they first met.

"What was that?"

"You called me a Nazi."

"And you think sexist pig is an improvement?"

"Don't you?"

"You must be growing on me, Schwartz. You're right, I'm getting soft."

The faculty had eventually sheathed their verbal daggers, curbed their egos, and resumed the activities they were paid to do. The board of directors stopped posturing for the evening news, settled down, and approved the budget and the elevation of the current dean for academic affairs to the vacant vice president's slot. Its mutineers pacified, the ship, metaphorically speaking, was back on course. Ruth had had to endure all of this while recovering from the surgery attendant on an automobile wreck that put her into a three-week coma and gave her a fractured skull, a cracked cervical vertebra, a ruptured spleen, and a broken leg. She had done what needed doing and—mission accomplished, to quote another more famous president of different time and place—she now slept like a log in the next room. That is if logs could be thought to snore, an affliction she'd acquired as a side effect of the broken neck. The doc said he thought it would go away when she began sleeping on her side as she used to. Ike thought that was easy for him to say. He didn't have to share her bed. But success in small things had extracted its price. To Ike, she looked about as worn out and beaten as he had ever seen anyone, and that included some pretty beat up folks from another time and another life.

He settled in a camp chair and looked over the Shenandoah Valley nearly a thousand feet below him. His A-frame in the mountains, the retreat he'd established when he first returned to the valley running from the bad times, the BR times—Before Ruth times—now served as a place of refuge for both of them. He, from the burdens and annoyances that attached his job as sheriff of Picketsville, Virginia, and she from the similar but heavier ones borne by the presidency of Callend University. How much longer the cabin could serve as their weekend hiding place remained to be seen. Too many people insisted they needed twenty-four-seven access to one or the other of them. And privacy, especially for those who serve in the public sector, whether as educators or police, had been slowly eroded away by the nonsensical notions that emerged first from an obsessed media hungry for information and disinclined to dig it out the hard way. More recently they dealt with the semi-informed, semiliterate blogosphere that maintained the public's "right to know" trumped any individual's right to privacy.

He wondered if the late Marlon Brando might not have had it right. Maybe he should follow his example and buy an inaccessible island out in the middle of the ocean somewhere and disappear from view forever.

◇◇◇

Charlie Garland had two telephones on his desk. One of them had a number that was accessible to the general public, if you knew where to start and looked for it hard enough. The other did not. The only calls he received on the latter were from the director of the CIA, and the rare calls forwarded to it from other venues that needed his attention. And then only after they'd been screened by an anonymous person sitting at a desk somewhere else in the labyrinthine corridors of the Company. It was the latter that chirped at him. It was distinguishable from the other by its array of buttons, or rather lack thereof. Where the first had the means of putting a caller on hold and the ability to forward calls, the later had only a single green button. Charlie did not like to use it.

He picked up and listened. A hello would not be required.

"Archie Whitlock is dead," the director said.

"How?"

"He fell off a cliff in New England somewhere. An island in Maine I think. I'll send you the details in a minute."

"It was an accident?"

"What do you think?"

"It's possible, but as it's Archie we're discussing, not likely. I thought we had tucked him away from the bad guys with a new ID and a new life."

"We did and he was. He went away as we requested and the last anyone heard, he'd purchased an old 'fixer upper' in Maine and planned on turning it into a B and B or some such nonsense. Can you picture Archie as a Yankee innkeeper?"

"He was crazy enough to try, by all accounts, but then I never thought I'd see an African-American as president in my lifetime. Do you remember Archie's obsession with weather forecasting going back a few years? Maybe the location offered a chance to take up the hobby again."

"You think? Maybe. Anyway, we picked up the report of Archie's death in a routine post from a county sheriff's office. A couple of local fishermen apparently retrieved the body. I'm not sure what fishermen have to do with falling off a cliff but I suppose there is a connection. Anyway, we inserted the background documents we'd ponied up for Whitlock into the feedback to the sheriff including the new ID. His office is satisfied Whitlock was the guy we said he was and that he fell—accident."

"So, problem solved. Two problems solved, in fact. The Maine cops are happy and won't press on with an investigation, and Archie is finally off the books."

"Yes, indeed, two down but still one to go."

"Sir?"

"I am calling you, Garland. Why do you suppose I am calling you?"

"Obviously, you don't want me to find out who shoved Archie of the cliff, that's for some other unit, I hope, and clearly not in my job description. Even if it were, and you wanted me to, I would need a task force and at least a year to do it."

"A task force?"

"I can think of at least a half dozen people in various intelligence communities around the globe, along with a small army of very dangerous arms dealers, drug cartel *jefes*, and several smoothies in industrial complexes who had scores to settle with Archie. Oh, and don't forget, he had four ex-wives and three times as many unhappy girlfriends, any one of whom would have been elated to send Archie to wherever dirty spooks go to die. No doubt there are others you can add to the list."

"I could. As you noted, it is not your job to figure that out. Maine cops say accident—it stays accident. What I want to know is how, Charlie? How did whoever, ex-wives, ex-spooks, gun runners, whoever...how did he/she/they find him? Who, besides the people in Identity and Relocation knew where he was? Someone leaked something. Find the hole in the fence and close it."

"It had to be inside? You're sure?"

"Not absolutely, but what are the chances of it coming from anywhere else?"

"Wikileaks?"

"Don't get smart with me, Charlie, I haven't had my breakfast yet."

"Okay, I'm on it. Any ideas where to start?"

"I don't know about you, but I'm thinking orange juice, then coffee, and pancakes."

"Thanks for that, Mr. Director, and a very good morning to you, too."

"I've sent you an encrypted file on the NTK net. Read it and get back to me this afternoon when you've had a chance to study it."

Need to Know File? Charlie hung up and drummed his fingers on the beat-up old oak desk he'd used for years. He'd been offered a new shiny steel one on several occasions but he'd refused the offer, said he had gotten attached to this one and in fact hoped they either let him keep it when he retired, or convert it to a coffin if death was the way he finally ended his government career.

Chapter Three

Ruth slumped against the rattan chair back and glowered at her scrambled eggs. She used her fork to push them around and then dropped it with a clank on her plate. She sipped her coffee and made a face. "Is it me or has the whole world gone nuts?"

"A little of both, I think. If I had to choose, I'd go with the world, but that's only my take. So, the problem is what? The eggs too cold, too runny? Coffee is...what? Too strong, too weak, too sour, too hot, what? Or is it the company? What's the problem, Goldilocks?"

"Not you, Schwartz, and not breakfast. Breakfast always smells good, even when it isn't. The eggs are...yellow and the coffee is brown. What more could I possibly expect from a cop who cooks? I guess I woke up really bitchy this morning and I don't know why."

"Bitchy...you think?"

"Sorry, yeah. I'm on vacation and I can't get into it. I keep waiting for the phone to ring and some stuck-up department chairperson to attempt academic blackmail in order to get me to assign him more space or full-time equivalents. Maybe some over-indulged fashionista, never ever previously challenged sophomore from Scarsdale or Tom's River with a fifty-dollar manicure, will inform me that Daddy intends to file a law suit claiming the college abused his darling because she got a B on her genetics term paper when she thought she deserved an A and now her chances for going to Harvard Medical school have been ruined."

"Wow, you really are in a funk, Harris. I think they call what you have a grand funk—very rare in these parts. We generally manage with a major funk or a brown study, whatever that is. I guess I am not surprised, only amazed it took you six months to get there."

"What? Get where?"

"You are obviously suffering from a very bad case of PT-ASS. That's post-traumatic administrator's stress syndrome. You have had a really bad year and it has finally caught up with you."

"What do you mean finally? I've been yelling at you for six months. I don't know how you put up with me."

"There's an answer for that but I generally don't like to sound mushy before lunch."

"Since when?"

"Since I almost went crazy sitting in the hospital last fall watching you do your comatose act. You were very convincing, by the way."

"That's sweet. How'd I look—comatose?"

"Terrible."

"Thank you for that. I would hate to think I was alluring while contemplating whether to wake up or not. So what are we going to do about my post-traumatic...whatever you said?"

"It's your vacation. For now, I say if the phone rings, we don't answer it."

"And that helps how?"

"We came up here to get away from the university and the office for peace and quiet. That's how it helps."

"What if it's for you? What if someone has taken an axe to their mother-in-law or something worse and they need good old Sheriff Ike to ride in on his white horse and collar the bad guy."

"In the first place, I don't have a horse, white or otherwise but I do have an old gray Jeep. It's not running at the moment but we live in hope. More importantly, I have very good deputies and they can handle axe murderers, speeding tickets, and their daily donut ration without my help. They do not need me. The bigger question is what if one of those prima donnas who play in your sand box calls and needs to have his a…nose wiped?"

"Point taken. Oh, Ike it used to be so wonderfully easy. Before the merger with Carter-Union we were on our way to becoming another Scripps College or Wellesley. Now it looks like we couldn't compete with a B-rated community college on a party weekend."

"That's not true and you know it. Your faculty has always been prickly. It's what the professional intelligentsia do. It's in their DNA. It comes with a vellum certificate declaring them smarter than people."

"I guess you're right, sort of. Remember, Ike, I used to be one of them before I became one of me."

"Pardon?"

"You know what I mean. I don't know, it's not that bad, but it's different and complicated. I must be heading to burn-out city."

"I've been there. It's nice in the springtime but I wouldn't want to live there. You know what? We need to get away. Not away like here, where everybody knows we hang out, but away, away. Some place where there are no phones, no TV, no Internet no—please God—no Twitter, Facebook, or, you should pardon the expression, social networks. Peace and quiet. Let someone else solve the case of the department chairman axe murders."

"We should go to Las Vegas. I've never been to Sin City. Who would ever think to find us there?"

"Almost anyone with the will to do so. Vegas is busy, but private it is not, in spite of the slogan suggesting otherwise. We need someplace really remote."

"You know such a place?"

Ike shrugged. "Short of Mauritius, no. Sorry. More coffee?"

"No, thanks. I do."

"Do? Do what?"

"Know such a place."

"Really? Where?"

"My Great-aunt Margaret VanDeVeer left me a cottage in Maine on an island that's, like, four miles off the coast or something, near Bass Harbor. It has no phone tower, no electricity, no…nothing. Strictly roughing it. Wood burning fire places and beds with fat duvets to keep you warm at night and all the fresh sea air you can manage. Is there more toast?"

Ike slid the last of the wheat toast onto her plate. "How come I'm hearing about this for the first time?"

"I received a letter from a Boston attorney three months ago. That was when I was up to my you-know-what in contentious board meetings, faculty focus groups, and all that other crap. I told the lawyer to go to probate for me. I sent him a POA and signed off. I said I'd contact him later. Then I pretty much forgot all about it."

"And this cottage is where again?"

"Atlantic Ocean off the coast of Maine."

"Sounds cold."

"So? Don't be such a wuss."

"Right. No wussiness for me. So, speaking about your you-know-what—"

"Later, lover. First things first. How much leave time do you have left?"

"A couple of weeks. If that's not enough, I could always quit."

"Forget that. I plan to sleep safe with the law on my side, not some unemployed bum. I'm due for some compassionate leave, don't you think?"

"Absolutely."

"So, I'll extend the week off and we'll go to Scone Island, that's the name of the place, and kick back for two weeks or so. What do you say? We deserve some R and R, right?"

"Maine in May?"

"Think about it…moonlight over the ocean, the previously mentioned wood burning fireplace, a fat duvet with my you-know-what under it. Is that sounding like Maine in May could be a go?"

"Late May. Okay, you have yourself a deal. What about Las Vegas?"

"If the island washes out, Vegas will be plan B."

"Check. I think we might want to clear this junket with a few folks first, don't you?"

"Yeah, yeah, and, hey, no calling Charlie Garland to tell him where you are. Every time that charmer calls, he gets you into trouble."

"I thought you said there were no phone towers."

"That's right. No phone, so no Charlie. Okay, we're good to go. Wait. He has access to all that CIA secret I-can-find-you-anywhere-in-the-world technology. You'll have to scotch that."

"No problem there. It's not like I have a chip implanted in my neck anymore—"

"Anymore? You mean you did at one time?"

"No, merely making sure you're awake."

At that precise moment, Charlie Garland had a slightly related thought. He had scanned the encrypted file for an hour and one name in particular jumped off the pages. Archie Whitlock, CIA field agent, before he became Harmon Staley, bed-and-breakfast operator, had several ops that had gone pear shaped. In each case, Ike Schwartz, the Company's best mop-up operative, had been called in to provide back-up and in at least one instance execute an extraction. Ike knew Whitlock back in the day. He might also know who Archie might contact in his new persona, if anyone. He needed to call Ike. More importantly, if Archie had in fact been pushed off the cliff, what were the chances that others associated with one or more of Archie's ops weren't also in line for an "accident?" He turned back to the reports scattered across his desk. The director did not want him to ferret out the killer, fine, but he still needed to know if any of the names were linked to those ops gone bad. Especially if agents like Ike might be at risk. Did Archie get nudged into free fall by a homicidal ex-wife, an angry former agent, one of the myriad nut jobs that haunted the Internet looking for conspiracies, or someone who had a problem with a particular operation? And would he now be in the hunt for other players?

Charlie picked up his phone—that would be the one with the listing, however obscure—and punched in Ike's number. He waited until Ike's voice mail came on the line. He left a message and wondered why Ike did not pick up. Then he remembered it was Sunday and Ike would not answer unless convinced the call was an emergency. Charlie never figured out how he knew what was and what wasn't an emergency without first asking. But he'd long ago concluded that Ike's mental configuration did not match any known normal pattern.

The call logger that recorded a time and date stamp for all calls in or out of the CIA, except on certain select phones, noted the time, duration, and number called. It would repeat the operation twice more that morning and only one of them would be made from Charlie's phone.

Chapter Four

Ike walked into the sheriff's office as the day shift rotated in and the night shift out. He nodded to the four or five deputies who were finishing their coffee and moving toward the door to start the day's routine. Ike gestured for Frank Sutherlin, his chief deputy and usually second in command to come into his office. He wheeled and waved to Frank's sister-in-law, Essie, who served as Dispatcher and general dogs-body, to do the same.

"I thought you were on leave, Ike. What are you doing in here this morning?"

"Not enough privacy up in the mountains anymore. You know where I am. Hell, everybody in town knows. Same for Ruth so we're moving out."

"I guess you're tired of hearing it every day, Ike, but how is Doctor Harris?"

"And as always, Frank, she's still recovering. It has been a very bad year for her, but you know all about that. The worst of the problems up at the university are over. It has taken its toll, however. She's had no time to recuperate from the attempt on her life. She jumped right back in the snake pit. Right now she looks ragged and worn and edgy. I'm thinking that if I don't take her away, far away, for a while, something might bump into her and she will shatter like expensive porcelain."

"So, is she taking some time off?"

"She is and I am. Do you two think you can manage here for a few weeks?"

"Sure, no problem. Essie and I can hold down the fort, I think. Can't we Essie?"

Essie gave them one of her hundred-watt grins. "Where are you going in case we need to get in touch with you?"

"See, that's the problem with you two."

"Problem? What's a problem? I only asked for a phone number in case there is an emergency. It's SOP, right?"

"Not this time. I asked if you thought you could manage for a few weeks and you said sure. Then you implied you couldn't, after all."

"How? All I did—"

"All you did was ask me for a phone number where I could be reached. Why? What extraordinary set of circumstances do you imagine would require a need to talk to me? You are a good cop, Frank. If I dropped dead, you'd be running this show. You do not need to be in contact with me."

Frank scratched his head. "Sorry. I see what you mean, but I'm thinking maybe you need your morning coffee, Ike. Essie, get the boss some of today's special before it starts to turn into something more useful for paving the street than drinking."

"Thanks, but no thanks. I am off to the Crossroads Diner in a minute, then I pick up the aforementioned Dr. Harris who is setting her mother up as gatekeeper at the university, and we will be off. I wanted to get here early enough to ward off any calls about to be dumped on me which will stop or slow down the process."

"If I tell the mayor that I have no idea where you are and the Martians land and take over the Kroger supermarket, he'll be really upset."

"And well he should. Okay, Ms. Harris and I will be traveling to a remote location. There are no phones there—none at all. Don't give me that look, it's true, there are no phones, no e-mail, really poor TV reception if you could actually turn the set on but since there's also no electricity you can't, and again, no phones, no cell phones, no land line, nothing."

"But—"

"But. Okay, in the event that the Martians do in fact attack us or Sarah Palin shows up on her motorcycle, you can send a message to the Hancock County Sheriff's Office in Ellsworth, Maine. Someone there will get a message to me in a day or two, a couple of hours if it's a real emergency."

"A day or…Ike, I'm serious."

"And so am I. I do not wish anyone to be able to find either me or Ruth. We want absolute privacy. You can run this office, and I expect you to do it without any input from me."

"But—"

"And that means no phone calls or contacts, especially from Charlie Garland, Essie. If he calls, you have my permission to give voice to every expletive you've ever deleted. He is like a sudden drop in barometric pressure. He calls and you know a storm is on the way. He brings trouble, complications at least, and I am not willing to put myself in his orbit anymore. He was a sweetheart during Ruth's hospitalization and I owe him for that, but for several weeks starting today, I do not know him. You are to tell him nothing."

"No to Charlie Garland. Got it. Suppose he says it's an emergency?"

"With Charlie it's always an emergency. He lives in a perpetual state of emergency. It is his life, but it is not mine, and he never seems to remember I do not draw a paycheck from his outfit anymore. In fact, I do not want to draw a paycheck from it, and I have absolutely no intention of allowing myself to be sucked into one of his dark plots, not now, not ever again. Tell him that."

"No dark plots, right. But you are going to tell us where you're going."

"Nope. Nothing beyond what I said, Hancock County Sheriff's Department, Ellsworth, Maine. That's all you get."

The phone rang as if on cue and Essie picked up. "Picketsville Sheriff's Office, how can I help?" She listened for a moment, then covered the phone with her hand and mouthed, "Charlie Garland."

"Tell him I haven't come in today, you don't know where I am, and he probably should try calling me on my cell phone."

Essie nodded and turned back to the phone. "I'm sorry, Mr. Garland, but Ike ain't here today. Him and Ms. Harris is taking some time off. Maybe you should try his cell…What?… No, don't know where he's gone to. He said something about a camping trip and he'd let us know later when he got to wherever that was at. Yes, sir, I sure will let you know as soon as I do…An emergency, right, I hear you. Matter of life and death? Really? Wow. Well, if he calls in, I'll sure enough tell him."

"Thank you, Essie. That was perfect. Camping trip? Terrific, keep it up for two weeks and I'll see about getting you a raise."

"How about Frank here, won't he deserve one too?"

"That will depend on how he handles the Martians down at the supermarket."

"Not Ms. Palin?"

"That lady can take care of herself."

Chapter Five

Charlie had to wait for the director to return his call. He spent the interval reviewing the sheets of paper in front of him. He shook his head in frustration. First he had been unable to track down Ike Schwartz. There were two other names as well that needed checking—Neil Bernstein and Al Jackson. They were involved in at least two of Archie's stickier operations gone south. Jackson's controller said he'd tell him what happened but did not seem concerned. That was the frustrating part. Unless Charlie could talk to the three of them privately, they could not know that they might be at risk. That was assuming whoever knocked off Archie Whitlock turned out to be someone connected to his old ops or holding a contract on Archie as a result. It was an untested, even sweeping assumption, but Charlie would rather let them weigh the risks than take a chance. As far as he was concerned, they needed to know and stay alert until the whole Archie business was resolved.

Then there was the phone log. Someone inside the building was tracking his calls. Was he being monitored by the director or by someone else in the Company who might be the "hole in the fence?" In any case, this conversation with the director would be the last he'd make using a traceable phone.

The phone rang.

"Director, could you please push the green button on the phone now?"

"What? You want to scramble this conversation? Garland, we are in-house and you are talking to me, not some field agent in Syria."

"Yes, sir, I know that. Could you please push the button anyway?"

"It's come to that?"

"'Fraid so."

Charlie listened for the soft squawk that told him their conversation would be digitally encoded, pushed the identical button on his phone and took a breath.

"Why?" the director said.

"Someone in the building is tracking my calls, Director. Unless you can offer a reason why I shouldn't be, I am worried about that. I called Ike Schwartz and shortly after that, so did someone else. That might have been you or someone running a parallel program. I don't know, but until I am sure what is going on or who is poking around in my stuff, I am not willing to take any chances."

"And you are afraid of what, Garland?"

"I don't know who killed Archie Whitlock, or why he was killed, and as you made clear, that is not my job. In fact right now I really hope it was an accident, but we both know it wasn't and it probably wasn't a random event or unrelated to who he used to be and what he used to do, either."

"You think it goes back to something he was involved in before?"

"As I said, I don't know. But if it is connected, then it's within the realm of possibility that Ike, Neil Bernstein, and Al Jackson may be in that same someone's crosshairs as well. I am not willing to wait until one of them turns up dead to find out."

"They are possible targets because…?"

"They share some history with Archie that was not so good for our side."

"I see. So have you contacted them?"

"That's my current problem. I can't locate Ike. His people tell me he's on vacation somewhere and they do not know where. They are waiting for him to call in with his location."

"You believe them?"

"I believe they believe him but, no, I don't. I called Ruth Harris…you remember her…as well, and also spoke to her mother. She didn't know anything either. But…"

"But what?"

"Well, she and I had a misunderstanding back in the fall and I don't think she'd volunteer anything to me anyway."

"A misunderstanding?"

"It's a long story and one for another day. But in any case I asked her to tell Ruth to tell Ike that Archie was dead and he should call in. I made her write it down. That's all I can do."

"How about the other two?"

"Coincidently, Bernstein is *in absentia* as well. I talked to Halmi, his control, who gave me the number of his girlfriend, Krissie somebody…wait, here it is, Kristine Johansen. I did manage to reach her. She said she wasn't sure, but she believed he was in Colorado someplace climbing rocks. Why do people take those kinds of risks, anyway?"

"Charlie, Bernstein was a field agent. Rock climbing would be pretty tame stuff compared, say, to running with Archie Whitlock."

"Right, sorry. This Krissie person didn't know where he'd gone for sure but gave me the name of a town she thought she remembered being nearby. I left the same message with her and put in a call to local cops to look for him. I told them I was his boss, and that 'there was a problem at the plant,' and that if they ran across him to please have him call in."

"And Jackson?"

"Better luck there. He's up the road in Baltimore with relatives. His guy will have him come in as soon as he connects. He should be pretty safe; he's using an untraceable credit card and his relatives have different last names."

"Okay, I can't think of anything more you can do. When they call, bring them all in until we're sure we have this thing sorted. Are we done here?"

"Yes, sir."

The director's phone went dead. Charlie hung up. He'd done what he could. The three either were in danger or they weren't. The immediate problem now was to fix the fence and that might coincidently lead him to a killer—or not.

Eden Saint Clare sat perfectly still for nearly a half hour, thinking about Charlie Garland's call. Her daughter was all she had left of a life spent as the wife of an academic who now teetered on the brink of oblivion—his mind, having succumbed to Alzheimer's, had anticipated the trip by several years. Ruth Harris reminded her of her soon-to-be late husband in many ways. She was stubborn, opinionated, tough, and brave. And stubborn often ruled the day. She said under no circumstances was Eden to tell Garland or anyone else that Ike and she were off to Aunt Margaret VanDeVeer's cottage on Scone Island. So she had dummied up when Charlie called. Then he left a message for Ike, it was very important that Ike know that Archie somebody…Whitlock… was dead. What was that all about?

And the other thing that bothered her a little was that Ruth had borrowed her American Express card. "Why," she'd asked, "don't you use your own?"

She'd only looked up and said, "So Charlie Garland and his spook friends won't be able to trace me." She seemed annoyed when she said that.

Eden had suggested that Charlie Garland was no dummy and if he thought about it for a minute the first thing he'd do would be to try "Saint Clare" in his search engine, wouldn't he?

Ruth stopped packing, a sports bra suspended in mid air, and nodded. "You're right," she'd said, "I'll only use it for emergencies."

So Eden had a secret and a mission of sorts: keep Garland and his people in the dark. Presumably that meant everyone in the sheriff's office as well. She poured a dollop of brandy into a snifter, warmed it for a moment with her palms, enjoyed the aroma and then downed it in one gulp. So much for sophistication. The brandy perked her up, she thought. Actually, a jolt of one-hundred proof alcohol, irrespective of the medium with which it is delivered, will anesthetize a substantial number of neurons and significantly reduce anyone's cognitive faculties, but Eden came from a generation that relied on a "pick-me-up" and therefore, science notwithstanding, she felt invigorated.

What if, she wondered, Charlie's message carried a subliminal warning, that Archie Somebody-or-the other is dead was actually code for some big and dangerous undertaking involving Ike and spies or terrorists? After all, Ike's past life had an uncomfortable habit of resurfacing. If Dead Archie meant something bad loomed in the near future, then might she be in peril as well? After all, if she knew where Ike and Ruth were and the guys in the black SUVs were on their trail, wouldn't they come to her ASAP? Wouldn't the goons in trench coats arrive at her door to ask? Visions of water-boarding and blinding lights crossed her mind, abetted somewhat more than she'd ever admit by the brandy. Once burned, twice shy, she thought, time to make tracks. Since Ruth had taken her AMEX card, she rummaged around and took Ruth's. Tit for tat. She scooped up the rest of her credit cards, packed a bag and booked a flight to Chicago. She had business there anyway, and who, besides family, would think to look for her there?

Charlie Garland would. He'd been there once before when she made the trip west. But she didn't think of that.

Chapter Six

"We're stopping for disposable cell phones." Ike pulled into a parking lot adjoining a strip mall.

"Isn't that a little over the top? I mean leaving no trail is one thing—kind of fun actually, but would anyone really go to all that trouble to find us?"

"Probably not, but as they say, 'old habits die hard.' I still suffer from 'residual spook paranoia.' I'm not as bad as I used to be, but you get me started on a maneuver like this and all the old routines kick in whether they make any sense or not."

"Okay, fine, but you seem to have forgotten, there are no phone towers on the island. You can't call anyone. What do we need these for?"

"I am not thinking about the island. If I have to, I will take care of that some other way. We are traveling by car. You are still in a neck brace and recovering from some serious trauma. No matter how much you play at being Plucky Petunia, you have a way to go before you are near to being your old self, physically. Consider this, if we have car trouble, a health set-back, or any unexpected nonsense on the trip up and back, I want to be able to contact somebody. Okay?"

"Gottcha. Safety first and all that."

"And all that. Wait here." Ike entered a drugstore and fifteen minutes later emerged with a plastic bag with numerous items.

"How many of those things did you buy?"

"Enough so that if one fails, can't be charged, runs out of minutes, or for any other reason turns out to be useless, we have backup"

"Holy cow, Ike, you really are in super spook mode. I'd have loved to see you in your heyday playing at being America's 007."

"No, you wouldn't. I promise I wasn't playing at anything, and believe me 007 is fiction."

"But fun to watch. Who do you think was the best Bond—Sean Connery, David Niven, George Lazenby, Roger Moore, Timothy Dalton, Pierce Brosnan, or Daniel Craig?"

"Who's George Lazenby? And David Niven was Bond? When?"

"Niven was in the spoof and Lazenby only did one picture, I think."

"None of the above. I liked the books okay, but the movies became sillier and sillier as they went on. Please, an invisible car? And don't forget diamond thread saws tucked into a Rolex. At the end they were more like *Get Smart* than Fleming's original. In any case, if that's your idea of spying, forget it."

"You would know. So, how are we traveling to Maine and when do we stop for lunch?"

"You're thinking food already?"

"I'm on vacation. I intend to eat and get fat. You got a problem with that?"

"Nope. We will take I-81 to I-66. It merges with the Washington beltway, and it feeds us onto I-95, which we will follow all the way north to Maine. We will take the appropriate exit to Mt. Desert Island and follow Jill—that's the voice on our Garmin—to Bass Harbor. Boat from there to the island, simple. As for lunch, when we hit the DC beltway, we'll pull off near the airport and find a place to eat, okay?"

"Goody. Now, if you have no objection, I am going to take the first of many naps. Please do not play the radio except classical music, and that softly."

"That is one mouthful of declarative sentences. Who appointed you captain of this ship?"

"I am the victim, remember. We live in an age of victimhood and, on this trek, I am the one to be pitied."

"Bullshit."

"Nevertheless." Ruth punched a pillow into submission and slumped against the door post and was asleep in three minutes.

"Victim, my sweet…" Ike glanced at the sleeping figure and smiled. She really did need to eat and get fat.

Scone Island had been so named by Scots-Irish sailors in the early 1600s because of its rough triangular shape and the fact it rose from the ocean as a low mound. Except for the cove at its southernmost end, it did indeed resemble a triangular scone. The long edge, the hypotenuse, if you will, faced the mainland, and the road that paralleled its western shore became West Road. The road on the northeast leg of the triangle was then North Road, and the remaining leg of the roadway, South Road. The designation as roads seemed something of a conflation, but at the turn of the twentieth century, the term road carried a different expectation than it does today. They had been named that way for something over a hundred years, and no one thought to change them any more than anyone wanted to change the island's ambiance from what it had always been. Some of the old-timers worried that a newcomer, like Harmon Staley or even that Barstow fellow, might start trouble. Newcomers usually did, but now Staley was dead, fell over a cliff, and Henry Potter, who'd retrieved the body, said he smelled like a distillery, so there you go.

The rough triangular shape which gave Scone Island its name had one flaw. The western edge had a semicircular indentation near its southernmost end, adjacent to the cluster of houses indicated on the map as Southport. It appeared as if someone had taken a bite from the scone. In 1910, when the newly formed Scone Island Association planned the community, naming the little cove became an early point of contention. How and by whom would it be used? Should it be declared a common area, or would control, that is to say ownership, fall to those who'd purchased the lots on its periphery? The rest of the island's shoreline had been so relegated. The residents of Southport, mostly lobstermen who were on the island well before the "foreigners" arrived, moored their work boats in it and made it crystal clear that they would not be moved irrespective of the Association's high-falutin' ideas. Franklin Cabot, that would be the original Cabot on the island with that name, insisted the cove be privatized and be delegated for the exclusive use of the property owners immediately adjacent to it. And, because he or his relatives owned the majority of those lots, he insisted the cove be named after him. The other owners objected to both the naming and the privatization and he was overruled. Then, in keeping with the scone theme and because it appeared as such, it became, instead, The Bite.

Summer residents referred to Henry Potter as the mayor of Southport. He accepted the honorific with as much grace a Down Easterner could. That is to say, he wasn't rude to the men who invaded his space every year with their sailboats and motor launches and New York accents. He would be the last of the Potters, he'd often declared. He'd never married, had neither siblings nor close relatives, and his parents had sailed to their reward years ago. When he died, there would be no more Potters on Scone Island or the near mainland either—well, none he'd claim at least. There was that librarian that he took to Pine Tree Island on Labor Day back in the day and who had had to leave town, but she'd never said anything so that was that. He'd lived all of his sixty-plus years on Scone Island in Southport with the other half dozen families who inhabited the island mostly year round. He was the proprietor of the island's general store and the operator of the battery-powered ship-to-shore radio that tracked the local fishermen, lobster boats, and could be used for emergencies to call the mainland and the police.

At the turn of the century when the fancy folks from New York and thereabouts first came to the island with their plans to buy up the land and turn it into a limited access summer resort, they tried to buy or force out the few families who lived in

Southport more or less permanently. Their efforts failed. Down East lobstermen and trawler operators were not impressed with city people, their money, or their plans for the island.

So, over the years, the little resident community had existed cheek by jowl with the summer folk. Work boats were moored beside expensive sailboats and motor yachts. In the winter the pleasure boats would be pulled ashore or stored on the mainland, but the work boats stayed. During the first two decades of the island's corporate life, a steam launch made a daily round trip from Bass Harbor, then known as McKinley, to Southport during the months of June through August. The stock market collapse of 1929 and the ensuing Great Depression occasioned by that economic cataclysm put an end to the launch, along with the luxury of live-in servants, plus many of the island's residents who hadn't the foresight to sell short. Thus, in the years following, the summer visitors came to depend on the locals for mail and grocery delivery and, of course, their ship-to-shore radios.

Chapter Seven

Much to Ruth's annoyance, Ike insisted he check in at the Hancock County Sheriff's Office in Ellsworth before they drove the last leg to Bass Harbor and the boat ride to Scone Island.

"It's professional courtesy," he'd said. "A cop thing."

"Then I should have dropped in on the people at the University of Maine, right? Professional courtesy, you know."

"Don't be ridiculous."

"Ridiculous? You think? Tell me, what's the difference?"

"Propinquity."

"Excuse me?"

"I'm on the ground, a cop *in situ,* you could say. Look, if a problem arises in the University of Maine or the local community college, the fact there is another university president in the area doesn't materially help them, but if something goes bad in the county, a crime is committed or attempted, another cop in the area is an asset the locals would like to know about. I would expect their sheriff to let me know if he showed up in Picketsville for any length of time."

"I could help a college in trouble."

"You could, but would they ask? Would you?"

"No, I guess not. So, what took you so long?"

"The sheriff gave me a rundown of the locals, residents—stuff like that. A man died on your island four days ago; did you know that?"

"Who? How?"

"Some man named Harmon Staley reportedly overextended his relationship with a bottle of bourbon and fell off a cliff at a place called Cliffside. Ring a bell?"

"No, don't know the name, but I remember the house. It's the big one at the north end of the island. I can't remember the name of the people who used to live there, but I'm sure it wasn't Staley. I haven't been on the island since I was a little girl and frankly I don't remember much about any of the people. There was a nice woman who was a good friend of my aunt. Um...I'll think of her name in a minute...and there were the locals, Mr. Potter and the two Gott brothers, but that's pretty much it. The police weren't suggesting foul play or anything, were they?"

"No, he wanted to give me a heads-up."

The last bit wasn't entirely true. The Medical Examiner's report had two or three puzzling entries that had the Sheriff scratching his head and he'd asked Ike to keep an ear to the ground and send back anything he might pick up. Ike said he would.

"Smithwick."

"What?"

"Mary Smithwick was the name of the woman I met who was a friend of Aunt Margaret. She has a place over on South Road near where a path that cuts across the middle of the island meets the road. I think that's right. She had a married sister who had the place next door to her. Funny how things come back to you—it was the sister who was mixed up in something that nobody would talk about."

"Really? What?"

Ruth shrugged. "I have no idea. I told you, nobody talked about it. When we were kids, we used to pretend the husband was a Russian spy and was hiding on the island. We'd snitch the grown-ups' bird glasses and watch him through the hedge."

"No one bothered to ask what a Russian spy would be doing lurking about on an island four miles off the coast?"

"It didn't seem important at the time. Hey, you can smell the ocean now. You used to smell more than ocean. The place used to be known as McKinley. It had a cannery and it smelled like fish when I was here last."

"With a name like Bass Harbor, that can't be true anymore. Any place that is called Bass Harbor has to be a yuppie vacation spot complete with outlet stores and wine bars, not a fishing village. If it were still fish it would still be called McKinley. Was it named after the twenty-fifth President, or somebody local?"

"The former. The story goes that when the government first established a post office in the town, they had to name it. I guess they wanted to do something for the sitting president. So, yuppies and wine bars? You are playing Populist ideologue again. What's up with that? You are a Harvard graduate and as much as anyone I know, a beneficiary of upper crustiness. Why do come down so hard on your own kind?"

"Two reasons, white privilege guilt and a father who, more than any living man, qualifies as a 'yellow dog Democrat.' It's genetic, I guess."

"Well it's unbecoming."

"Here's the pier and that must be your Walter Gott looking at his watch. Are we late and is there such a thing in these parts?"

"We are and there is. People who fish and lobster for a living live by the tides. You miss one and your day is shot. Lateness is not much admired." Ruth eased out of the car and hobbled over to the lobsterman when the wind gusted up and nearly blew her over. "Whoa, there's a breeze today. Captain Gott, I'm sorry we are late. Ike has never driven this distance and calculating time and traffic got away from us."

"Yawp. Is that there your baggage?" Ike had begun offloading the bags and boxes from the trunk and rear seat. "Sure is a lot of equipment for a week or so, ain't it?"

"My goodness, Ike what is all that stuff? I packed a bag and so did you. What's in the boxes?"

"A few extras. Mr. Gott—"

"Captain," Ruth said.

"What?"

"The correct address is, Captain, Ike."

"You're serious?"

"I am. And as a resident or as a visitor, we must observe the niceties."

"Fine. Captain, I understand from *Doctor* Harris here that the few appliances in the cottages run on propane. Is that correct?"

"Yawp."

"And there is ample supply at Doctor Harris' cottage?"

"Henry Potter said they was."

"And is the means of tapping the line for additional units, should I need one, also available?"

"Can't say as I rightly know. All them houses is different. You fixing to install something or another?"

"Yawp, I mean, yep. Is there a hardware store in Bass Harbor where such a device can be had?"

"McEachern and Hutchins out on Tremont road will have her, I expect."

"Good. Then if I need one, you could fetch it out to the island for me on one of your grocery runs?"

"I could, yawp."

"Fine. Let's get aboard and see this wonderful island of yours."

"'Tain't mine, you know. Belongs to a whole bunch of folks including the lady here."

"Indeed."

"Ike, you did not answer my question. What's all this stuff?"

"Things to make your stay pleasanter, madam."

"You brought an ice cream machine, a case of booze, and a crate of chocolate bars?"

"Better."

"What could possibly be better than that?"

"Patience. Captain, cast off, or sail ho, or whatever."

Walter Gott piloted his boat and his two passengers out of the harbor and windward of the Bass Harbor Light and set a course east nor'east to Scone Island. Walter and his brother, when they weren't attending their lobster pots, provided ferry service to the island for the summer folk. They also picked up and delivered grocery orders the folks would give him every

Monday, Wednesday, and Friday mornings. He inspected Ike and Ruth out of the corner of his eye. "Looked like city folks," Walter would say to Henry Potter later. "That there couple don't strike me as your typical pair. First off, the lady looks like she needed a good meal and a dose of the wife's tonic. Worn to a frazzle is what she is. And the man, well he looks a puzzle and that was for sure. Big fellah, no doubt about that. Maybe a gangster or something. Tough, if I'm guessing rightly."

Henry told him the lady was the niece, some removed, of old Miz VanDeVeer who died last winter and left her place to her, and she'd been in the hospital or something. The fellah with her was her whatchamacallit, her significant other. And Walter should show some respect because he heard he was maybe a police.

Chapter Eight

The jeep bounced over the last stretch of dry streambed, its motor straining against the grade, wheels spitting rocks into the underbrush. Neil Bernstein clenched his jaw against the shocks that rocketed up his spine. Another twenty yards and he would be back at the clearing and could make camp. Tomorrow he would tackle the rock face that towered five hundred feet above him. But right now, he only wanted to stop, unload the jeep, pitch camp, and settle in for the night.

He had been coming to this remote stretch of the Rockies off and on for years. This particular climb was a favorite. It is not a smart thing to climb solo no matter what your skill level might be, so he often brought Krissie Johansen along. As a single parent she was reluctant to take the sort of risks that could have made her daughters orphans. But to please him, she'd tried climbing once. After an hour in which she managed to scale perhaps twenty-five feet of an easy climb and ruined a twenty-five-dollar manicure, she'd given up. The exhilaration he felt when he pitted his body against an uncompromising sheer stone face eluded her. She could not understand how people would put themselves through such a bone-wearying exercise and take the risks involved. But she did understand its importance to Neil. So, on the occasions when she could send her girls to their grandparents for the weekend and accompany Neil, she'd stay back at camp and read, sunbathe, and watch him as he advanced slowly upward like a bug on a wall. With the both sets of grandparents unavailable, she'd begged off this time.

It was just as well, he thought. Something…the tickle on the back of his neck, a warning perhaps…nothing substantial, but Neil had survived a decade with the Company because he paid attention to those little tweaks and tingles. He didn't like to think he might put Krissie in harm's way. It was probably nothing, but you never knew. Premonition ran in the family, in fact. His grandfather, he remembered, could tell you what the weather would be by the ache in a knee shattered at Guadalcanal in another age and had claimed he'd predicted the Jets winning Super Bowl III. Neil wondered about that. Earlier in the week, Neil's neck seemed to be saying, "You need to get out of Dodge," and as he had leave time accrued and because Halmi told him it could be weeks before he had anything new for him, he drove west to his rocks. He decided not to mention to Halmi he'd be alone. He didn't need the lecture about how stupid it was to climb solo.

He pulled up in the dry, shallow creek bed and killed the engine. Off to his right the ground rose gently to the rock face. At its foot, nearly three acres of treeless mountain meadow glistened in the late afternoon sun. Neil clambered awkwardly from the jeep, his legs and back stiff from the long drive. He stretched, threw his arms back, and took a dozen deep breaths to work out the kinks. Grabbing his bedroll and backpack, he climbed the embankment and turned to the slight rise forty yards away where he usually made camp. A new stand of shrubbery and aspens bordered the creek bed and effectively screened it from the meadow. Neil stepped from this cover and paused. In front of him the rock face rose almost perfectly perpendicular. He walked toward it absorbed in its majesty, in its challenge. At the campsite he paused only long enough to drop his equipment and glance around. He thought he saw movement in the trees edging the far end of the meadow. Probably an elk cow and her calf inspecting the meadow grass for possible danger.

The rock face captured his attention again. He stood and stared, only vaguely aware of the bird's songs, the rustle of the aspens in the afternoon's gentle breeze and the rumble of a motor, probably an airplane, in the distance. He walked to the face and looked straight up—beautiful. Tomorrow at first light he would pit his skill and strength against it, but now he only wanted to study and admire it, to plan his attack. To his left, twenty or thirty feet up, he saw a seam that rose diagonally across to his right. He would work his way along that, he thought, and then take the next fifty feet with pitons straight up. He stepped back to improve his view. The details higher up eluded him. He would have to go back for his binoculars. No bother; he had the rest of the afternoon and evening to work out the ascent. Neil strode back toward the jeep to retrieve the rest of his gear.

The clearing was quiet, but the motor he'd heard before, if it was the same one, seemed nearer and more distinct. Now he recognized the pulsing chock-chock-chock of an older model helicopter and wondered idly what it was doing way out here—police, Forest Service? He paused at the campsite to smooth out his ground cloth and spread his bedroll.

Sunlight glinting off something metallic brought him up short. He could make out the upper part of the jeep through the trees, but the flicker seemed to come from a point further down the track. He searched the underbrush but failed to see anything. Frowning, he quickened his pace. As far as he knew he was alone, but that did not mean someone else could not be there. Although remote, this particular rock face was fairly well known to the climbing fraternity.

He saw two men when he got to the edge of the meadow and trees. They were working their way up the ravine toward him. Their appearance disturbed him but he couldn't think why. Both wore camo, the new digitalized version, and looked more like soldiers than hunters. But nowadays, who could say? He'd seen an ad for camo diapers—for newborn survivalists, he supposed. Both men sported a beret bearing some sort of insignia.

Neil had run across all kinds of people in the wilderness—many odder in appearance than these two. Ordinarily he would not have been concerned. A camaraderie exists among hunters, climbers, backpackers, and outdoors people generally that transcended politics and personalities, especially deep under the forest's canopy. In that environment, they all shared a common set of values and goals. That special *bonhomie* did not, however, extend to the dirt bikers, snowmobilers and the other occasional noisy, beer-swilling intruders into the wild that one came across at its fringes. But in a remote place like this, the chance meeting of another human being did not constitute an occasion for alarm. Even so, Neil felt a sudden stab as the two men approached.

He hurried the last few feet to the jeep and began unloading his gear. Somewhere in it he packed his government issue Sig Sauer that he always carried on the road, "to shoot snakes" he'd explained to Krissie. She couldn't know that a M-11 provided an awful lot of fire power for snake killing. He could not remember which of the duffels he put it in—not a mistake he would normally make. A quick glance over his shoulder revealed the men were now only thirty yards away. And now Neil also realized what had disturbed him before. The men were not carrying backpacks; they were not carrying anything—no canteen, no compass—nothing. You did not get this far into the wild without something. And they were fresh—as though they had just stepped out of a taxi around the corner, their pants creased and neatly bloused in their boot tops. Then he saw the guns holstered at their hips.

The helicopter hovered somewhere nearby, perhaps over the ridge. He could not tell where exactly—the sound of its engine seemed to bounce around, first here, then there.

With his panic growing but still under control, he yanked open the first bag and searched frantically among the cold steel of the pitons and C-rings and the rough coils of rope. Wrong duffle, no pistol. He heard the scrabble of rock dislodged by an approaching boot. He turned to face his visitors empty-handed.

"Afternoon," he said, he hoped casually.

"Afternoon." The man to his right said, but it could have been either one. They were as alike in stature and appearance as to be interchangeable. Both stood about six feet tall, were trim, and sported sandy moustaches. Aside from the fact that one had blue eyes, the other brown, they could have been twins, right down to the 1911 Colt .45 at their hips.

The men stopped. One squinted at the sun, absorbed, it seemed, in the clatter of the helicopter. He turned and faced Neil. The other simply stood unblinking, staring at a spot six feet behind Neil's left eye.

"Nice day for a trip to the mountains, wouldn't you agree, Agent Bernstein?" the first one said. Neil heard but could not place the accent.

"What?" Neil was taken aback by the familiarity. "How do you know me? Who are you?"

"Friend of a friend, you might say."

"Really? Who might that be?" Neil nurtured the unlikely hope that these two men were forest rangers sent to find him and deliver an urgent message. Unlikely, since no one knew where he'd gone except Krissie, and even she did not know his exact location. And who knew to address him as agent? This could go south. He wondered if he was quick enough to get the second bag open and the M-11 out before one of these Bozos drew down on him.

The man smiled and nodded.

"Well, as a matter of fact, there is, now that you mention it. You can stand real still and not make a fuss and I might tell you who." These last words he accompanied by drawing and chambering a round in his pistol. The steely blue eyes, mirthless in spite of his sunny, good-natured smile, froze Neil in his tracks. So much for the Sig Sauer.

"Look," he said, hoping these two were thugs, not what the hair on the back of his neck suggested. "I haven't got much, some camping equipment, a couple of bucks." He left his gold and stainless steel Rolex off the inventory, hoping his sleeve stayed down and they would not notice it. "Take them, whatever you want, and point that thing somewhere else."

"Not interested in your stuff, son, we came to have a chat, you could say, with you."

"A chat with me! Why me? I'm nobody."

"Oh no, Sonny, you're definitely somebody. Luckily for us, we found you."

"Us? Who's us?" Neil choked. "You must have made a mistake. I'm not an…what did you call me? An agent? What, you think I sell real estate, insurance? I'm a consultant for a local government agency, that's all."

"Local government agency—that's a good one," the man said to his companion. "He says he works for the local government, Bob."

"Funny man."

"Too true."

Neil studied the men. If he could figure out what, or perhaps who these guys represented, maybe he could talk them down. Their blank eyes told him nothing. They were military in dress and demeanor, but not Army or Marine. He tried to make out the insignia on their berets. It appeared to be something like a number, fifty-one or seven centered in a star. It meant nothing to Neil. The helicopter chattered in. The sound doubled and then the machine loomed suddenly above the cliff face, rose a few feet, dropped gracefully into the valley, and beat its way toward them.

The man gestured with his pistol.

"Let's go," he shouted over the din.

"Go? Go where?" Neil yelled back.

"You're going for a little ride in the chopper." The second man spoke for the first time. Hey, don't worry," he shouted over the chopper's clattering, "It'll be a very short ride."

Neil thought irrelevantly that he had been wrong. The two were not twins at all. This one had really bad teeth.

Chapter Nine

The sun glowed orange and deep lavender to the west as Scone Island loomed on the horizon. Twilight framed it and the trees, which dominated its silhouette, grew progressively darker as they drew near.

"We will moor at the pier in The Bite, won't we, Captain?" Walter Gott merely nodded and kept a close eye on the current. The tide was on the ebb and he had to be careful where he put the keel of his boat. "The pier is very clever, Ike. Since the tides can run twelve feet or more and the bottom in the harbor shelves out a ways, the pier is built in two pieces. No, make that three. Guess how it works."

"Judging from the map I'd say there is a long arm that extends past the low tide line and a T-shaped platform at the end floats rises and falls with the tide. Then there must be a ramp or ladders from it to the permanent portion. Am I close?"

"Smart ass. You cheated."

"I did my homework, if that's what you mean by cheating. That habit has kept me vertical when others have fallen on their faces, often never to rise again. Do not knock it. Cheating saves lives."

"You are the only person I know who can make a virtue from a recognized vice and get away with it."

"I'm not the only one, just the only one of your immediate acquaintance."

"Who else, then?"

"Obviously you've been too busy to read the newspapers. When we get settled you can start with the entertainment section and witness how an adoring public celebrates the drug abuse, infidelity, greed, and theft of their idols. Then move to the business pages and—"

"Okay, okay, you are at it again. It's a vacation, Ike, come on, lighten up."

"You asked. So, can you see your cottage yet?"

"I think it's in the middle of that row to your left, the one with the widow's walk."

"Port."

"Maybe after dinner sure, but not now. The way this boat is rocking you might spill it, and I don't think Captain Gott would appreciate that."

"I thought you were a Down Easter."

"Oh, I am, whaling stock, "Down to the Sea in Ships" and all that."

"Then you should know that port means left on board a boat, not wine."

"Right. I mean left. I knew that. I was testing you, landlubber. Port, starboard, abaft and abeam and other nautical stuff."

"Amazing. Hang on, we're about to nudge the pier." The boat's motor picked up sound as Walter briefly threw the screw into reverse and then it gently bumped the pilings, which restrained the floating portion of the pier. Walter stepped quickly off the boat and dropped the aft and forward mooring lines over the small bollards at either end and signaled for Ike and Ruth to alight. Ike handed her up and turned his attention to the bags and crates stacked on the deck.

"You're gonna need some help lugging that there gear all the way to your house, Miss."

"Thank you, I guess we will. Is there anyone on the island who could do it?"

"Coupla young fellahs over at the LaFranc's place. If you don't mind paying, I'll fetch them."

"You do that," Ike said. "Some of this stuff is pretty heavy, and I'm whipped. We'll take the bags with us and the guys can bring the rest along when they can."

"Yawp."

Ike and Ruth extended the handles of their roller bags and headed up the ramp to the pier and then toward the shore.

"I have a steak and salad stuff in this plastic bag and you have the booze, right?" Ruth grinned and they set off. "A fire, a steak and salad, a couple of drinks, and who knows what therapeutic effect that will have?"

"We will soon find out. As much as I am savoring this wonderful salt air, it is getting dark and cold. Here, give me your bag. We can move more quickly if you don't have to lug that thing over this poor excuse for a path."

"It's a road."

"And I am Frank Lloyd Wright."

"Come on, Ike, get in the spirit of the thing."

"Right—feeling more spiritual already."

"Look, the moon is clearing the horizon. You can make it out in that gap between the big island and Pine Tree Island."

"You didn't tell me about the little island."

"No? Well, it's a really nice place for a picnic. When the tide is out, you can walk over to it and if you eat fast, get back before the tide comes in again."

"And if you don't?"

"Then you camp out for another nine or ten hours."

"I'll pass."

"No spirit of adventure?"

"More than once I've spent hours wet and shivering in the dark. I do not have any intention to ever do it again. So, no spirit of adventure. This whole junket is rough enough.

Charlie knew he needed to pack it in and go home, which meant a condo near Alexandria and a night spent looking at reports. He had one more thing to consider, and he wanted to do that in the relative security of his office rather than outside in a Denny's or the pizza joint on the highway. There were possibilities that lay somewhere other than with Archie Whitlock's angry exes or professionals motivated by revenge. What if it was someone inside? Charlie did not believe the director would order a hit on Archie, but there were agencies and groups that ran operations that paralleled the CIA, and all of them were understandably shy about mentioning what they were up to. Had Archie stirred up something or someone in one or another of those dark basements and did that someone, with his or her access to the agency's server, decide to send a wet squad out and snuff Archie and any future embarrassment he might cause them now that he was no longer under the agency's umbrella?

Charlie considered that possibility and realized it was equally possible the director could order such a black operation. Then it would be good cover for him to task Charlie to find a leak where there would be none. It would serve to keep Charlie occupied and out of the game while the cleaning detail did what they were ordered to do. The director knew of the relationship Charlie had with Ike, and so diverting him made sense. He did not like this new thought, but he had been in the business long enough to know that some secrets could be kept only if sent to the grave along with their keepers. Sentimentality and the "old school tie" would play no part in a decision to proceed if the risk was deemed real and the decision to eliminate made. If Archie had to go, he would be terminated and anyone who might have an embarrassing memory about him and his work would be fair game as well.

Charlie decided he would exercise option BBB, his code for going Behind the Boss' Back. He didn't like it, but there were times and occasions when one had to cover areas and possibilities others would as soon you forgot.

And in a business not known for making them, Ike was his friend.

Chapter Ten

Ike managed to broil the steaks in the antique range, barely. If they both hadn't liked their beef rare, the evening would have been a disaster. With a pre-mixed-in-a bag salad and a not quite soft, not quite done baked potato, he and Ruth dined by candlelight on the cottage's screened back porch.

"That tasted very good, all things being considered."

"By all things, you are referring to the cooking, the appliances, or the circumstances?"

"All of the above. It can't be easy to cook on this old oven, and cops aren't known for their culinary skills, are they? Then there is the fact we're both bushed. So, as I said, all things considered."

"What do you mean no culinary skills? I'll have you know I am extremely skillful, culinary wise."

"How come I've never seen any evidence?"

"Cooking takes time and patience and a settled life. Neither you nor I have a surfeit of the above."

"So when does one acquire them?"

"One must be in a domestic situation."

"And we are not domesticated."

"Not as yet, but we live in hope. The cooking arrangements will soon be better."

"Really? How so, oh mighty chef?"

"I am not a chef. A chef knows what a *confit* is. I haven't a clue. I am a cook, not a chef. To answer your question, I brought some things to make this enterprise somewhat less trying."

"That would be the booze and the chocolates?"

"No. Better. I will show you in the morning. Right now I am tired, cold—getting colder and could use a shower."

"It will take a while for the hot water heater to get us enough for a shower."

"You don't have a shower. I looked. You have a Procrustean tub with a rubber hose that has a sprinkler head on it. The hose leaks, by the way. I am willing to forgo a shower tonight. I prefer the thought of a fire in the bedroom and one of your duvets."

"I'm game if you are."

"The operative word is game."

He would demonstrate why he'd hoped there was an auxiliary tap on the propane tank in the morning. As it happened he'd found there was one and it would soon come in handy. Camping out held no attraction to Ike. Too many years spent in cold, barren hillsides, basements, and caves in what he referred to as "his other life" had created a permanent abhorrence to living rough, unless it became absolutely necessary. As far as he was concerned, this trip was not one of those occasions.

Charlie Garland tried his three contacts one last time and failed. Ike had not reported in, his deputy on duty said. Neither Halmi nor Krissie Johansen had heard from Bernstein and didn't expect to, and Al Jackson's contact had to attend his nephew's graduation in Hackensack. He didn't seem worried, though, and said he'd track Al down first thing when he was back on station.

Charlie fumed. His job involved enough probing into dark places. He shouldn't have to babysit one ex- and two active operatives. Of course, the director had reminded him of that fact earlier. It was not his job to look after them. His job was to find the leak in the system, if it was internal, and if not, to say so. Someone else would look outside to find who killed Archie and why. Or perhaps they wouldn't. Archie was off the books, out of the system, and no longer a person of interest to the agency. His demise was convenient and certain to be ruled an accident with even a slight tip of the hat in gratitude to whoever gave Archie a shove. Problem solved. Fair enough. But if he didn't alert the three men at risk so they could at least secure their perimeters, finding and fixing the leak would be meaningless on the one hand, and far more difficult on the other. That is, if the death of Archie Whitlock was, in fact, related to his past employment.

He waited five minutes and then went to the call logger to check if these last calls had been tracked like the earlier ones. They had. Now he needed the software to track the tracker. He'd been promised it the next morning. He turned out his lamp, stood, and left his office allowing the door to lock automatically. The file he'd neglected to put away still lay on his desk. He went home and slept soundly.

He nearly always did.

◇◇◇

The sun was well up before Ike woke and higher still before he realized where he was and why. In the past, this would not have been the case. In his former profession, being instantly awake and alert often was the difference between staying alive and disappearing into the black hole reserved for failed covert operatives. This morning he felt pretty good about it. It had taken a long time, but he had finally achieved the level of sleep induced fuzziness afforded normal people. It would not last, as it turned out, but on that bright May morning in the crisp chill air off the coast of Maine, he felt really good.

Ruth was no more than a soft lump completely buried in the duvet, most of which she had managed to wrap around her body, leaving Ike with barely enough to cover his considerably larger frame. Only her right hand protruded from the mound. He gently tucked it back and received a muffled grunt in response. So she wasn't dead—always a good sign. He rolled out and headed to the kitchen. He would brew a pot of coffee in the relic of a percolator and then get to work on the propane line. Chester LaFranc's sons, Ronny and Robby, had delivered the remainder of his baggage the previous night. While he waited for the coffee to cough, he set about unpacking them.

He had the major items out and assembled when Ruth, still swathed in the duvet, limped into the kitchen forty-five minutes later.

"Is that coffee I smell? Why do I have to ask? Coffee has a distinctive aroma and that, though close, is not it." She peered in the pot. "It's brown and hot. It'll have to do. Maybe we should have brought instant. I hate instant, but it can't be any worse than this stuff. What are you doing?"

"Well you might ask. Drink or do not drink out of that pot. Either way it is the last dark brown liquid—I will not dignify it as coffee—we will ever brew in it. Later this morning we will have an appropriate memorial service and consign its remains into the sea like a Viking warrior, or something less noble like Osama bin Laden."

"Are you telling me you bought a new pot for the stove?"

"Better. Check out that big box on the table."

Ruth removed a smaller box from the larger one and looked at it closely. "You're the town idiot. You can't put this on the stove. What were you thinking? This is an electric pot."

"Root around in there some more."

"Ike, this is a radio and an electric frying pan. Someone saw you coming, Bunky. You did remember that I told you there was no electricity on the island?"

"The town idiot does remember, but as he has told you on countless occasions before, he does not like roughing it, fireplaces and fluffy duvets notwithstanding. You see this apparatus here? You asked what I was doing. I am installing a generator. In a few minutes, if all goes well and the instructions, which were obviously translated from Chinese, are correct, we will have electricity. That means we can perk a decent pot of coffee, fry an egg, or read a book after six PM."

"Electricity. You mean I didn't have to bring an extra battery for my laptop after all?"

"Wait, you brought your laptop? I thought we agreed there would be no work done on this vacation."

"I wasn't going to work really, well sort of, but nothing urgent, you know. Some odds and ends I thought I could work on when you were taking a nap."

"Me, a nap? When have you ever seen me take a nap?"

"I thought you might want to start. Is it ready?"

"Let's see. Plug that lamp into this first outlet and I'll open the gas line and start it up."

The little generator he'd bought in an RV outlet store huffed to life and the lamp lit.

"Gimme that coffee pot."

Chapter Eleven

Tom Stone, whose tenure as a Hancock County deputy sheriff totaled six months the previous week, wandered down to the Bass Harbor pier looking for one of the Scone Island captains. He would be taking the launch to Scone shortly, but he thought he might get lucky and find a Gott or a LaFranc in port. Sheriff Harvey Breckinridge told him he believed it would be a good idea for Tom to "mix and mingle."

Tom looked confused. "Mix and mingle? Sorry, I…"

"Okay, Tommy, it's like this. You're new here, fresh, well almost fresh, from the police academy. The way law enforcement works here, and everywhere else for that matter, is when the guys who have to enforce it become part of the community in which they work. You need to get out and talk to people, and Scone Island is yours for the time being."

"Okay, I can see that. What do I talk about?"

"Right. You need a reason. So, I'm looking at the coroner's report on that accident out on Scone, and something smells a little off, you know. Like lunch meat that has been in the meat keeper a tad too long. Suspicious, but not a health hazard yet."

"Something's not right?"

"Well, maybe. That's not important. It's a reason to talk, see?" Harvey picked up a manila folder. "A fall of sixty feet onto rocks," it says here, "doesn't leave much in the way of bruises that can't be explained as resulting from the fall, but—" Harvey looked up with raised eyebrows. The *but* caught Tommy's attention. A *but* could mean a lot of things. Did the coroner have some doubts? Or was there too much tissue damage to tell anything, but the lab tests were inconclusive for alcohol in spite of what the man who retrieved the body said and maybe there was a thing or two needing a look out there? No thoughts about changing the investigation's outcome, of course, but asking a few questions couldn't hurt. Whatever the cause, substance abuse or stupidity, it would stay on the books as an accident. Unless the *but* converted into hard evidence to the contrary.

"But what? Did he see something that shouldn't be there?"

"Maybe. The description we were given of the body's position suggests…"

"What?"

"Patience, son. It's a long shot, but the report said this guy, Staley, was lying face down on the rocks. If he didn't hit anything on the way down, then there is a really bad contusion on the back of his head that has to be accounted for, that's all."

"On the back of his head. Not front? So the doc is saying that the victim might have been sapped from the rear and dropped over the cliff. That a killer might have assumed the fall to the rocks below would cover any wounds he might have received beforehand?"

"He's not saying, Tommy, but that was my thought. We can't possibly support a conclusion outside of accidental death without more evidence."

"What kind of evidence?"

"The coroner says the wound on the back of Mr. Staley's head looks like it could have been made with a pipe or round, heavy metal object."

"A pry bar, tire iron?"

"Possibly. I'd rule out tire iron. No cars on the island, not likely there'd be a tire iron."

"So you want me to what? Look for a blunt instrument… investigate?"

"No, not really. I think you should keep your ears open, naturally, and a hypothetical knock on the head is enough to give you an excuse to slip out there and talk to the locals, you see? Maine folk are not given to idle chit-chat, as you know, but if you have a reason…"

"Right, chat with the locals, get the feel for the place and who knows, something might turn up."

"Talk to Miss Smithwick. She found the body. Maybe she will remember something we didn't pick up on before."

"Boss, for the record, do you think it wasn't an accident?"

"Didn't say that, son, but you need to think like that. Otherwise you will appear to be wasting taxpayer's time and money. These folks are quick to pick up on someone who isn't telling the truth."

"So I need to believe it wasn't an accident."

"Classic police work, Tommy. Always assume there is something else until the case is cold. And even then, keep an open mind. You'd be surprised at the stuff that pops up sometimes years after we've closed a file. Oh, one more thing. There is an out-of-town cop out there. You might drop by and introduce yourself. His name is Ike Schwartz. I gather he's worth knowing."

"How so?"

"I called his office and then Googled him."

"You Googled a cop?"

"Yep. Interesting guy if the crap on the Internet is halfway right. And he doesn't want anyone to know he's out there. A cop has enough trouble taking a vacation as you will soon discover. So, off you go."

The police launch, its twin Chrysler marine engines throbbing, gentled to the pier. The exhaust made a small dent in the chronic smell of fish that harked back to the town's packing days. It was mostly tourist now, but the lobstermen and fishing boats still worked from the little seaport on Mt. Desert Island. High tide made the approach easy.

Tom Stone spent the better part of the morning in Henry Potter's Store, the one-room combination mail-drop, bait shop, and necessaries—Potter's term for the odds and ends he carried for people who forgot to order groceries on time. The array of goods available in that category assumed people could survive on packages of peanut butter crackers, stale potato chips, and Spam. He also had coffee in plain brown packages and three kinds of beer. All of his goods were priced anywhere from 80 to 120 percent above the same goods in Bass Harbor which, in turn, were significantly higher than nearly anywhere else. All this was true except for the coffee. Since it had no label, comparisons could not be made.

Tom discovered that Potter had some very decided views about the death of Harmon Staley. He thought that Staley might have been part of a secret organization at one time, he said.

"A secret organization? What kind? You don't think he was running a terrorist cell or anything, do you?" Tom wondered why he even asked. Terrorist cell?

"Naw, nothing like that, Deputy. See, when I went out there after Miz Smithwick told me about him taking a nose dive off the cliff, like, I am pretty sure I saw a big old radio antenna out behind the little house and—"

"Little house?"

"Oh, yeah. He had two houses out there. The big house is all gone to rack and ruin, but the little one, it was a guest house in the old days, is where he was living while he worked on the repairs on the big one. 'Course never happen, then or now."

"What would never happen?"

"Fixing the big one up. He said as how he was into making it into a bed and breakfast or something like that. Never happen. Who'd come out here and pay to stay in an old broke-down house with no electricity, telephone, and such?"

"You live here."

"But I ain't no tourist, neither. No sir, the summer folks come here exactly because they like the no phone and electricity thing. No accounting for taste, they say. But you think some New York fella'll come up here for a stay like that. Don't seem likely."

"You said you saw an antenna?"

"Oh yeah. I did. Then yesterday, I was up that way to check on some of the empty places, the Dankos and the Banks and them, and I took a stroll out to the end of the point and, bingo, no antenna. So what does that mean?"

"Wind knocked it over?"

"No, sir, some of his people came and cleaned up the mess."

"You think?"

Potter laid a finger on one side of his nose. "Not for nothing the Island was used by the Army intelligence in World War II."

"It was?"

"Yawp. Not everybody knows it, but it were."

Tom left Potter and his conspiracy theories and after getting directions from the old man, set out to find the sheriff from Virginia that his boss had Googled.

Chapter Twelve

Al Jackson credited the United States Army for turning his life around. He insisted on that point in spite of the fact that during his tenure in the uniformed service he'd narrowly missed being blown apart by an IED in Iraq, received a nasty thigh wound from friendly fire in a place in South America he was not allowed to talk about and to which the DoD denied ever having deployed troops, and there was an incident with a drill sergeant early on that landed him in the stockade for six days before his talents were recognized and he was passed along to a group that knew how to use them. He liked that life even better.

All this started inauspiciously enough. He'd flunked out of Morgan State University after one semester and seemed on the verge of being absorbed into the west Baltimore gang culture when a judge offered him a wholly illegal choice, but the judge was an old-fashioned man and also not up for re-election. "Go to jail or join the Army," he'd said. Since Al had no priors, the Army was available. He took the deal and reported for basic training a week later. The judge was able to expedite that as well. The Army trained him in skills he'd never dreamed existed. Special Forces, sniper school, jump school, and in the midst of that and the action it engendered, he discovered he had a facility for languages. That led him to more schools, some deep JSOC initiated covert action, and eventually all the way into covert ops with the CIA.

To anyone who asked, he'd say he was muscle. Operatives, field agents, they had the brains and they ran the ops. Al's job hinged on how much shooting and explosive work needed to be done—at what range and what order of magnitude respectively. He found his new life, played out in the dark and violent world of covert operations, exactly what he seemed best suited for and he hoped he'd live forever or, failing that, cash in his chips while on some exotic operation in a hail of bullets. He was a romantic that way, you could say.

The SEALS got the Osama gig, a fact which annoyed him immensely, and now, as business seemed slow with the new Administration in Washington, he'd been told to stand down. He knew that being placed on extended leave meant either going slightly crazy or getting into trouble. For anyone else, leave with pay would be considered a soft berth. Not for Al. He feared getting rusty. Yet in his line of work, there were not many opportunities for him to practice his skill set outside the confines of the Company. Organized crime could use him and the gangbangers he knew as a youth could too, but he did not see either as a healthy option. Then there were a dozen petty despots around the world desperate to hold onto power at any cost, another possibility, but Uncle Sam still paid his bills and as long as that was so, he would not stray—not far, at least. If the conditions of his employment were to change, however… Anyway, he worried he might have lost a step. Maybe he was not as quick as he should be. And maybe that is why he ended up very dead in Pig Town one Saturday night.

He'd taken in a twi-night doubleheader at Camden yards—Chicago White Sox and the Orioles, and had left during the fifth inning of the second game. May nights, irrespective of the hype from Major League baseball, were not warm enough to play night games, at least not in Baltimore. He was cold, and his team had already nose dived into its expected position at the bottom of the American League East. He, as well as a dwindling fan base in the city, blamed that fact on the "Lawyer." The man had bought a team that in the old days regularly went to the playoffs and the World Series and he'd turned it into a mediocrity. He mourned for his Birds.

He'd parked some ten blocks away from the ballpark, thinking the exercise would keep him sharp, and had been walking back to his car when he was gunned down. The police only knew Al as an ex-GI with gang connections going back a few years. He had no visible means of support, albeit he had money in his pocket when they found him in a pool of blood in Traci Adkins Park near Ramsay Street. They ran a sweep of the neighborhood, talked to the two witnesses who came forward, and classified the case as another drive-by, probably gang-related, and figured they'd never find the shooter.

It was the weekend and Al's control had been caught in a ten-car pile-up on the New Jersey Turnpike. He was one of a half-dozen people sent to local hospitals for treatment of minor injuries and whiplash. It is the sad consequence of a life that requires you to be invisible that you tend to remain that way even after you die. Al Jackson would remain unknown and unmourned for three days, until his control finally tracked him down in the Baltimore city morgue wearing a toe tag that could have belonged to anybody. This lapse would prove critical, but not the way one would expect.

◇◇◇

Eden Saint Clare had room service deliver a bagel and cream cheese, orange juice, and coffee to her room. She sat, nibbled, and sipped by the room's only window and contemplated Lake Michigan. She shivered. The mere act of looking at the lake could give you a chill, especially in the fall and early spring. In the winter, when the ice piled up on the breakwaters, the experience shifted from chilling, to cold, to arctic. She'd not spent enough time in Chicago during the summer to know if a lake view ever felt anything but gelid. After this last trip, she would probably never have a reason to find out. She pulled her robe tighter around her shoulders and turned her attention to her complimentary copy of *USA Today.* If anything big and important was in the news, it would be in the paper, she thought, and maybe then she could figure out if Charlie's call was merely social or carried the scent of danger. She smiled—scent of danger. A nice turn of phrase, she thought. An editor might disagree.

The paper, as usual, had all the same-o, same-o stories she'd read in one version or another for the last decade or so; trouble in the Mideast, economic woes, the myriad shootings here and there across the nation, political guesswork by people who denied they were guessing but who in fact were. Pundits. The trouble with *USA Today,* she believed, was that it did not carry the comics. A crossword puzzle it had, and Sudoku, but no easy relief from the dreariness brought on by the contents in the remainder of the paper. At least the *Chicago Tribune* had funnies. Years spent trolling the slightly Marxist halls of academe had biased her against the *Trib*, naturally. In fairness to it and papers like it, she believed one could make a case for the editorial page being a sort of an auxiliary to the comics. Her Tea Partying sister-in-law had become quite angry when she'd said as much at their last meeting.

Her husband's body was a heartbeat away from following his mind to wherever it had gone years before. Heaven or hell, she didn't know. Religion did not play importantly in her married life before, and now it did not offer the comfort it might have, had she been open to it. For a brief moment she wondered if maybe that had been a mistake. Lawyers, hairdressers, and piano bars provided poor sources of solace. She brushed aside these too-deep-for-nine-in-the-morning thoughts, set aside the cup and bagel ends. It was time to dress and head to the lawyer's office to meet the sister-in-law. Why couldn't people just die and be buried? Why must the surviving relatives fight over everything from who gets the rose medallion bowl to the burial allotment from the Social Security Administration?

She had the bellman call her a cab and waited inside the revolving doors and out of the chill until it drove up and the doorman signaled to her. Had she turned around and glanced at the desk, she might have noticed the tallish man in the blue suit inquiring after her at the desk. But she didn't turn and didn't see him.

Chapter Thirteen

"Now that we have settled into almost livable domesticity and have the promise of uninterrupted time, maybe we can take some of it and plan what happens next. This summer we could—"

Ruth put her coffee cup down with a loud click—the sort of gesture that signaled she wanted the floor, and looked up from the papers in her lap.

"I've been reading this book I found in Aunt Margaret's desk. It's something the residents put together years ago and—"

"Did I hear a change of subject?" Ike had been careful about using the "W" word while Ruth healed and waged war with her barons, his name for the department chairpersons and deans who vied for space, money, and attention from the Queen, that is to say, Ruth. Now, as he floated plans for a wedding they, like the proverbial trial balloon made of lead, sank.

"Okay, okay, Ike, I promise, when we get back to Picketsville, we'll have a serious talk, weddings I mean. But we're here on this little island recuperating. We are alone, well mostly so. We have no responsibilities, no one knocking on the door, no cops with problems, no academics with complaints, no students with roommate issues."

"No cops in sight, true, no student or faculty either, but it's you who's recuperating. I'm along for the ride and the pleasure of your company, of course."

"Baloney. You had a bad patch of your own to go through only yours was political while mine was—"

"All of the above. But do not forget that the political took a back seat to a friend in a hospital bed."

"Sorry, you're right. Were you really so strung out?"

"Me? Hah."

"Right, my man of steely nerves and true grit. Did I ever thank you for being that for me?"

"How could you? You were asleep, remember?"

"You can't remember being asleep. Only going there and waking up."

"No dreams?"

"Many, but none remembered or worth repeating. We'll talk later, Ike, okay?"

"Okay. For now we live in the moment; *carpe diem*. Tell me about your book while I mop up the last of my breakfast with the last of your toast."

"The book is called *Scone Island Stories*. Clever, huh? They're all from the years between the two big wars, amazing fish caught, things that happened at the annual Fourth of July picnic, snipe hunts. Gracious, does everybody get snookered into a snipe hunt sometime before they're ten? And there are some legends. The island was once thought to be named… I can't quite read this. I think it's *Wôboz* something. Native American, I think it means Deer Island."

"There's another island with that name south of here, I think."

"I expect it's a pretty common name up and down the east coast, the Great Lakes and points south, west, and north, but that's not the point. The legend is that Indians would canoe out here once a year to hunt. There was a herd of deer on the island. God only knows how they, that is the deer, managed to cross over four miles of ocean to get here. Anyway, the island was like a deer ranch. They'd paddle out, shepherd the deer to the narrow end of the island, thin out the herd, smoke it, make jerky, whatever, and pack it back to the mainland. The remaining deer would then breed and make more venison for the next year."

"Fascinating. What other amazing stories have you for me?"

"You are such a clunk."

"A what?"

"Clunk. This form of hunting is very interesting from a historical point of view. Cattle tending of any sort would be unusual in this culture and at that time. Only a clunk would miss that."

"The clunk inquires, how is this example different from plains Indians chasing buffalo over a cliff?"

"Don't be difficult. It is different. The bison were running wild and were hunted across miles of prairie while the deer were limited to…never mind. It was different"

"If you say so. A difference without a distinction…or is it the other way round?"

Ruth turned some pages while Ike rinsed and stacked the dishes. "The other way round. Okay, here's one you'll love. It's titled *Indian Romeo and Juliet*."

"Don't tell me. Let me guess. It's the legend of two star-crossed lovers kept apart by unfeeling parents who tragically die rather than submit to a callous disregard for true love?"

"You've already heard it? Yep, they ran away one night while the hunt was on when the tide was out, and fled to Pine Tree Island. That's the little island I pointed out to you when we arrived. You can see it on the map down near Southport. So, they went to the island at low tide only it had a different name then, naturally."

"Verona."

"Don't get smart.

"*Two households, both alike in dignity, in fair Verona, where we lay our scene…*"

"Very good. Can you recite more? Never mind. I don't want to hear it. Aunt Margaret's husband, Uncle Oscar, could recite all of Shakespeare's sonnets by heart."

"All?"

"That's what he said. I never called him on it."

"My father said he knew a rabbi once who could recite all of David's psalms that way."

"And could he?"

"Well, since he did them in Hebrew, how could you tell? Abe never knew for sure how many if any. But he said he was impressive to listen to."

"No doubt. So, back to the story. The tide roared in. It can run up to fifteen feet sometimes. The parents couldn't get to them to stop them from you know what."

"I can imagine."

"Of course you can, and then some. So, when the tide went out again and the hunters ran out to the island, they found them dead in each other's arms."

"Wow. Why didn't the parents paddle out to the little island in their canoes and fetch the naughty children home?"

"I don't know. Why can't you go along with the story?"

"Right. Very touching. Anything else in that book I should know about?"

"Well, someone, Aunt Margaret I guess, penciled in a list of names of the Coast Guard officers and men who served on the island and…let's see, shore artillery personnel, ditto. They were written in by hand. You think Aunt Margaret might have had a suitor?"

"I thought you told me the summer residents did not use the island during the war."

"Oh, right. Well, I thought so, but here are the names. Someone wrote them down for a reason, don't you think? I wonder why."

"Ah-ha. The Hardy Boys and the Mystery of Scone Island. Did you check the closet for old love letters, treasure maps?"

"Don't get smart."

"Dumbing down. So, what's on tap for the day?"

"I think we have enough stuff here to make sandwiches. I found bottle of red wine with a good year in the pantry and we can stop at Mr. Potter's store for some chips. This afternoon we'll pack a picnic, sun screen, and blankets and go out to Pine Tree Island like the lovers."

"What if the tide comes roaring in? You did say it roared."

"I did. No problem, landlubber, I have a tide table. We will go out to the island on the ebb and return before the flood, we'll have had our fun and walk back, simple."

"Whenever I hear someone describe a thing as simple, I worry. Okay, picnic it is, but add another purchase at the store. I think it might rain. I want a poncho at least."

"Rain? Poncho? Not a chance."

Chapter Fourteen

While Ruth manufactured sandwiches and scurried around looking for another corkscrew and blankets, Ike adjusted the fittings on his generator, checking for gas leaks and randomly plugging and unplugging the several appliances he'd packed in one or other of the crates the LaFranc boys left on Ruth's front porch. He didn't expect a knock at the door, and the sound startled him momentarily. Ruth managed to beat him to the front of the house to answer it.

"Good morning," the guy said through the screen door. "I am Deputy Thomas Stone, and you must be Ruth Harris."

"Must I? Well, I suppose I must. How do you do, Deputy Stone? Is there something I can do for you?"

Ike perked up. What had brought one of Harvey Breckinridge's deputies out to the island? Had Frank called? Was there trouble that he couldn't handle? That didn't seem likely after the lecture he'd given Essie and Frank before he left. It would have to be something really big. He rounded the porch and headed for the front door.

"Deputy," he said. "Did Harvey send you?"

"Excuse me, but are you Sheriff Schwartz?"

"Yes, and you have news for me?"

"News?"

"You're here. I assume your boss sent you for a reason."

"Well, yes he did."

"And?"

"And what?"

"This conversation is enormously entertaining," Ruth said. "But informative it is not. Let's go inside, drink decent coffee, and Deputy Stone can tell us why he is here." She ushered the two men into the parlor and set the coffee pot to strong. "Can I ask a personal question, Deputy?"

"What? Oh, certainly."

"How long have you been a Deputy Sheriff?"

"Well, not very long, actually."

"I only ask because I spent most of last October and November in a hospital where all the physical therapists and doctors looked like they were maybe twelve years old. It is a function of advancing age, I guess. Any way, you fall into the barely over a decade plus category."

"Me? I assure you, I am not twelve, Ma'am."

"No, of course you're not. I am sorry. That was rude of me. It comes from spending too much time with the old sheriff here."

"Don't pay her any attention. She's off her medication. When she gets like this we have to send her to her room for an hour or two."

Tom Stone looked from one to the other like someone who had courtside seats at Wimbledon. Finally he said, "You two have been together for a while, am I right?"

"Mercy, how can you tell?"

Stone started to answer and then thought better of it. "I think you asked me a question a while back…before you began your SNL skit here. Sorry, but I forgot what it was."

"Right. I asked if you were sent out here for a reason and do I need to hear why?"

"For a reason? Well, yes. The sheriff wants me to get to know the people on the island, especially the year-round residents. Actually they're not really year-round. Most of them come to the mainland in the fall, especially if they have kids in school, but some of the old-timers stick it out, they tell me. See, I'm new to the area and I need to get familiar with the island and the people on it."

"And you need to get to know them because…?"

"Oh, for the time being, the island will be my responsibility, my beat you could say. And so I need to 'mix and mingle.' That's how the sheriff put it."

"So you're here to talk to the locals. We are not local. You are here. Is there a reason for that?"

"Um…I'm not sure what you mean."

"Deputy, I left instructions with my people back in Virginia that they could reach me through your boss if there was a huge emergency. You are here. Is there an emergency?"

"No, sir, none that I know of. Wait, you thought…Oh, I see. Sorry. No, the sheriff, he Googled you and told me if I was to get a chance, I should look you up. So here I am."

"I was Googled?"

"Sounds positively salacious," Ruth said.

"It does, doesn't it? Well, Deputy. I've been Googled and you have found me. What can I do for you?"

"The sheriff said he mentioned the death we had out here to you and asked if you would kind of, like, keep your ears open."

"A Mr. Staley did a swan dive off the cliff after a having a close relationship with a bottle of whiskey, yes he did."

"Did he mention the ME's report to you?"

"Not really, the final hadn't come in. Is there something in it I should know?"

"Oh, crap, here we go." Ruth put her coffee mug down on the table with a bang. Some of the liquid splashed out and on to *Scone Island Stories*. "Ike, don't you dare go off and play cop. We are on vacation and you promised."

"I have no intention of doing anything but lie around the house being useless. I am merely chatting with my young colleague here. He has a job to do and I am only showing a courteous and professional but dispassionate interest in it."

"Bullshit."

"If an academic type arrived at our door, some history wonk itching to discuss the phenomenon of aboriginal deer herding, you would jump right in, march all over the island looking for campsites, pottery shards, or whatever, vacation or no."

"It's not the same."

"It is. So, relax. You spilled your coffee all over your book, by the way. Deputy, go on."

"Well, I…"

"Don't mind me," Ruth huffed. "I am the hostess here. I will get a rag and more coffee. Pray continue. But, I warn you, Ike, if I hear even a hint of police procedure, you will…there's a second bedroom you know, and it may not have a duvet."

Ruth left the room.

"Go on, deputy. What was in the ME's report?"

"Nothing solid. A question about a wound to the back of the head that had to be explained if the man had fallen free to the bottom of the cliff. See, he was face down so—"

"Unless he hit something on the way down that flipped him, he might have been helped over the edge."

"Yes."

"What do you know about him?"

"Not much, really. His name was Harmon Staley. He arrived about a year ago and bought the place at the end of the island. He said he was going to fix it up and turn it into a tourist thing."

"Relatives, family, heirs?"

"None that we can find. Born in Kansas someplace on a farm or something, parents dead, no siblings, not married and no connections anywhere. That could create a problem or two right there. I mean what happens to the property? And then there was a guy out here trying to buy up places and he's sort of stuck. Captain Gott told me he was real anxious to get the dead man's house and all."

"Buying? Who?"

"A man named Frank Barstow. According to Mr. Potter, he pestered Staley a lot. I guess he wanted his place especially or something."

"Pestered?"

"That's what he said."

"Well, I don't know about the Maine law on abandoned property, but I'm sure they will sort out the business at probate. There must be a statute on the books that covers it. When they do, Barstow… you did say his name was Frank Barstow?"

"Yes, sir."

"He could acquire it then. It might take some time, but if he really needs or wants it, he will be able to get it. Anything else?" Ike frowned. Barstow, he'd heard that name before but could not remember where or when, but definitely in the last year. Frank Barstow—something like that but different. Not an ordinary name

"Nothing…well, it's pretty off the charts, but Mr. Potter thinks he saw a radio antenna on the place when he went out there to see the body and then it was not there later."

"A radio antenna?"

"That's what he said. He thinks Mr. Staley was a spy or conspirator of some sort."

"Does he really?" Ike sat and stared at the coffee stained booklet on the table. It was all too neat—the biography, the fall, and Barstow. An antenna? How likely was that? "Maybe you and I should take a walk out there and have a look around."

"Ike, you do and you sleep on the porch." If looks could kill, Ike thought.

"It's only curiosity, Ruth. No police anything. If you don't believe me, come with us. You need to exercise that leg. Then you will see for yourself that I really am on vacation."

"You think you can bluff me off with that old move? I know you, Schwartz. You bet I'm coming, and I have my eye on you, too, Deputy Stone."

"Yes, ma'am."

Chapter Fifteen

The Las Vegas Police Department responded to a 9-1-1 call from a frantic tourist at four-thirty AM, He reported the body of a middle-aged woman lay in an alley near Circus Circus. He thought she might be dead. He did not leave his name nor remain on the scene for the police when they arrived. The LVPD did not consider that unusual. Tourists in Las Vegas have little enough time to get into trouble without wasting any of it in a police station giving statements. What did seem unusual, if anything in Sin City can be so described, was that the body had been reported so promptly. The usual drill would be for folks to step around an inert figure. It wasn't that they were callous. They either didn't want to be involved or assumed it was another drunk or a homeless person. Probably both. Their vacations were short enough, and reporting a body and spending time with the police could cut into what little time they had left.

The location of the body also struck the homicide cops as odd because it was in a well lit and often frequented throughway paralleling a parking garage close to the casino side entrance. Surely there had to have been witnesses. But no one came forward to admit having seen or heard anything. The woman's purse and any ID she may have been carrying was missing, of course. Her clothes were all new and the labels in them were the sort found in any low budget clothing store in the country. Even her shoes could have come from anywhere. Gone were the days when a drycleaner would mark his work or when a piece of clothing, a scarf, or glove could be traced by its label to the store where it had been purchased and thence to its wearer. Mass marketing, Internet buying, and nationally franchised stores had effectively blurred the lines of consumer society. For all the impressive new techniques used to identify suspects and victims that advanced forensic science had introduced into the art of detection, it seemed capitalism had removed nearly an equal number. All anyone could venture to surmise was she'd apparently been mugged and robbed, a distressingly common occurrence in modern urban America. An autopsy might provide more information, but the detective who'd pulled the case doubted it.

The local CSI team arrived, documented the scene, and had it cleared for pedestrian use in record time. It is not good business to have bodies, robberies, and murders this close to the Strip. If tourists start to hear about or experience that sort of thing, they could stop coming to Vegas, and that would mean they would spend their vacation savings somewhere else. This latest victim was packed into an ambulance and borne away. She would lie on a cold slab in the city morgue waiting for the ME to do an autopsy. In the meantime someone would be sent to flash her picture around in the nearby casinos and ask some perfunctory questions, and her finger prints would eventually be run through AFIS. Her DNA might or might not be sent through the system as well, but in any case it would take three weeks to get any analysis if they wanted it, and would cost money from an already thin operating budget. Sending the DNA sample out would be a last resort. The sensible course of action, and the one that had always yielded results in the past: the Department would wait for the inevitable missing persons bulletin to arrive in a few days or weeks.

It never failed. Some desperate relatives in some Midwestern city—Minneapolis, Chicago, Urbana-Champaign, wherever—would have failed to hear from a missing wife, aunt, mother, or daughter, and they'd would have gone to their local cops who in turn would forward the MPB to Las Vegas, the destination to which the missing person had indicated she was headed. When it arrived in a day, week, or month, they'd connect the dots and a grieving child, spouse, nephew, or parent would arrive, identify the body and make arrangements to have her shipped home in a box, large or small, or as likely, leave her behind in a local columbarium. As the slogan goes, "What happens in Vegas stays in Vegas."

Nothing changes.

Cora Dinwiddie had watched the television drama *CSI* since its first episode aired on October 6, 2000. Thus, the fact that the Las Vegas police consigned her body to a refrigerated shelf at the Las Vegas city morgue could only be described as ironic. Cora was born in Eureka Springs, Arkansas, forty years previously. After high school she married a classmate who joined the Marines, and after his basic training they had moved about the country as service families do. When he was posted to Okinawa, she stayed behind. Absence makes the heart grow fonder, it is alleged, and in Cora's case it made her grow fonder of Earl, an over-the-road trucker. Her Marine forgotten, she traveled across the country with Earl to Los Angeles, where she discovered her new love already had a wife and two children, none of whom he was prepared to abandon. Cora contemplated her options and settled on a career as a bartender, rather than the steadier but more perilous work available on the streets.

Dinwiddie did not strike her as an appropriate name for southern California. She changed it, more or less legally, to Sharpe. That name she borrowed from the title of a novel one of her customers left on the bar. She thought the extra E on the end looked classy. It was some years, and a few more job changes later, that she met Archie Whitlock. Their time together, she would tell to anyone willing to listen, had been exciting, maddening, and frequently dangerous. It lasted long enough for them to marry and separate. She didn't bother with the formality of a divorce from Archie because, first, she had grown to fear him and what he might do if she pressed the issue, and second, she hadn't bothered to get divorce from her Marine earlier and thought that fact might emerge in a court hearing. So she simply walked away. But she kept her married name, Cora Sharpe Whitlock—classy.

Imagine her amazement then, when she'd seen Archie, after all those years, in McCarran International, on his way east, he'd said. He told her he'd retired and was living on an island in Maine. She didn't know whether to believe him or not, but in any case declined his invitation to take up where they'd left off. He looked awful, and besides, she didn't want to risk another go-round with him, his drinking, and the crazy things he did when he lost his temper. She'd almost forgotten the meeting until the man at the blackjack table where she was playing happened to ask about Archie. He said they had "a mutual friend." He looked pretty hot, as her friend Deloris would say, so she agreed to have dinner with him and who knew? Over coffee and during their subsequent chat, she said she was done with the old spy and good riddance.

That was almost a month ago and she'd forgotten all about both the man and Archie Whitlock. Then a guy stopped her in the alley and mumbled her name. She stopped, turned to run, but ran head first into another guy who was bigger and faster. She was processing that fact when everything went black. She never made it back to Circus Circus.

Chapter Sixteen

West Road did not appear any smoother north of Ruth's cottage than the more southern portion she and Ike had taken from the pier. Ice or some manifestation of the snowfall, frost at least, had lifted up large clumps of dirt and gravel and created what looked like the reverse of potholes, which gave the road the appearance of a plowed field. Ruth still suffered from a low-level foot-drop, which worsened as she grew tired. She had to be careful where she stepped so as not to trip. Her expression suggested she was having second thoughts about accompanying the two men on this excursion, but the thought, however remote, of Ike being drawn into a police investigation drove her on.

"How are you doing there, Gimpy?"

Ruth, who was lagging behind the other two ignored Ike, and gritted her teeth against the ache in the muscles of her still healing leg.

Ike turned back to Stone. "How much farther, Deputy?"

"You can see the roof from here. That's the big house. The guest house, where Staley actually lived, is to the left."

"Where did Mr. Potter say he saw an antenna?"

"I think it was behind the guest house or something."

"What," Ruth wondered aloud, "would the man need a radio antenna for?"

"Mr. Potter thought he might be signaling ships at sea or sending messages out."

"To whom and why?"

"He didn't say. I think he had thoughts of terrorist cells or gun runners."

"You have a lot of that up here in Maine? Gun runners and terrorists?"

"No experience with gun running, for sure. We leave that to Arizona and the Feds, but we have a pretty porous border up here and an easy one for folks to cross over from Canada. The Canadians aren't as touchy about who comes and goes as we are."

Ike smiled and stopped in the path to let Ruth catch up. "You okay?"

"Dandy. So, he's saying that this dead bed-and-breakfast guy is sending messages to illegals on the other side of the state?"

"Meaning no disrespect to Mister Potter, our village sage, I rather doubt we will find an operating radio antenna or any evidence of one. If your man wished to send messages surely he would use a phone."

Stone frowned. "Well, that would be mighty fine, Sheriff, but I reckon you forgot there's no service out here."

"Would be if you wanted it."

"How's that possible?" Stone kicked idly at a pebble and missed.

"Yeah, how's that possible?" Ruth had caught up and the idea of a phone had her attention.

"An Iridium phone."

"Say again."

"A satellite phone. You can speak to anyone, anywhere in the world with a satphone. It doesn't need towers or lines, just a clear path to the satellite and a means of keeping the batteries charged. A generator would do that."

"You think he had a phone?"

"No, I don't. I said if he had wanted to communicate with anyone on the outside, a radio would be the least likely option. So, antenna also not likely."

"Why don't we have one of those, what did you call it?"

"Satphone."

"Exactly. Why don't we have one?" Ruth had barely heard of the devices and their availability to people generally. Her preoccupation with all things academic meant she had not caught up with the twenty-first century's latest societal menace: the rapid dissemination and easy availability of military-grade technology throughout the global economy. It was a phenomenon many thought posed a greater danger to society than drug trafficking. Weapons, sophisticated communications equipment, explosive devices, anything an army might have or need to wage a modest scale war was now equally available to any crackpot or crazy who could visit a gun show, knew someone who knew someone, or who had the cash pay for it. Navy SEALs were not the only people in possession of the means to extract a perceived enemy from a foreign country. The Air Force was not the only entity capable of launching a missile, not to mention the SAMs, SCUDS, and other acronymous weaponry that might in turn threaten a commercial airliner, factory, or power plant anywhere in the world. Indeed, Air Force One could be brought down by an unemployed plumber with anger issues. It was a sobering thought.

"If you had a working phone, Ruth, it would be only a matter of time before you would use it and then all the careful maneuvering we did to find privacy and protection would be gone. I thought you wanted to be incommunicado."

"I do. Still it would beat all those throwaways you bought on the way up."

"They are for emergencies and they do not work out here."

"Okay, okay, I'm just saying."

Three moderately experienced rock climbers from Denver found a body at the foot of the cliff sometime shortly after dawn. One of them had to walk down the dry streambed for a mile and found a signal strong enough to call 9-1-1. It was another two hours before the Barratt police department's forensics team and ambulance showed up. Technically, although the area was in a federal preserve, accidents in this area were routinely handled locally. They deployed their people and quickly vetted the area.

The dead man's camp, they noted, had been hastily set up. There was no evidence of a fire, for example. They concluded that the dead man must have rushed his climb.

The Barratt police department had experience with these accidents. City people with little or no experience thought they could graduate from a climbing wall to a real monster like this one without any intermediate training or testing. Every year, it seemed some idiot fell and broke a leg, an arm, or worse, like this one, where the fall was fatal. They took statements from the Denver people, cautioned them against trying anything too difficult too soon themselves, and guessed by the look of the three climbers that the chances were pretty good they'd be back the next day to pick up another corpse.

Corporal Sandy Ansona circled the grassy plain before they left, in the off chance he might stumble across something the others had missed. Sandy was thorough to the point of being a major pain in the ass to the rest of the team.

"Come on, Sandy, this dude thought he was Spider Man and cashed out. Let's pack this in right now," his partner yelled.

Sandy waved and continued his circuit. He spent a moment studying the odd disturbances in the grass at the grassy area's center. He stopped and inspected the grass. Before he was a cop, he was a grunt in Iraq and he recognized the swirl pattern a helicopter makes when it lands. What he couldn't do is tell how long it had been there. The presence of a chopper in the area might or might not be important. He took a picture. Satisfied he'd seen everything and that he'd correctly identified it, he headed back to the crime scene van. He stopped one last time to look at the creek bed, frowned, removed his pocket camera and shot three pictures of the sand in the center. He walked fifty yards farther along and did it again. Then he rejoined the others and they drove off with the remains of Neil Bernstein, late of the CIA, in the back of the van.

◇◇◇

The police ran Neil's fingerprints through the usual databases all of which yielded nothing. His driver's license eventually led to an address of convenience in the suburbs of Washington, D.C., but there was no missing persons bulletin on the wire about him. The chief did not like the way all of this was beginning to shake out. Unless he was a fugitive, any normal person should be easily connected with family or employer or someone one way or another. But this guy—it looked like he was deliberately off the grid. And there was that call from some guy named Garland. What if they connected? He inspected Bernstein's belongings and then called in the lieutenant. Two guys in fatigues showed up later and spent some time in the chief's office. An hour later, to no one's surprise, and without an autopsy, the men left after a final word with the chief. The body was picked up by an out-of-town mortuary the next morning. Bernstein's file disappeared. The chief seemed pleased with the outcome.

Corporal Ansona watched the whole thing out of the corner of his eye and said nothing.

◇◇◇

Charlie finally heard from the station agent in Chicago. Eden Saint Clare was at the Fairmount. He sent a message to keep her under surveillance and to trace her phone calls. He brushed aside the question about a warrant to do so. He did not have time for that. Chicago demurred.

"If you think you need one, get one, but start the traces now." He hung up. New kid on the block, he thought. He'll learn. When the phone rang twenty seconds later, he sighed and picked up. "Yes, that is what I said, now move."

Chapter Seventeen

There wasn't much to see at Cliffside. As expected, the two houses were so rundown as to call into question what their late owner had in mind. To renovate them and open a B-and-B seemed very unlikely. There was no sign of an antenna, radio or otherwise.

"Well, I guess Mr. Potter was seeing things." Stone looked slightly embarrassed at having dragged Ike and Ruth, especially with her bad leg, out to the end of the island.

"We should check the back yard." Ike led the way around the house toward the farthest reach of the island. A rusty and very twisted framework that in better days could have been a mast of some sort lay in the grass.

Ruth found a nearly flat tree stump and sat down. Somewhere nearby a fruit tree was in bloom. She did not know her scents and could not tell if it was an apple, pear, or peach, but it marginally brightened her day. "There's your radio mast, Deputy, but I don't think it will send any messages any time soon."

"Not a radio mast." Ike stepped over for a closer look.

"What is it then?" Ruth said.

"I'm guessing it was part of, or a precursor to, the Maine Mesonet at one time."

"The what?"

"Mesonet is a weather data collecting system that consists of towers like this one here and all sorts of recording apparatus. They are strung across the country in most states and record wind direction and velocity, temperature, barometric pressure, stuff like that on at various locations. The data is fed into computers. If you wish to, you can find out what's happening weather-wise on or near those locations or across the whole net. There are two of these towers on Mount Desert Island and a bunch of others down the coast and inland."

"I doubt that that thing ever sent a computer anything."

"No, probably not. It looks like it was put up decades ago. Maybe the previous owner ran an amateur weather station at one time or another. Lots of people did. Before computers and the establishment of the net, information would be logged in manually and mailed in."

"From here," Ruth said, "it looks old enough to have been part of the military presence during World War II."

"A distinct possibility, certainly."

"Potter said it was up when he came out to check on Staley after the accident, but the shape this mess is in, I don't see how that could be." Stone gave the wreckage a kick and one cross bar dropped away from the base.

Ike walked the length of the apparatus.

"I'm guessing Staley found it lying in the grass and tried to set it up. You can see where vines once grew up and around it but they've been cut away. Then there's a rope attached near the top that he strung over that tree limb," Ike waved at a gnarled oak twenty feet away. "It looks like he tried to hoist it up. Anyway, it must have blown over sometime afterwards. You can see it fell in not quite the same place where he found it."

"Why would he want to re-erect the thing?"

"That's a question for another day. Either out of curiosity to see what it looked like or, maybe he hoped to shore it up and put it back into working order. More than likely we'll never know, unless it was...umm"

"Unless it was...umm, what?" Ruth had massaged her calf back into a semblance of normal. When Ike started musing like that, she knew, it usually meant he was spinning the Rolodex in his brain for a memory or a connection that would be important later. The mast that was not a radio antenna had suddenly become interesting to him.

"Nothing. A passing thought. I was reminded of something that I saw once when...but that was a long time ago. Let's go look at the cliff."

They walked toward the fence that marked Staley's property. Stone led them to the east cliff face which, he said, was where Staley fell or was pushed. Ike stood for a long moment and gazed out to sea. He stepped so close to the cliff edge that Ruth thought her heart had stopped beating.

"Be careful, Ike."

"No problem. I needed to check something."

"What?"

"Well, I was thinking worst case. Deputy, let's assume the ME got it right and the victim was clonked on the head. What did his assailant use to do the clonking and where is it now?"

Stone thought a moment. "If it were me that hit him, I'd chuck it over the cliff into the ocean."

"So would I, but let's say he didn't where would it be, then?"

"It could be almost anywhere."

"Precisely. You said the ME suggested blunt force trauma probably executed with an iron bar or something similar."

"Yes."

"If he's right about that, then Staley was tossed off the cliff rather than accidentally falling. Also, he had to be forced to walk this far. To make him do that, the killer, assuming there is one, would doubtlessly have had a gun. Wouldn't he have used the gun butt to hit Staley? And since this is so remote from the few other residents on the island, why not simply shoot him?"

"Got it," Stone frowned. His casual "mix and mingle" appeared to be turning into something more than he bargained for.

"Wait a minute," Ruth said. She'd been following the conversation with a mixture of fascination and horror. "If a man is facing a gun and realizes his assailant intends to force him to the cliff in order to shove him off, wouldn't he refuse? I would. I'd flop down on the grass and make him use the gun. No way

I'm going into free fall because the bad guy wants me to do his dirty work for him."

"Point taken. Most people, however, will go along for a while. They may be in denial or hopes the bad guy will make a mistake, maybe trip, let down his guard, change his mind, or make himself vulnerable to a countermeasure, gain some time. The instinct for survival will click into place. He would wait for a chance, stall. I would, and I think the deputy would, too."

"But what could you possibly do?"

"Oh, I don't know. It would be a matter of chance, luck maybe. If it were my choice, I would probably drop to the ground and do a leg sweep somewhere along the path back there and… wait here." Ike retraced his steps along the track they'd followed from the weather tower, stopped and moved to his right ten feet, on a line to the porch, and inspected the ground. "Deputy Stone, come over here and look at this."

Stone and Ruth walked over to Ike and stared at the ground at his feet.

"What do you see?"

"The turf been disturbed."

"There's been a struggle. I don't know who your Mr. Staley was before he went into the B-and-B business, but he knew enough to try the 'drop and sweep.' It looks like it worked. Over here you can see where someone else fell and then over there, see that thin line of indented grass?"

"You mean where some of it is yellowish rather than green?"

"Exactly. Unless I am mistaken a piece of something like rebar lay there until a few days ago. The guy who was knocked down felt it, picked it up, and before Staley could run or attack, he hit him with it. Then, if the rest of this mess means anything, he half dragged him to the edge and shoved him over."

"You think he came back and threw the weapon over the cliff?" Ruth was now completely absorbed by the puzzle and, she would deny it later, enjoying it as well.

"Would you? No, I think whoever did this was feeling pretty cocky about having pulled off the perfect murder. He retraced his steps, picked up the bar and tossed it into the bushes." Ike faced the house, pretended to lean over and pick something up. He swept his arm in an arc and pointed. "If he's right-handed it'll be over there and if he's a lefty," he pointed in the opposite direction, "it's that way."

Stone stepped into the underbrush to Ike's right. "I'm going with the percentages and say he's right-handed." After a few minutes he bent over and, using his handkerchief in lieu of gloves, held up a rusty iron bar.

"It would appear, Deputy, that you have an active murder case on your hands. I expect you will want to go back and report this good news to your sheriff. Come on, Ruth, as promised we are done here. We need to get back to the house and rest up if we are going on that picnic."

The three made their way back to West Road. In front of Ruth's cottage, Ike turned to the deputy.

"As a matter of curiosity, Deputy, do you know how old Staley was?"

"In his sixties, I think. Thereabout, anyway; his bio wasn't very extensive. We were still looking for information when we closed the case as an accident. Why?"

"No reason. I was wondering how many people could have pulled off that leg sweep, and of that number, how many could do it at age sixty?"

Chapter Eighteen

At eleven-thirty that morning, Ruth and Ike stopped by Potter's Store and helped themselves to some chips and sunscreen. They left what they hoped would be enough money to cover the costs. Ruth couldn't remember what the sales tax was, if any, so they added an extra dollar and headed out to Pine Tree Island. The tide had not cleared the interval between Southport and the little island standing to the south and a little west.

"Now we can wait for the tide to go all the way out and then walk, or we can wade on over, it doesn't look too deep."

"You're sure about this tide business? That water looks pretty menacing to me."

"You're one of them good ol' suth-ren boys, Ike. Now us New Englanders know about tides. Whaling stock and all that."

"Okay, Ahab, we wade. If you disappear beneath the surface, remember it was me that said 'I told you so.'"

"You didn't though."

"I'm doing it now. I told you so."

"Shut up and follow me and hold the cooler up high. I don't want soggy sandwiches."

The water was colder and deeper than either expected but they managed to reach the island and clamber up its bank. The dry land formed a low mound with a cleared flattened area at its center. Evidence of old camp fires dotted the space. Ruth dropped her bag and blanket next to the largest of them.

"We could have a fire and toast marshmallows."

"We don't have any marshmallows. We could heat up our sandwiches but I can't imagine why. My feet are freezing and my slacks are wet practically to my waist. How about we heat them up."

"You go find us some firewood and kindling and we can both dry off and so on."

"And so on?"

"Do you need a map? Go."

Ike went in search of firewood. He found some pieces of driftwood along the shore where a higher than average tide had deposited them. There were plenty of pine needles for kindling and, true to the nature of pine trees in general, enough dry branches were scattered about on the ground and clinging to the trees to make a nice fire. Ike got it blazing. Ruth sat on one side, her bare feet extended toward the flames.

"It's really too cold to sunbathe." She sounded disappointed.

"Don't let that stop you. The view from here is certainly nice, but you in full sunbathing mode would be nicer still."

"You are a dirty old man."

"Yes, I'm proud to admit, I am, but you're right, I don't think you should risk pneumonia for the privilege of inducing early skin cancer. Let's eat. Maybe it will warm up if this breeze dies down, and then you can be my dessert."

They unpacked their sandwiches and Ruth uncorked the wine. "What's so important about a sixty-year-old guy doing the leg thing?"

"That is an excellent question that I hope the young man asks as well. I knew there was a reason I made you a deputy."

"You made me a deputy last year to cover your ass from too much pillow talk."

"There was the CYA motive for sure, but mostly I needed your first-class brain to talk to every now and again and besides, it gives me an excuse to talk shop off duty."

"So, it's my brains you find attractive, sailor?"

"Oh, indeed. Maybe the sun will warm up and you can tan your 'brains' after all."

Ruth unbuttoned the two top buttons of her sweater and sang, slightly off key, "Dah-de-dah… boom…dah-de dah…"

"As I said, pure genius. Pass me a sandwich and pour me another dollop of that almost drinkable wine, please."

Ruth lay sprawled on a black and red Hudson's Bay blanket. Ike wondered how she could manage that. His remembrance of Hudson's Bay blankets, at least the ones he grew up with, was that they were wool and very scratchy. Since another manufacturer now made them under license, he didn't know if it was still true. But wool is wool even under the best of circumstances. Ike turned the pages of *Scone Island Stories.*

"Here's an interesting bit," he said. "Here, take a look at the list of names your aunt or someone penciled in the back." He handed her the book opened to the back. "Check out the captain of the Coast Guard Station."

"Gustave Staehle. Do you think his pals called him Gus?"

"Can't say. That's not part of the name I find interesting."

"No ? Why?"

"Come on deputy, I am counting on you to help me here."

"No dice, copper. We're on vacation, remember?"

Ike glanced at the sky. "Shouldn't we be moving back to the mainland? The tide will be coming in soon and it looks like rain."

"No rain. I already told you, not going to happen."

"You know that, or you hope that?"

"It's the silver maples. When it's going to rain, they turn their leaves over so the silvery side shows. See, they're not doing it; *ergo* no rain."

"It's good to know you are grounded in all things natural and botanical."

"Go see for yourself. We have plenty of time."

Ike walked back to the embankment where they'd climbed out earlier. The water swirled near the topmost edge. Ruth was pulling on her sweater and gathering the picnic materials when he returned. The fire was out, the air had turned chilly, and the sky dark.

"Let me see that tide table of yours."

"What? Okay, here." She handed him the narrow booklet. "It's open to today's date."

Ike studied the pages. A frown creased his forehead. "Did you notice that the times are printed in both italics and standard type face?"

"I did. I wondered about that."

"Umm… not enough, I'm afraid, oh ye of olde, spelled with an extra *e*, whaling stock. The type face is important."

"Really?" She walked over to him and stood so that she could read over his shoulder. She smelled like pine needles. "What's so important?"

"The italicized times are AM and the regular are PM."

"Oops."

"We need more firewood, we're here for another five hours, maybe more."

"Well, at least we have an almost full bottle of wine. Let's drink it and then put a note in the bottle, 'Help, stranded on a remote island. Send more wine.' What do you think?"

"For someone who is usually a type A compulsive, you are taking this remarkably well."

"Yes, I am. I keep telling myself, it's the new me. But I am cold. Firewood first, then the wine. Thank God for these blankets. They are really itchy, though. You should see my back."

"I'll take a rain check on that, thank you. Speaking of rain, is it getting darker?"

"I told you, no rain,"

"Right, silver maples. Is that bit of information stored in the same place as your how to read a tide table?"

"Lighten up, Schwartz. Do you have an important meeting to attend? Build us a nice fire and we'll cuddle and sing camp songs."

"Firewood. Be right back."

When he returned, he encouraged the remaining coals to flare up and soon had a reasonably decent fire blazing. He turned and headed out again.

"Now where are you going?"

"I break out in a rash when people sing camp songs, and you need to finish drying out. The temperature is dropping and you do not need to add pneumonia to your list of medical problems."

"No cuddling either?"

"Ah, as to that. Warm up and dry off. I won't be long. We will need more wood soon and while I am gathering it, I'm going exploring. This island can't be more than thirty yards across. Let's see what the natives left. Maybe I'll stumble across your Indian Romeo and Juliet."

"Maybe we will both freeze to death and they'll find us in the morning entwined in each other's arms like them."

"It's May, for crying out loud. You're not going to freeze."

"I'm going to stay here by the fire. I don't think my leg is up to exploring. Bring back lots of wood when you're done playing Nimrod."

Chapter Nineteen

Charlie finally reached Neil Bernstein's girl friend, Krissie Johansen, a second time. Things were becoming tight. She told him she still had not heard from Neil since he left a week earlier. She hoped she would have by now, but guessed she really didn't expect to. She didn't sound so sure about that part.

"He didn't call you when he traveled out there to climb? I would think climbing solo is dangerous enough but to not check in would be foolhardy."

"Where he goes, you know, out there in the mountains, there's not much in the way of a signal for a cell phone. So I don't always expect calls. Most of the time, when he's by himself, he'll walk around and sooner or later he finds a few bars and calls me. Not always when he arrives, though, but maybe later."

"He hasn't called at all so far?"

"No. So, like I said, it's not unusual, only it's not like him either. Like, it's been a week." Charlie heard the worry in her voice.

"So where exactly does he do this climbing, Miss Johansen?"

"He calls it his 'special place.' It's not like it's really his, you know. Other people go there, too, but he likes to think of it as, you know, sort of his. I can't tell you exactly. The times I went there we usually stopped at that little town I told you about before to gas up and get sodas and stuff before we turned into the mountains. Do you think something's happened to him, Mr. Garland?"

"I called out there earlier and they had no news. I guess I should try again. Anyway, let's hope he's okay." Charlie thanked her, hung up, and Googled Barratt, Colorado, and studied its website for a few minutes. There wasn't much to be learned. He called the police department a second time and again asked if they had any new information on a Neil Bernstein. The local cops wanted to know who was asking. Charlie hesitated. He was unwilling to tip his hand yet and the caller's voice on the other end sounded distant, like this call was not one the Barratt PD either wanted or expected. Charlie lied and said he was calling for Bernstein's employer. It wasn't entirely untrue. But in any case, it didn't seem to work. The cop on the other end said they had no information to offer about any accident or disappearance of a Neil Bernstein and hung up.

"That," a very frustrated Charlie said to the wall, "has all the characteristics of tuna salad left too long in the sun."

He was on the verge of calling out a special unit and tasking it to drop in on the cops in Barratt when his phone rang. Al Jackson's control. They talked for ten minutes. It was not good news. Charlie made another call to another police department. The Baltimore PD, unlike the one in Colorado, was more than happy to talk to a fed who would assume responsibility for one of their murder books. Charlie promised that someone would be over to clean up for them.

Where the hell was Ike?

It didn't take long for Ike to circumnavigate the island. It didn't offer much in the way of excitement, though. Not even any interesting flotsam in on the tide. Except for a square concrete box-like structure near the southernmost edge, there was nothing to see. He might not have seen it either because of the dense foliage and honeysuckle which grew around and over it. He caught sight of a corner which peeked out. Had he not paused in the path and looked around to get his bearings, he would have missed it. He studied the box. It appeared to have been constructed from poured concrete. It had a coffin-like lid attached by two massive hasps with corroded brass locks at either end of the rectangular box on which it rested. Some lettering had been painted on one side at one time which was now nearly indecipherable.

What the heck, he thought, why not? He wrestled the lid back, not without considerable effort and couldn't have moved it at all except the padlocks that held two hasps in place at either end had been so corroded by decades of sea salt air that they fell away when he banged on them with a rock. Enough light remained for him to see that he had opened a concrete enclosure that appeared to line a pit at least five feet deep. He also saw in its depths, green, crusted, and corroded copper plates to which the leads from a three-stranded cable had been connected. He stood and sighted toward the west and then pivoted and looked the other way. It could be. If he guessed correctly this cable had to lead to the ocean floor and thence…where?

He replaced the lid, repositioned the broken locks so that at a casual glance they looked intact, and shoved the underbrush back in place. He stepped back and squinted at the results. Exactly as it was before. Good. As he turned to start back he barked his shin on a stump. Not a stump. A pole about a foot in diameter had once been sunk in the ground next to the construction and then apparently sawn off a foot above ground level. He pushed back some nearby brush and thought he saw what could have been footers two or three feet distant from the enclosure's four corners. They might have been intended to anchor a small building. Something had been planned for this spot. He saw no evidence that any construction had actually been done. Whatever someone in the past had intended for the site had been abandoned a long time ago. He gathered an armful of firewood on his way back to rejoin a shivering and somewhat distraught Ruth.

"I wonder…" He dropped the wood into a untidy pile.

"You wonder what?"

"Nothing. Well, maybe something. I wonder if what Barstow was pestering Staley about was out here on this island, not at Cliffside."

"I don't think I want an answer for that very cryptic remark right now. Come over here. Help me drink this wine and then keep me warm until the tide turns."

It started to rain.

◇◇◇

"I am soaked to the waist and freezing, Ike."

"That's what you get for putting your trust in maple trees. Oaks I could understand, but maples?"

"The leaves turned. You saw them."

"They did, after the rain started. That's a confirmation, not a warning, and it was coming down hard enough to make the confirmation superfluous. Besides, here's something for you to consider later at your leisure. Those were sugar maples, not silver."

"A maple is a maple."

"Yeah, yeah. A rose by any other name may smell as sweet, Juliet, but a tea rose is not a wild rose on any day of the week. Besides, I offered to carry you across the rising tide, but you put on your women's equality armor and, bad leg and neck notwithstanding, refused my offer. So I will not feel sorry for you. You need to go upstairs and see if you can get your hose-shower to produce enough hot water to warm you up."

"What about you? Aren't you freezing too?"

"Some, but I have a higher waist. I will towel off and put on dry duds. Besides I had the foresight to carry antifreeze with me on this trip."

"Antifreeze as in…"

"A bottle of moderately expensive sour mash bourbon. I will pour me a few fingers, add some of this marvelous spring water, and warm myself from the inside out."

"Good. All the more hot water for me."

"Which is not saying very much, as it happens. Meanwhile, I will light a fire, allow myself to become very mellow, and with any luck will not be late for dinner."

"There's dinner? Where?"

"If there is to be a meal, and that will depend on my relative sobriety, there is a can of Spam in the pantry, four more-or-less fresh eggs, and enough bread to make a pile of toast which, with butter and jam should hold us until breakfast. What we will do about that is another question."

"A trip to Mister Potter's store."

"And pay a king's ransom for some for pancake mix and powdered milk? The man is a thief. Here," he handed her a half filled glass of bourbon. "You can get a head start with this, and be careful in that tub. The floor is linoleum and slippery when wet."

"I didn't know they still made linoleum, or do they?"

"I think it went out with Ipana tooth paste. While you are soaking and boozing I want you to think about buying the island from which we narrowly escaped."

"Whatever happened to Bucky Beaver anyway?"

"Bucky retired about the time Ipana disappeared from the shelves. I don't know which came first. Maybe he developed a cavity, which would be very bad for business."

"Tough luck for Bucky. As for me, booze and a warm bath. What could be better?"

"A double tub and endless hot water?"

"Not on this island, Bunky. If you wanted bath time erotica, you should have opted for Plan B. Face it, Scone Island is lost in time, a nineteenth-century idea of adventurous living. All very Edith Whartony."

"As you say, but—"

"But?"

"Nothing. I was just thinking about Pine Island."

"Okay, on that *non sequitur*, I will leave for warm water."

Chapter Twenty

A few hundred miles to the south, in Langley, Virginia, Charlie Garland sat at his desk drumming his fingers. The cadence was intended to be that of Scott Joplin's "Maple Leaf Rag," but given Charlie's notoriously bad sense of rhythm, it could have as easily been the "1812 Overture" or the theme to "Gilligan's Island." He stopped when his index finger caught an errant paperclip and sent it flying across the room. He reached for the laptop's keyboard and began tapping on it instead. He opened a recently created file, clicked on the tool bar, and then PRINT. Charlie, unlike the majority of employees at the CIA, had permission to use his own, that is to say, personal laptop. He had a government issue machine sitting on his desk as well, and it would normally be the one in play. But because his position as internal watch dog required a measure of flexibility and privacy from the eyes of even his colleagues, there were times and programs he needed to run without the knowledge of the rest of the agency, with its constant, nearly paranoiac monitoring. For the same reason, he had his own off-line printer.

When the printer stopped bzz-bzzting, he removed the sheets and returned attention to the computer. He took one last look at it and then wiped the file from memory. A simple delete would not do. He did not want anyone to discover at some later date that he had wandered into the director's hard drive when he'd run tracking software in his effort to discover who had been snooping around his phone logs. He'd been told to look for an internal leak. That was all. No directive had been sent his way to do anything else. But he had software that could back-trace hackers, and the program had, in fact, done what it was designed to do, but it wasn't what he'd hoped for or could comfortably use. After some more reflection, he also erased the print history from his laptop. A guy who'd been in his office for a job interview had showed him how to do that. Charlie hadn't hired the guy but wrote a glowing letter of recommendation to the HR department at NSA, a venue he thought the guy's skill set more nearly matched. He felt slightly foolish erasing the history, but under the circumstances, he felt he had no other choice. If the answer to a question he would soon put to the director came out wrong, his days with the agency might well be drawing to a close. It was not a happy thought.

He shoved the paper copy into his middle desk drawer and slammed it shut. If this were a Humphrey Bogart film, he thought, he would now open the right-hand desk drawer and remove a glass and a half-filled bottle of bourbon. Bogie would have pronounced it bore-bon. But no bottle or glass sat in that drawer, and he wasn't the late Humphrey Deforest Bogart, either. He settled, instead, for one-half of a Mounds Bar and dialed the director. It was getting late, but he knew his workaholic boss would still be at his desk. Among other things, he needed to tell him about Al Jackson.

And then…

◇◇◇

Ruth put her glass down and stared at Ike. "Wait a minute… did I hear you say you…you want me to buy Pine Tree Island?"

"You did."

"Why do I want to buy Pine Tree Island? And with what money, by the way?"

"I understand the relative poverty imposed on those dedicated to a life of self-sacrifice in the halls of academe so, consider it a wedding present, pre-nup so to speak, for me. I'll give you the money."

"Let me get this straight. You want to give me money to buy you an island that's not even a third the size of a football field and give it to you as a wedding present? Why don't you buy it yourself? And what on earth do you want it for?"

"I read in *The New York Times* that within the president's proposals to raise revenue and reduce the deficit, he suggested selling islands, courthouses, maybe even airstrips, not to mention generally idle or underused vehicles, roads, buildings, et cetera. Among the listings is Plum Island, N.Y., by the way."

"I don't believe it."

"You don't believe the government is selling surplus property?"

"No, I don't believe you read the *New York Times.* Were you in a hostage situation" What?"

"Doctor's office, smarty pants, and a week-old copy at that. So, if I understand the procedures for the purchase of government surplus property, and I'm not saying that I do, local interests have the right of first refusal when a property is for sale. You are a property owner here on Scone Island, you have that right. I am not, so I do not. Not yet, anyway. You can do this for me."

"Government surplus property? The government owns Pine Tree Island?"

"I think so. There were painted markings, almost completely obliterated, on some construction I found on the island that looked like *Property of U.S.C.G.* That would be the United States Coast Guard. I'm guessing the construction was started and then abandoned toward the end of World War II. I want you to buy it for me, for us, as an investment. That is if I'm right."

"Right about what? You want to fill me in on the big secret?"

"Both Staley and this guy Barstow were attempting, in different ways, to develop the island. Barstow wanted to build a first-class resort and Staley a bed-and-breakfast. He may have been old and cranky and currently dead, but I don't think he was stupid. Both had spent money, a good deal of money I think, on property and who knows what else. I think each in his own way thought he had an edge. Barstow intended to buy up as much as he could, spring his surprise, and resell at a huge profit at least. He was on his way to see Staley the night of the murder. I think he wanted to make a deal."

"What kind of a deal?"

"Not sure, but I think a quick look through Staley's things will turn up the answer. I'll have a look tomorrow. Who knows, we might get lucky."

"You'd break into Cliffside? You're a cop. You can't break into a house."

"I can if it's a crime scene."

"It's out of your jurisdiction. I'm no lawyer, but I'm pretty sure you're out of bounds here."

"Didn't you hear Deputy Stone ask me for help? I'd be helping."

"But what are you looking for?"

"A hydrological survey, among other things."

"'A hydrological survey, among other things?' What the hell is that supposed to mean?"

"Part of a puzzle that is bugging me and might be useful to solve for a later day."

"Still not with you, Schwartz."

"Trust me."

"Ha!"

Ike pumped up the Coleman lantern. It began to hiss and he lit it. The mantle caught and glowed a bright white. He snuffed the candle he'd been holding and placed it beside the lantern on the table.

"There," he said, "isn't that almost romantic?"

"Almost."

Ike stretched his legs out and sipped his drink. "It's a shame we can't use the light I brought."

"Next time you shop, remember to put light bulbs on the list. By the way, I thought I saw a duffle in the car that you didn't bring over to the island with us when we arrived. What's in it?"

"A tent."

"A what?"

"Two-man, sorry, a two-person tent. It's one if those pop-up things."

"So, you brought a tent, or did you buy it? And why, she asks knowing full well she is not going to like the answer."

"Behaviors, good and bad, become habit and, even after they are no longer needed, automatically pop up when you get involved in a particular task or bit of business, like our running away from home. You know, they kick in with the right Pavlovian stimulus."

"I still don't follow. To what behaviors do you refer to, Dr. Pavlov?"

"Spook survival. Once we set in motion the actions we wanted to assure that we could not be found, by Charlie in particular, I went into a 'leave no trail' mode. Behavior from another life."

"Like the disposable cell phones?"

"Exactly. So when I picked up the generator and stuff to bring some measure of civilization here, I also bought the tent on the assumption that if anyone who might be on our trail discovered the other purchases, he'd have a little information about our destination. Not much, but some. If he was quick enough he might figure it out. So, I bought the tent. Now, if the tracker is on the scent, he will assume we went camping. People don't go north to camp at this time of year. He'll look south. You see how it works?"

"You were thinking all this in the store as you stockpiled this junk?"

"I wasn't thinking about the items at all actually. I reacted automatically and the next thing I knew the clerk was ringing up a tent. Besides Essie told Charlie we'd gone camping."

"And all this to evade Charlie Garland?"

"No, of course not. Charlie would have to be really desperate to go to the trouble to put a search in motion. As I said, it was a conditioned reflex. I started the process with an eye to making it difficult for anyone to trace us. The rest followed—like riding a bicycle. So now, whether we need it or not, we have left a false trail that could, in more perilous times, buy us hours, days, weeks even."

"That is amazing. Terrorists with bombs, angry ex-faculty, guys you put away in the slammer, bill collectors from Netflix, none of them can find us now. Wow. Congratulations."

"Thank you. It's always a treat to know you're appreciated."

"Un-huh. Did it ever occur to you while you were plunking down good hard cash for a two-person tent, not to mention all this other stuff, that you were spending the kids' inheritance?"

"Kids? I think you may be a little ahead of yourself there, kiddo. But, if that is something you'd like initiate, we can take this almost romantic lantern upstairs and get started."

"Alas, due to the wonders of research in reproductive physiology and the easy availability of modern pharmaceuticals, it will require a little more in the way of planning than a quick hop in the sack. Sorry about that."

"Gone are the days, alas."

"Were they good old days or bad?"

"Scary, I think. No social commentary tonight, please. Please stay focused on the progeny of our loins, as the Good Book would put it. And don't forget, before we bring a scion into the world, we must first contact the admissions office at Harvard to see which year they will have an opening for the inevitable prodigal we will produce."

"Oh, indeed. Maybe we should sort that out now—just in case. One doesn't like to rush into things and miss the opportunity on the rise. Imagine the poor tyke's disappointment if Mummy and Daddy were to miss the year and she would have to settle for Yale."

"Dreadful. Another drink?"

"Yes. Let's drink to a very confused Charlie and the promise of eventual children—note the plural, I was an only child, as were you, and I do not recommend that circumstance for any of ours."

Ike started to say something, bit his lip instead, and smiled. Whether or not she would admit it later, Ruth had moved significantly off the dime when it came to the formalization of their relationship. One did not speak of children, even in jest, without the concept infiltrating one's thoughts, like Indians in an old Western sneaking up on the cavalry's fort and thus changing the balance of the equation. It was a mixed metaphor but he liked it anyway, especially the image of Indians creeping into Ruth's fortress.

Chapter Twenty-one

The director of the CIA, as Charlie and everyone else who paid attention to the news knew, had come to the agency after nomination by the director of National Intelligence and with the advice and consent of the Senate. He had moved to that point from a career as a general officer in the United States Army. And he had risen to the rank of general by surviving several combat tours of duty in the Mid- and Far East and more emotionally grueling ones at the Pentagon. Four stars come only to those who show bravery in the field, firmness of purpose in their career, and the ability to avoid the long knives of their comrades in the E Ring. He had done all these things, but at the expense of his marriage, his health, and not a few of his friends. He had been waiting for Charlie Garland's call for two hours when his phone finally rang.

Charlie would not have known that, of course, but he wouldn't have been surprised to find it out. Whatever else could be said of the director, political appointee or not, a limited intelligence wasn't one of them. That claim could not have been made of one or two of his predecessors, one of whom went on to become a presidential candidate.

"What have you got for me, Garland?"

"Some bad news and a question."

"What's the question?"

"Bad news first. We found Al Jackson, or rather his control found him through the crime stats of the Baltimore Police Department. He's dead. That makes two—Archie and now Al."

"How did Jackson die? And are you sure the two are related?"

"As to the latter, no. The Baltimore cops have it reported as a random drive-by shooting."

"And I take it you don't think it was."

"Oh, I think it was a drive-by shooting, all right, but not random, but the truth is, I really can't say, director. They found ticket stubs to the ball game at Camden yards in his pocket, a twi-nighter. He'd parked several blocks away, I'm not sure why. It appears he left early and was going to his car when it happened. It's dark and he's a black guy in South Baltimore walking along the streets near a neighborhood that used to be called Pig Town. To the north of where they found him is West Baltimore, home to all kinds of bad guys, if I read the papers correctly. Also, he was connected to some of those same bad guys in the past—before we got him. Could it have been random? Sure, but with Archie dead and Neil Bernstein missing, what are the odds? I don't like coincidences, at least not like this one."

"No, you're right. No news from Bernstein either?"

"His girlfriend, partner, whatever, hasn't heard from him since he left. She says he usually checks in, and he hasn't."

"Maybe he's romping in the sand somewhere with a new playmate and doesn't want to tell her."

"Halmi would know and he says no. He says Neil went west to climb a rock. So, is he incommunicado or will we be collecting another body, this time from Colorado? I don't know, director. I called the Barratt police and talked to the cop on the desk out there, without tipping who I was, of course, and I received very suspicious answers."

"What do you mean, suspicious?"

"It was weasely, too pat, too smooth. They're hiding something."

"You think? Find out. What about Ike Schwartz? Do you still think he is in danger?"

"Assuming these deaths are connected and not accidents either of time or place, I do. Listen, this may all end as a tempest in a teapot—a series of coincidences that defy logic and statistical probability, but I don't like it."

"So, have you tried to track down Ike? You did say he was out of the loop."

"I did, and I have tried, as you well know."

"Pardon? I know?"

"Yes, sir, and that leads to the question I have to ask you before we talk anymore."

"A question?"

Charlie slipped the sheets of paper from the middle drawer and spread them across the desk top. "As I told you earlier, I discovered my phone calls were being monitored, hacked actually. I borrowed, you should pardon the expression, a program from a colleague over at NSA that back-tracks hackers, and I traced the source."

"Yes, so, who's your Peeping Tom?"

"You are, sir. The program dropped me off at your doorstep, you could say."

Sandy Ansona considered himself a good cop. He resented the jibes he and his small-town colleagues received from people passing through the town, tourists and the stuck-up folk from Boulder. He never understood that—the Boulder business. And bikers on their way to some idiot rally where they'd all get stoned and show off the mess they'd made by customizing their expensive Harleys. The worst happened when the locals started referring to him and the other guys as Buford or Barney. But the real trouble lay with both the chief and the lieutenant who, sadly, deserved the abuse. If they weren't fixing tickets for the mayor's teenage daughters, they were rousting various citizens—those of foreign extraction mostly—for anything from free donuts to favors of a more intimate nature.

He really did not like the business about the stiff they brought down from the mountain. The guy was wearing a steel and gold Rolex that mysteriously disappeared from the deceased's inventory along with his M-11. The pistol was important,

Sandy knew, but wasn't sure how. He'd spent a little time in the MPs and he knew government issue when he saw it. Since the chief now sported the Rolex, he assumed the gun went to the lieutenant. Spoils of war, they would say. More like grave robbing—without the grave.

He wheeled his cruiser around and started back along Main Street. Patrolling Barratt was a matter of form. Nothing much happened here except tourists on their way through and cowboys drinking too much once a month. If it weren't for the occasional speed trap the chief set up, the town would dry up and blow away. He passed Frank's Diner and glanced in the few windows not yet steamed up. The lieutenant was chatting up Gloria, the new girl down from Wyoming. Would she or wouldn't she? And would the lieutenant's wife hear about it?

He reached the town's limits and pulled over on the shoulder to think. What kind of a guy goes rock climbing in one-hundred dollar sneakers and wearing a gold and steel Rolex? Whatever else Neil Bernstein might have been, Sandy did not think he was a fool. He didn't fall off that cliff, either. And what was a helicopter doing in that mountain meadow? Who could he talk to who would not immediately blab to the chief? His brother, of course. He was a state trooper. If there was something crooked going on in Barratt, they'd be the ones to investigate. But his brother stood pretty low on the totem pole, or was it high? He'd been told by someone, he couldn't remember who or when, that the place of greatest honor on a totem pole was at the bottom, so maybe high was it. Either way his brother was on the wrong end. All he would do is tell his sergeant and it would go up the line and land right back on the chief's desk. Then Sandy could say goodbye to his job and career in law enforcement. That's how things worked in "the Thin Blue Line" he knew. "We cover our own," the chief had said to him when he joined the force after came home from his last tour in Afghanistan. He knew that. Besides, his brother would tell him to forget it and that "you have to go along to get along."

Sandy tapped his breast pocket where he'd slipped the bullet he'd taken from the lab after the ballistics test had been run on the Sig Sauer. You never knew. The lieutenant with a drop piece that belonged to someone else was not a good thing. Hanging onto the slug could be a good thing, given who now owned the Sig. Gloria from Wyoming had better watch her step.

He pounded the steering wheel in frustration and then pulled back onto the road, did an illegal u-ie, and headed back toward town.

Chapter Twenty-two

For what seemed an eternity Charlie waited for the director to respond. He imagined he could hear the wheels spinning as his boss processed what he'd said.

"My doorstep, you say?"

"Yes, sir."

Another long pause and time ticked away. Charlie wondered if indeed early retirement didn't lurk just around the corner. He thought it could be worse. There were things he always wanted to do besides skulk around the agency's basement. A little time in the sun, Barbados or the Seychelles. He'd heard they were very nice, like Bali when it was still the Bali he'd read about in his old copies of *National Geographic*. And then he would…what would he do? The truth about Charlie—he didn't really want to do anything other than what he did. He loved his job. He may have been the only person in the metro-DC area who did.

"So, you think Ike Schwartz may be at risk?"

A shift in the direction of the conversation. The director did not want to talk, it seemed. Okay, they would play that piece as a duet. "Yes, I do."

"You've been trying to track him?"

"As I said—yes, until now."

"You're not trying to find him anymore? Why?"

"Sir, given what I have told you, if you were me, would you?"

Another long silence. More thinking on the part of the director. "Garland, I can't talk about the monitoring right now.

You will have to trust me on this. Now, what do you plan to do about Schwartz?"

"Nothing, sir."

"Nothing? I thought you said he might possibly be in trouble."

"I did, but to trace him through our system would be counter-intuitive under the circumstances."

"Explain."

"Sir ? Okay, for the sake of continuing the discussion, I will concede that the monitoring may have some purpose other than that which seems obvious to me. Nevertheless, if I haven't been able to find him using up all the leads I currently have, what is the chance someone else, with fewer, will?"

"You mean if you can't find him, no one can?"

"Sort of. I am not arrogant enough to believe that I have the edge here. But I believe that Ike is safer this way than running the risks associated with continuing to search for him with someone watching."

"You don't think he needs to be warned?"

"I didn't say that. I said under the current circumstances, he's better off if he stays wherever he is and hidden."

Once again the director's response seemed glacially slow in coming. While he waited, Charlie reflected on his own words. His choice of vocabulary and sentence structure, he realized, shifted to a more impersonal and formal mode when he was suspicious of his listener. He wondered if the director noticed. So what if he did? Not only was Ike his friend, but the director owed Ike for a few close calls as well.

"What about his fiancée?"

"Ruth?"

"Yes. What about her? They could get to him through her."

"They are together. Both out of sight."

"Her mother, what's her name, Evie Saint Something?"

"Eden Saint Clare? No problem, I have a man babysitting her everywhere she goes."

"Okay, then that will have to do for now."

"The monitoring from your office, too?"

"We're done, Garland."

The line went dead. Something was clearly out of whack. Charlie, for the first time in a long time, felt afraid. He called his man in Chicago and told him to move in very tight to Ms. Saint Clare. If necessary, keep her clear from "friendlies." The guy didn't sound too happy about that part.

He locked up but didn't go straight home. There were too many loose ends flapping about that he needed to think about. The director had left the answer to his question hanging. It was too important a question to brush off, but that's what he'd done. Charlie knew that the director held Ike in high regard, but he also knew that being director of the CIA meant he had many balls in the air, and sentimentality in determining which stayed in play and which were allowed to fall would not be factored in when making the choices. If there was something about Archie Whitlock that needed to be permanently erased, for example, the director would order the erasure and any ancillary problems, theoretical or human, if necessary. He wouldn't like it, but he would do it. Collateral damage, within certain boundaries, was considered SOP. And, if the director thought too much had slipped from his control, Charlie might find himself included in it as well.

That said, it should be obvious that if the director knew something needed to be done about Archie or Ike and the other two, it probably needed doing. And Charlie was enough of a realist to know that he would look the other way if Ike were taken down by someone on the inside. For the first time, Charlie began to question his job.

He pulled into an all-night diner and slouched to a back booth. A waitress dressed in a pink-frilled poodle skirt brought him coffee. He ordered a slice of pie à la mode which he did not eat. He needed to think. There had to be some other way. There had to be.

His ice cream melted.

◇◇◇

Ike turned the gas in the Coleman down, and the lantern's hissing abated and slowly shut down leaving only the glow of its mantle to light his way to bed. He managed to slip under the duvet as the light faded to insignificance. King-sized beds had not found their way to Aunt Margaret's cottage—nor had queens. Double beds, for those used to something roomier, take some getting used to. Ruth hitched over.

"So, do you wonder if Charlie is still looking for you?"

"Still?"

"Didn't you tell me he called as you were clearing out of your office?"

"Oh, I guess I did say that. Yes, he called. That's when Essie told him we were camping. If he ever looked, Charlie will have given up by now. He should know that no matter what sort of emergency he can dream up to lure me back into the Puzzle Palace, it won't work."

"Still, he gets you all the time, Ike. He calls. You pretend not to care about his problem and then you go rabbiting off to save the world."

"I can count on the thumbs of one hand the number of times I have rabbited off in what could even remotely be described as saving the world."

"You're being modest. You know what I mean."

"Ruth, when you were playing Sleeping Beauty back in the fall, Charlie was there for me and, I might add, for you. He was there for me when I couldn't sort out what happened in Zurich. So was the director, as a matter of fact. Charlie was there for me when I needed him. I try to reciprocate."

"But you are hiding from him now."

"Ruth, if Charlie really wanted to find me, he would. If he hasn't by now it can only mean he has no real reason to and he is respecting our wish to be alone."

"What about the tent business?"

"I don't for a minute think that would fool Charlie. That's for lesser minds. I told you, spook paranoia. No, Charlie would have jumped right over the tent trick and headed north. Since he hasn't, there is no reason to expect he'll showing up at our doorstep looking for breakfast."

"You're sure?"

"Positive."

"You don't sound positive, pal. Okay, and you're done playing policeman with Deputy Stone?"

"Almost."

"What do you mean, almost?'

"I want to check out Staley's house and look for that water study. Since the house is connected to his murder case, still on it, one could say."

He said it and he believed it, but something still nagged at Ike about the Staley business besides the presumed hydrologic study. Something about that tower was buried deep in his memory—where nightmares go to hide, and when you think you're done with them, they jump out and ruin a peaceful night's sleep. He wished Charlie *would* show up. Perhaps he could help him remember. He wanted to ask him why a weather tower seemed so important. Oh yes, and why did the name Frank Barstow also set off alarm bells? Little ones to be sure, but large or small, a warning should never be ignored. More paranoia, he guessed.

He would tell Ruth he wanted to take a walk over to Cliffside in the morning.

"I can hear you thinking, Schwartz. It better be about me under this duvet in a short nightie and not about crime and punishment in one form or another. It's very cold, dark, and lonely in the guest room."

"I was thinking it's time to Google you."

"Oh, you are a dirty old man. Hey, watch the leg."

Chapter Twenty-three

Charlie felt that anyone witnessing the next hour's activities would brand him as paranoid or moderately stupid. But caution, a trait he'd developed in his early years at the agency, convinced him not to go straight home. He went, instead to a Walmart. There he bought a few items of clothing, toiletries, a disposable phone, a note book, and a screwdriver. A second stop produced a decent bottle of Scotch. He used the screwdriver to switch the front license plate on his car with one he lifted from a sedan parked next to his. People rarely checked their plates, and if they did the odds were it would be the rear one when they loaded their groceries or, in this case beer or bottles. His last stop was a motel on New York Avenue toward the Maryland line. It was not a very attractive neighborhood, never had been, but at the same time it wasn't the sort of place where anyone looking for him would go. He booked a room, paid cash, and backed into his parking spot so that the Massachusetts plate on the front bumper would be facing the street.

If asked, he would describe the room as tired—worn bedspread, frayed carpeting, an excess of yellowed caulking around the tub rim where the grout had cracked and the wall behind begun to flake away. The whole place was in serious need of a coat of paint, new curtains, and furniture that didn't look as if they had been Goodwill Store rejects. But, on the plus side, it was clean and quiet. The traffic along New York Avenue somehow did not seem to penetrate its walls. Someone had, in fact, made an effort to make it as attractive as possible with a sprig of forsythia in a cracked vase and, importantly, all three door locks worked. Good enough.

He took a shower, turned on the TV, and poured three fingers of the Scotch in the plastic cup that came wrapped in cellophane in the bathroom. His other choice was the Styrofoam version that came with the in-room coffee machine. Somehow Scotch in Styrofoam didn't work for him. Plastic seemed marginally better. At least it looked correct.

He had some serious thinking to do. He did not turn on his new phone. Not yet. He frowned at the advances of technology that made the world a safer place but at the moment were making his life difficult. He wished he'd kept his old Nokia. That one was made before manufacturers, in a moment of public spiritedness, put geo-positional tracking chips in their cell phones. He could have left the old Nokia powered up. He made a mental note to scour second-hand stores and garage sales and find one. A nontraceable phone had its occasional uses, and in his line of work probably justified the extra monthly expense. He doubted the phone provider would put one of those old clunkers into service, but he knew a guy who could do it for him, for a price. Then again, maybe the guy could simply disable the chip in a new phone. That seemed like a better idea. Ike had introduced the guy to him years ago.

Ike. Where was Ike?

He pulled out the shiny new notebook and started writing—lists. The first began with the report of Archie Whitlock's alleged accident. He worked at that list for an hour, dredging through his memory for details he'd read, conversations he'd had. He put that one aside and began a second, a to-do list this time. He needed to find Ike before the director, or whoever for whatever reason they were looking, found him first. That tent business might fool some folks but he knew Ike. He'd headed north. But where? He had no answer for that. He scratched at the paper for another half hour and then, satisfied with what he'd accomplished, he turned off the light and went to sleep.

◇◇◇

The LVPD's fax machine beeped to a halt and night duty officer picked up the stack from its out tray. He skimmed them quickly and then walked through the squad room pausing at various desks to deposit one or more of the sheets. Robbery, homicide, missing persons, and so on. He wasn't sure what to do with the last bit of paper so he put it back in the tray for the day clerk to deal with. Identifying the Jane Doe down in the morgue would have to wait a few more hours and then depend on the relative devotion to duty by the day clerk due on duty in three hours and who, at that particular moment, had regretted the four margaritas he'd downed in a fast forty-five minutes on a dare from his drinking buddy and brother-in-law. Thus, it would be several more hours after he came on duty, before anything as mundane as delivering a fax to the appropriate cop would rear its head through the fog and pain of an Olympian-sized hangover. So, even though the LVPD now had the identity of their mugging victim lying in the morgue, it wouldn't make it to her toe tag until sometime the next day.

It was an hour before dawn, Ike guessed. He hadn't lived at this latitude long enough to work out the difference in sunrise and sunset times between those in Maine as opposed to Picketsville. He checked the luminous dial of his watch and discovered he could not quite make out the exact position of the hands. His doctor back home had suggested he get his eyesight checked.

"When was the last time you had your eyes refracted?" he'd asked.

Ike couldn't remember. He'd never had a problem, always been 20/20.

"You know, as you age," the eye doc had said, Ike thought condescendingly, "the lens begins to harden and the muscles that change it weaken. You probably will need reading glasses at least."

Ike had thanked him and had promptly forgotten the conversation. Now as he squinted at the blur in front of him he thought the doc might have been on to something. He got up and padded across the room to the door where he'd hung his field jacket. He slipped it on against the chill and eased his way downstairs, being careful to avoid the step with the loud squeak. In the parlor, he rummaged through the boxes and bags until he found the toss-away phones. He turned one on to check for reception. He knew there should be none but he'd seen a tower as they cleared the harbor, and some of the newer phones, even the cheap drugstore numbers like this one, had a greater range than they used to. No luck. He repacked the phone. Tomorrow he'd head to Cliffside and check out Staley. Dead or alive, the old guy was beginning to bug him. Charlie was the only person he knew who might be able to find him some answers. Certainly not Deputy Stone, the Boy Scout posing as a policeman. He climbed the stairs and reentered the bedroom. In his absence, Ruth had sprawled across two-thirds of the bed. Getting back in without waking her was going to be a problem. He lifted one arm and laid it across her chest. Then he carefully shifted her leg—the bad one—and slid in between the covers.

"Where have you been, Schwartz?"

"Been? You think I've been somewhere?"

"I heard you thumping around downstairs. What were you doing?"

"Bathroom. I am developing the old man's syndrome."

"Yeah, right. So, how come I didn't hear a flush?"

"You've forgotten or are still slightly comatose. We have an outhouse up here, remember. Short of a hurricane, outhouses don't get flushed."

He waited for her response, and when he heard her regular breathing, he guessed he wouldn't get one. He needed to get back to sleep before she rolled onto her back and began to snore. Love may be blind, but it isn't deaf.

◇◇◇

Across the Potomac River in Virginia, two men sat ensconced in a black SUV parked outside Charlie's condo. They had been there all night. As the sun rose yellow-orange over the capitol they reported that Garland had not returned home and asked what they should do next. They were told to sit tight until they were relieved. Under no circumstances were they to let the place out of their sight.

Chapter Twenty-four

The director of the CIA had too many things on his plate to have to worry about some damned-fool Congressional hearing. He called in the assistant director for public affairs and briefed him on what to say and where to dissemble when he met the solons on their own turf. He dismissed him with a caution not to let the bastards try anything funny, and then he called in his personal aide.

"Good morning, Director. Bad night?"

"Pure crap. What explanation did you dig up for me to explain why Garland's software pointed him to me?"

"Still working on it. We have time. These guys are clever; I'll say that for them. Luckily, they do not yet know that I have been shadowing Charlie for two months and so whatever they do to him will have no effect on our ongoing operations."

"Do to him? I don't want anything to happen to him, you understand?"

"Yes, sir.'

"You say we still have time? How so?"

"Garland has dropped out of sight. He didn't return home. Do you suppose he really—?"

"Thinks I'm after Schwartz? Of course he does. He's no fool. The question is what will he do in response?"

"Maybe we should tell him."

The director slapped his desk and spun around to gaze at, but not see, the woods that circled the building. "Can't do it.

Not yet. I need to get these guys, and as much as I hate to do it, Ike Schwartz has to be the bait. So, how did the program send him to me?"

"We had to fiddle with it. NSA helped. Charlie is too much of a bulldog to let it go otherwise. If he had identified who was on his trail, he would have moved in on them before we could set the operation in place. So we picked you. We didn't believe he'd believe it either, but, well…"

"He'll figure it out after a while. Right now, if I know Garland, he's working on ways to avoid me and any threat to him and Schwartz I might pose."

"So, what shall we do?"

"Can't do much. Tell your people to keep an eye peeled for him at his favorite places. Track his cell phone, and wait. In the meantime, double your efforts to root out those SOBs. Garland is too valuable to lose."

"What about Ike Schwartz?"

"Love the guy, but he doesn't work here anymore. I can't waste assets on him. I'm sorry. He's supposed to be hiding somewhere, for reasons of his own, I guess, so he'll assume he's safe enough for a while."

"If Charlie turns up, what do I do?"

"That has a fifty-fifty chance of happening at best. Feed him something soft and gooey. He won't believe you, but it should convince him that what is in play at the moment is sufficiently important to shut him up."

"Let's hope so."

"Yes, let's."

◇◇◇

Charlie checked out of his motel and drove to Prince George's county. He found a hole-in-the-wall restaurant that served breakfast all day. He managed two poached eggs with corned beef hash and a side of wheat toast. Fortunately the ketchup was plentiful, and therefore the meal more or less edible. At least the coffee was good. He switched his front license plate back and dropped the borrowed one—he didn't like to think of it as stolen—into a mail box, but not until after he'd wiped it.

His next stop, the Vietnam War Memorial, where he spent an hour strolling along its length, stopping from time to time to put a face to a name, a memory. He'd lost some friends over there. It wasn't his war. His came later, in the deserts of Iraq—the first sally into that ungrateful land. A few of the names on the wall were people he knew or grew up with, a school teacher who had a wife and baby, the guy who used to serve kids burgers at the drive-in, the older brother of one of his own friends and who'd been brought down himself in the desert not quite two decades later and who'd perhaps someday have his name etched into another wall in another mall. Perhaps not; who knew? The public is fickle and their memories short. When this latest series of deployments finally ended and the men and women made it home, would they be forgotten as well? Or only until someone decided to make political hay about the lack of a monument to their service?

He loved his country but there were days when his tolerance for the state of things in Washington drove him crazy. He also knew the country suffered from a serious blind spot. The people of the United States were distressingly ignorant of their own history. Few if any could tell you the difference between the War of 1812 and the Revolution or even knew there was a difference, blithely running Francis Scott Key in with Betsy Ross; Jefferson with Admiral Perry, and all of them in with Natty Bumpo and his Mohican friends. These same people would also insist their country stood as a bastion for peace around the world while ignorant of the fact that during its relatively short history, it had been at war somewhere, somehow, nearly continuously since its beginnings in 1775. That the longest stretch during which no American servicemen were deployed into combat of some sort was the two decades between the First and Second World Wars. Other than that bright moment, the country had been at war at some level—against foreign powers, France, Spain, Germany, its own citizens, north, south, Native Americans, in the Philippines, in Cuba, in Haiti—the list seemed almost endless. He shook his head. He needed to clear it. He'd always hoped that working for the CIA would somehow ameliorate the need to send men and women away to die. So far he had seen precious little movement in that direction, but still, he hoped.

Charlie had a Silver Star and a Purple Heart along with a few campaign ribbons tucked away in a dresser drawer. The miniature versions of three of them were more or less permanently attached to his dinner jacket. On the rare occasions he was summoned to a formal affair, he wore them, not as a display of his bravery and service—Charlie had no ego issues—but in the hope that people seeing them would stop and reflect, perhaps remember, and think about their country's bellicose history. And then think about who they really wanted for their Commander in Chief and why, think about who should sit in Congress. Who should be entrusted with life and death decisions about the nation's youth. War not only sapped the vitality of a nation more than pestilence, he thought, but it injured everyone, civilians and combatants alike. Surely, enough was enough. He turned and left the memorial. Too much darkness, too much introspection there. He needed some light and an inspiration. He had a problem to solve.

He found a bench and sat staring vacantly off into the distance. He rarely had simple problems to solve and this one wasn't one either. Was the director into something that could end badly for Ike, or was he covering for someone else, perhaps equally high up? He turned over the proposition; had someone tampered with his tracking program to create mistrust, misdirection? The bench was hard and still damp from the morning's dew. He wanted to be seated at his desk. He wanted direction, reassurance. He wanted Bogie's bottle. And he needed a plan.

Chapter Twenty-five

Ike fed Ruth a lunch that consisted of turkey sandwiches and several glasses of oenologically incorrect red wine. They were out of white but Ruth insisted she didn't care about conventions of that sort anyway. A half-hour later she declared the tryptophan was kicking in and she was going to try napping as she'd promised and would stretch out for a few minutes. She was asleep at once. Assured she was dead to the world, Ike headed to Cliffside and Harmon Staley's stuff. What had that old bird been up to?

As he expected, the door to the guest cottage was not locked. He searched it quickly. He found a cache of papers and letters. One asked for a geological survey of the island, another for a water assessment. So he had been thinking about expanding the scope of the house. But why a geological survey? He could understand Barstow wanting one, but Staley?

The surveys themselves were not in the guest house. He walked to the main house and that door was locked. Ike kicked it open. The house was a shambles already; one more busted door couldn't hurt. He'd make it up to the new owners, if and when—or not. Maybe he'd buy the place himself. No harm done if you break down your own door.

If the guest house was a mess, the main house was a disaster. He moved from room to room, all three floors and found nothing. All the closets, cupboards, and possible storage places were bare. He turned to leave ready to give up when he spotted the piano. It was an old Steinway grand in the same state of disrepair as everything else and covered with dust. Well not entirely. The dust on the lid showed had been disturbed. Hand prints...Staley's or his killer? He lifted it. What he saw almost made him drop it. The interior was largely devoid of strings and hammers. In their place were papers, a small duffle, and a holstered Glock. The papers included the expected hydrological survey, a topographical map of the island, and two hard cases that could only have held weaponry. He riffled the duffle. Not *a* gun, several guns! Pistols, shotgun shells and...a satphone.

Who the hell was Harmon Staley?

Ike checked the phone's charge and decided it was time to test it. He stepped out on the porch, headed up the path, and away from the house. He did not know if any of the nearby cottages were occupied but in any case he didn't want anyone to know he had the phone.

He switched it on, gave it a second or two to power up and locate a satellite, then called Charlie.

After an hour in the park, away from the Wall, and a stop for lunch at a restaurant on the Potomac's waterfront, Charlie headed across the river toward Langley, a decision made, and turned his cell phone back on. He could only guess at would happen when he arrived back at the agency, but he felt he had no other option. Either he would trust his boss in spite of what he knew, or he would quit. And though common sense suggested the latter to be the sanest choice, he wasn't quite ready to accept it. He turned his car toward the office and a possible showdown.

A mile and a half from the waffle-faced buildings of the Langley complex, Charlie's cell phone buzzed. He glanced at the number. He didn't recognize it except it was not beyond the possibility it identified a satellite phone. He pulled to the side of the road to answer. Charlie did not like it when people thought they could drive and manipulate a phone at the same time.

"Charlie, I need some information, but I can't talk long."

"Ike? I'll call you back." Charlie snapped the phone shut and tried to calculate how long the connection had been live, one second…two? Not long enough surely. He drove as fast as he dared back across the Potomac and into a parking lot near a busy office building. If anyone was scanning for calls, they'd get an earful. He dug through the paper bag on the passenger seat and found his "throw-away." Part of his second nature, or perhaps his years of experience, endowed Charlie with a sort of photographic memory. His short term memory could store scraps of information, numbers, names, dates and times, for twenty-four to forty-eight hours. Outside that time frame the gift failed him, but at the moment, he had Ike's number. He dialed back and waited.

"What the hell was that all about, Charlie?"

"Long story. Listen, Ike, I have to tell you something."

"So what else is new? Charlie, before you start, I need some information from you ASAP. I need you to look up a name for me, Harmon Staley."

"Who?"

"Harmon Staley."

"Ike, where are you?"

"No way, Charlie. I'm on vacation but there is something fishy going on and I need to know who the guy was."

"Okay, first you listen to me. It begins with the news I have been trying to get you for days. Archie Whitlock is dead."

"Archie is dead? Too bad and I should care? Why?"

"Stay with me. Neil Bernstein is missing and Al Jackson's also dead."

"Okay, they are dead. You think there is a connection and maybe I am in someone's cross-hairs, too. Is that about it?"

"Most, but not all. Archie was retired and under deep cover. Someone found him, and he was killed. I was tasked to find an internal leak, an assumed leak. Somehow whoever bumped Archie knew how to find him."

"So, why do I care how Archie was dropped?"

"Officially?"

"Actually."

"The cops are treating his death as an accident, but we think he was pushed off a cliff."

"Off a cliff? Wait, where did you tuck Archie away?"

"Some place in Maine—an island, your island if I'm guessing right."

"Scone Island. His new name was Staley, wasn't it?"

"Yes. Now you know."

"Good Lord, Charlie, he was my almost neighbor, and it wasn't an accident."

"How do you know?"

"Oddly, the scene of the crime. Mr. Staley—that's Archie, right? Staley took a piece of rebar on the back of the head before he was dumped into the Atlantic."

"You're really on that island where Archie was killed? This isn't some kind of shell game someone is playing with me. Because if it is, I want it to stop."

"No games, Charlie. I am on the island. Ruth needed a clean break. The A-frame had become a little like living at Graceland. We needed to go away, far away. She owns a cottage here, so here we are for another week at least."

"Why are you on a satphone?"

"Why are you on something other than your cell and what's with hanging up and using a different phone?"

"I asked you first."

"There is no phone service on this rock. I found this one in Staley's, that is Archie's, stash. I ask again—"

"Long story. Tell you in a minute. I need to get back to Archie. We're letting the local cops believe it was an accident. The director would rather no civilian interference in this one."

"Tell the director it's too late. The locals know Archie was murdered."

"How?"

"I told them. By the way, old Archie put up a fight. Almost took his killer out. If the iron bar hadn't been right at hand, I think he'd have won that one. So what's with your off-line phone?"

Charlie filled him in with what he'd found in his search for the person or persons tracking his phone calls. What he suspected, but could not confirm about the deaths of Archie, Al Jackson, and Neil Bernstein.

"You really do think someone is after me?"

"I wish I knew for sure. Until I get a different read on the other two, yeah, I do. I think they are hunting you, Ike. You must have seen something or done something with Archie back in the day they want forgotten. You know that if they find you they will also have to take down Ruth. No witnesses allowed. There's really no phone service?"

"Nope."

"Cripes, how do you manage?"

"Very nicely, thank you. At least up until this minute when you announced I have a bull's-eye painted on my back. Now, not so hot."

"You need to move."

"Why? You are the only one who knows where I am."

"True, but if they trace the satphone, they can get a fix on your location."

"How will they do that? If it's registered at all, it will be in Staley's name not mine, and you and I are talking on a temporarily dead-end circuit, and what are the chances Archie as Staley used either name to register the phone, if he registered it at all?"

"If they were monitoring my phone, they may have had enough time to track all or nearly all of your number."

"Charlie, they had what, a second, two max, and that's being generous. Even so, if you think about it, it might be useful."

"How's that?"

"Not sure, a feeling perhaps. Tell me the rest."

Chapter Twenty-six

The room received light only from a single grimy skylight, glowing computer screens that lined one wall, and a lamp on a desk at the center of the room. Men sat hunched staring at an array of monitors watching images as they scrolled across the flickering blue-green surfaces—images of streets, offices, or long shots of hillsides, all currently under surveillance for one reason or another. The frames changed every eight seconds. A second man sat apart at a desk in the center of the room shuffling through a stack of reports, one or two of which appeared official, others scribbled in pencil, but all bearing a number in their lower right hand corner.

One watcher looked up. "Garland received a phone call. I'm pretty sure it was from Schwartz."

"Can you trace it?"

"Not enough time. He answered and immediately said he'd call back. I have to wait for the call."

"Idiot, he won't use that cell phone. Garland is on to us. He'll go to a call box or an alternate we don't know about."

"We have all his phone records, financials, everything. If he has another phone, we'd know."

"Unless he went to Wal-Mart in the last twenty-four hours and bought a pay-as-you-go-phone. Use your head, man."

"He would have had to pay cash."

"Check his ATM withdrawals."

The first man typed for several seconds, squinted at the words on the screen in front of him, and shook his head. "He withdrew the max last night in Arlington."

"He won't get far on three hundred bucks."

"Wait, he took another three hundred this morning in DC from an ATM on New York Avenue."

"Jam up his bank account—no wait, cancel that—too obvious. Keep a watch on his financials. I want to know everything he does. If he's going to run, he'll need money and credit cards. Watch all of them. But right now I want you to get after his call. Try scanning the area for any signals coming from within the area of the towers that serviced the last call."

"Yes, sir. Don't worry, we'll find him."

"You'd better or there will be hell to pay by you know who."

Ike fidgeted while Charlie spoke for another ten minutes. He detailed what he knew and didn't know about Barratt, Colorado, Krissie Johansen, the Baltimore PD's guess about Al Jackson, and the difficulties he faced with the director. He also mentioned how he'd spent the previous night.

"If the Company's in this, you just gave them a bad night, Charlie. Okay, you think the director's putting the target on my back?"

"I think it's a possibility. I don't know why and I don't want to believe it, but what else could it be?"

Ike walked around the big ramshackle house and to the cliff's edge on the island's most northern point. The sea air was crisp and briny and blew steadily in from the northeast. He did not notice it or the spectacular view across to what he supposed could be Nova Scotia. That is if it were possible to actually see that far.

"Okay, I need time to think this through but here's my quick take. The director wants to find me because he wants to use me to bait a trap he intends to set to nail Archie's killer or killers."

"He wouldn't do that."

"He would if he had a reason. It would have to be a pretty big one, but he would, and you know he would."

"You're right, he would. This is over my head. Next question is why? Why did whoever is behind this need to rub out Al Jackson and Neil Bernstein? Blowing Archie away, I can understand. There must be dozens of people who had a motive to kill him. Or even if the boss ordered the hit on Archie, I would understand. I wouldn't like it, but I'd understand. But why the others and why you?"

"You said it, Charlie. Something must have happened on one of Archie's debacles. What you need to do, if you can, is pull reports on all of them that also included the three of us. There can't have been that many. In fact, I don't recall but one, wait… two…I don't know, not many. Dig them out, Charlie, and find out what makes the people involved in them a potential liability to someone. That someone will be your man."

"Okay, it will mean going in to the office and that may be the end of my road."

"Can you access the records remotely?"

"Not me. As far as I know, no one can."

"Do you remember Sam Ryder? I think she's married now. She used to work for me in Picketsville and is now at NSA?"

"Tall red head with the big…overbite? Yeah. I remember her."

"If push gets to shove, call her. I'll give you her home number. Tell her it's for me. Tell her about the target on my back, and then tell her what you need. She'll get the files if anyone can."

"You want to hack into the CIA?"

"It's that or you go in and sneak the files out yourself."

"I'll try that first. There are more ways in and out of that building than most people know. If I must, I can slip in and out without the director knowing—at least for twenty minutes or so. That should be enough time to suborn a file clerk or two. What will you do?"

"Figure on being the bait, I guess. Only I will be the one setting the trap, not the director."

"We're assuming that is what he's up to."

"I have no other choice, Charlie. If these guys found Archie, Al, and probably Neil, they have access and assets. They are good, and they will find me, too. That being the case, what other choice do I have?"

"You could come in. We'd protect you."

"Listen to yourself, Charlie. You have to sneak into the building or perhaps hack into the records, and you think I should come in?"

"I'm thinking of Ruth, Ike."

"Thanks for that. But for the same reasons, I'd much rather trust Ruth to the Picketsville sheriff's office. Besides, if I'm right, the director would turn around and toss me under the bus somewhere else. He's after something big and you and I are expendable. With regret, of course. I don't have a plan yet, Charlie. As I said, I need time to think this through."

"And then what?"

"Then I will set my trap, and either I will get them or they will get me. One way or the other, it will be over."

"I don't like this, Ike. Come in."

"Bad juju there, Charlie. In the meantime, you should go to work, make nice with the director and try to figure out what's in those files that has everybody acting weird and pretend all is well in heaven and earth and so on."

"*There are more things in heaven and earth, Horatio, than are dreamt of in your philosophy*. Be very careful, Ike, before you do anything that can't be undone."

"Thank you for that, O Prince of Denmark. I'll be careful. Tell you what. We need to talk some more. Do your thing at the Company and then go have lunch where we celebrated my engagement to Eloise. You remember?"

"A long time ago. Yes, I remember."

Ike closed the connection and stared out to sea. When she found out, Ruth was going to be really pissed, apoplectic more like. Well, it couldn't be helped, and at least they hadn't gone with Plan B. Las Vegas was no place to attempt a double-cross to trap a killer.

Chapter Twenty-seven

The view from the director's office window was shared with only a select few. Indeed, the location of his office and therefore the view would not be something one would find on a tourist map, were there one to be had, which, of course, there wasn't. In an age of ridiculously easy access to illicit arms purchases—everything from hand grenades to shoulder-held rocket launchers—putting a crosshair on a particular window, however protected from the exterior, was deemed a bad idea. As it happened the window out of which he now gazed included a clear view of the parking lot that had an assigned space for Charles Garland. His assistant waited until he turned his attention back to the room.

"This is very odd, Director. Once he powered up his cell phone, we were able to establish that Garland was on his way here. Then, he received a phone call which lasted something like five seconds and he high-tailed it back across the Potomac. What's going on?"

"Who knows? Best guess? Ike Schwartz contacted him. It would be nice to know why. Okay, something has gone south. I suppose it would be asking too much for the call to have been traced?"

"Sorry sir, there wasn't enough time. We couldn't even capture the caller's number. We've kept the tracker on in case he calls again but so far, nothing."

"You won't get anything more. Not anytime soon. Garland is no dummy. Five seconds and he hangs up? What does that tell you?"

"He knew we're locked on to his phone."

"Exactly. You can bet that if there is to be any more chat, it will be on safe phones."

"What if Garland comes in? I mean, he can't stay away forever."

The director turned and refocused his gaze on Charlie Garland's parking. "Oh, you can bet a week's pay he'll be in, innocent as a baby, all smiles and cooperation and leaving no tracks in the sand, I promise you. We've lost our edge, Mark. We'll have to try something else. Pull the surveillance on his apartment."

"Sir?"

"New ball game, son. Charlie's on to us, and for some reason, it looks like Schwartz is or soon will be in the game but on his own terms. I don't know how that happened. Sometimes that guy is positively uncanny. Either way, unless I'm really off base, we will be playing this one by Ike Schwartz's rules. Let's hope he can pull it off."

"And if he doesn't?"

"Then we go back to the proverbial drawing board. We need to put a lid on this business and pronto. The Senate confirmation that could blow up in the President's face could happen as early as next week."

◇◇◇

Ike returned to the big house and did a quick inventory of Archie Whitlock's duffel bag. It appeared the old man had emptied out one of his caches. Every field agent—well many of them—had small collections of arms, passports, cash, and credit cards, and false IDs tucked away in the event he or she needed disappear for a short while—or forever. Where Conan Doyle's characters had bolt holes, wary spies had duffels and lock boxes filled with necessities. It appeared Archie had brought one such to Scone Island with him. Why? What was he up to? Ike knew he'd need to figure that out, but it would have to be later.

He laid the items out on the piano lid. There was enough equipment in the bag to mount a small war. Very convenient. It would make what he had to do a lot easier. But first he had to talk to Ruth, get her off the island and back home or out of sight. Then he'd need to call the office and set up an around-the-clock watch on her. Nearer at hand, he'd need to recruit the Gott brothers, Henry Potter, and finally get a message to Stone and his boss over on the Mainland. Stone first. He'd need some serious help and felt sure he couldn't count on any coming from the agency, although he was sure they'd show up afterwards to tidy up.

He spent the next twenty minutes pacing through the big house, checking the rooms on each floor. There were good lines of fire from most of the windows. He remembered from his trip to the cliff's edge where Archie took his nose dive into eternity that the east cliff face had crude stone steps cut into it that led to the narrow beach and the remains of a long washed-away pier. The path from that point was clearly visible from the east windows. Would they come that way? If so they would have to come in on the ebb tide, the only time the beach would be sufficiently wide enough to allow a shore party to land without risking their boat's bottom on the rocks. More likely they'd arrive as summer renters or drop by sailors. The Bite must be a popular stopover for locals cruising up and down the coast. One boat more or less in the harbor would not attract any attention. Maybe this early in the season it might, but he couldn't be sure of that and there would be no way he could check on them if they did anchor. But Stone could, and he guessed Henry Potter didn't miss much.

With its limited access and closed society, there were clear advantages to making a stand here on the island, but even on the best of days, operations like this one more nearly resembled Swiss cheese than cheddar. The trick would be to cover all the possibilities with a single answer so that no matter how and when his stalkers arrived, he would be covered. Easier said than done.

It was time to face Ruth.

Charlie made his way back to Fairfax and then CIA headquarters. He would keep his phone off until he finished what he had to do in the building. Only when he'd finished what needed to be done, would he make his presence known. First, he had to check out some files. He entered the building through one of the "back doors" he'd mentioned to Ike—he hoped without attracting any attention. He managed to work his way to the records morgue and pull all the files that met the criteria he'd established. They had to be ops which included at least two of the three men either dead or at risk. After he'd copied several onto a thumb drive, he exited, circled around, and reentered the building, this time with his phone on, and making a conspicuous stop at Reception to swipe his ID card and have his image recorded on the surveillance camera. As he told Ike, there were ways into the building that did not necessarily require this last ritual if you knew them and were willing to run the risk of being challenged or at the very least reprimanded. Shot by a conscientious guard could be the worst case. That had happened only twice during his tenure.

He went quickly to his office and waited. He guessed the director would stew a while before he called. He made a duplicate thumb drive by copying the files from the morgue. He'd need something for them to confiscate if they guessed what he'd done. While he waited he skimmed through the files. There had to be something in one of them that was the clue to why Ike and the others were being hunted. And if the director or his aide had been monitoring the parking lot, there would be. Meanwhile he would need to work on his story.

The director did, in fact, wait ten minutes before summoning Charlie to his office.

Chapter Twenty-eight

Ruth was furious. Ike listened without comment while she stumped around the room aiming her invective first at the CIA, then Charlie, the Republican Party, politicians in general, Wall Street, and finally Ike for being a damned Boy Scout. Why did he have to stick his fork into every idiotic dish that Charlie Garland put on their table? And what was the big idea of having a phone and not telling her about it?

Ike let her vent while he poured them each a stiff whiskey. He had enough ice to cool but not seriously dilute the alcohol. That would be important when Ruth finally ran out of targets and energy and sat down to listen. He needed to explain the predicament they were in, and soon, because he had a long list of things that needed doing before he called Charlie back. Not the least of these involved getting Ruth off the island and safely back to Picketsville without attracting the attention of the goons were who were after him. And then there was the problem of her mother, wherever she'd disappeared to.

Finally, Ruth's ranting shuddered to a halt. Ike handed her the drink and explained in detail what had happened, that it had nothing to do with Charlie and his bad habit of involving Ike in his problems, that the situation was, as nearly as anyone could tell, historical and, given the director's odd behavior, serious. And, by the way, the phone was not his, but one he'd found at Cliffside and whose owner happened to be the source of the mess they were in.

"But why, Ike? Why did you call Charlie in the first place?"

"It goes with the tent."

"It goes with the tent? What the hell does that mean, it goes with the tent?"

"My previous employment has rendered me permanently bent out of shape, irretrievably twisted by too many years playing secret agent in too many covert operations. You push the button that puts me in spook mode and everything else follows instinctively—like buying the tent. Look, something seemed noticeably out of whack over at Cliffside. What kind of a sixty-year-old man drops his assailant with a classic leg sweep? I mean who can do that at age sixty? You have to wonder. So, I went back over there, as I promised, to look for the various studies I talked about—hydrological and so on. While I was rooting around looking for them, I found the phone with a bunch of other stuff."

"Other stuff? What kind of other stuff?"

"A cache of weapons for starters and ID cards, money...At that point, I knew the set-up had more to do with my past than I cared to think. The only people I know of who travel with that kind of baggage are either bad guys or the people who work with Charlie. So, I thought I'd better ask before something happened that I couldn't control."

"Why would you have to be in control?"

"You miss my point. The piano was stuffed with enough lethal junk to give Davey Crockett the means to win the battle at the Alamo. That is not something you can overlook."

"But why Charlie? Why not call the kid cop, Deputy Stone? It's his jurisdiction, his problem."

"I might have done except I felt certain that bag of goodies belonged to an agent, current or past. Charlie needed to know that one of his people was here and had become a victim or killer. Either way, something bad went down here. What I didn't expect to hear, that the dead guy was Archie Whitlock and that his murder was not the only one in the last several days, that the killings might be connected, or that there might be one more in the offing."

"One more? Who?"

"Me."

◇◇◇

Charlie Garland would never make anyone's best-dressed list. His friends said he looked like he'd been dragged backward through a keyhole. A more generous description was that he looked like an unmade bed. Some thought it was an affectation, a ploy used to make him blend in, to seem unimportant. In fact, his general mien and dress did produce that effect and played significantly in his success as the *de facto* internal affairs officer for the CIA. That, incidentally, was not his title, nor did he have one. The in-house phone book listed him as a public relations specialist and sometimes he even showed up in that part of the building which housed people given that task. This usually happened when he needed a favor, not when he was engaged in his job.

Part of Charlie's rumpledness, whether contrived or real, consisted of cuffed trousers. He may have been the only male in the DC area under sixty-five to have cuffs in his trousers. He occasionally found them useful, as he did this time when he received his summons to the director's office. One copy of the files he'd downloaded before making his very public entrance into the building went into his right pants cuff. He patted it as flat as he could and put the drive in his jacket pocket. He took the elevator up from the basement where his office with its battered desk and steel filing cabinet were located.

The director waited with an aide. Charlie knew the aide only slightly and only by his first name, Mark. Their previous encounters had not been positive. He nodded to the two men and waited. They could start.

The director stood staring out of his window. "Garland," he said without turning around, "you took a long time getting from that car of yours to your office."

"Pit stop, Director."

"It's a prostate problem then?"

"Very possibly. And I need to say hello to one of the women in finance. It's her birthday."

"Who would that be?"

"Name slips my mind. Young pretty girl, blonde and new. Wears her hair in a ponytail."

"That could be any of a hundred or more women in this building."

"Yes, I suppose it could."

"You knew it was this girl's birthday, what she looked like and you can't remember her name. Have I got that right?"

"On the money."

"How is that possible?"

"Might it have something to do with the prostate?"

"Okay, enough fun and games. Where were you from the moment you left that pile of junk you drive to when you appeared on station?"

"As I said—"

"I said no more games. Empty your pockets. Mark, pat him down. Unless I miss my guess, our friend here has been wishing his birthday greetings in the file morgue. And that lady is neither young, nor pretty and wears her hair in a bun, not a ponytail."

Charlie laid the contents of his pockets on the director's desk and allowed Mark to pat him down. If you don't know cuffs, you don't look for cuffs. Mark didn't on both counts.

"Nothing here, sir."

"Then whatever he lifted must still be in his office. Send someone down and confiscate every memory stick he's got. Charlie, as of this moment you are off-duty. Tell me a reason why I shouldn't furlough you."

"Can't think of any. How about this, since I couldn't find your leak inside, even if I wanted to, how about I try to find out what happened to Bernstein."

"We found the leak. You're off that task."

"Really, who?"

"Cora Dinwiddie, aka Cora Sharpe Whitlock."

"One of Archie's ex-wives?"

"Exactly. The Las Vegas police have her body in their morgue. The best guess is she met up with and told, possibly sold, Archie's location to his killer. How she knew it, I can't imagine. But knowing Archie, he may have gotten lonely and looked her up. Who knows? Okay, go find out what happened to Bernstein."

"That would put me in Barratt, Colorado, right?"

"Yes. Track Bernstein down, find out who did what to whom, and, by the way, take at least a week to do it."

"Right. I'll stop by my office and pick up a few things and—"

"Like hell you will. You are to leave the building immediately. You will do all your communications with the agency from outside the front door. Got it?"

"But my ID, files…how will I manage?'

"Files, exactly. No files. Okay now, stop your whining, Charlie. I know perfectly well you have access to any and all if you want it. Now, beat it."

Charlie didn't want to get into a pissing match with the director, but he needed confirmation. "So you are using Ike as bait and you want me far, far away?"

"Go away, Charlie, now."

"But that leaves Ike hanging out to dry."

"He's a big boy. He made the decision to act like the Lone Ranger, right? So, he gets his wish. He's on his own and I don't want you playing Tonto, got it?"

"But—"

"Charlie, I said go. So, go."

Tonto—very apt. Help is on its way, *Kemo Sabe.*

Chapter Twenty-nine

Ruth poured herself a second drink and glowered at Ike. Clearly, he thought, this will be a long and difficult day. "So what happens now, Ike?"

"Now? We figure out what to do. Charlie assumes, and his interaction with the director confirms, that to get the men who are knocking off my former colleagues, a trap needs to be set with the right bait."

"Bait? What kind of bait?"

"The director believes the best bait would be me, I think. Something happened on one of Archie's operations and apparently the people who are after me believe Archie and the people who worked with him saw, heard, or surmised something that someone wants buried—literally."

"But why now? You haven't done any of that crap for years. What's so important now that a bunch of people have to be erased?"

"I honestly don't know. Charlie was going to try and pull the files that might provide a clue. If he was successful, we will know soon enough. In the meantime we can't stand around and do nothing. They're coming for me irrespective of the reason. You need to pack and get a move-on."

"I need to pack? You mean we need to pack."

"Not me, you. You need to get back to Picketsville. I will call Frank and have him set up a round-the-clock watch on you."

"Round-the-clock…on me? Why on me? On you, you mean."

"No, I mean round-the-clock on you. I am afraid that whoever wants me will conclude the easiest way to get me would be through you. And they'd be right. But if you are covered, they will have to come directly at me. I don't want you involved in this. That goes for your mother, my father, and anyone else who might be deemed a bargaining chip."

"And you will boldly walk the streets of Picketsville drawing their fire like…what's his name in that movie?"

"What what's his name in what movie?"

"You know that old black and white thing you made me sit through when you were explaining what made a movie a classic. They had a big shoot out, and the pretty but really dopey bride ends up killing the last bad guy."

"*High Noon.*"

"Whatever. Is that your plan?"

"Not even close. I will wait for them here."

"Here? Are you nuts? There is nothing and no one here to help you. You'd be a sitting duck."

"That's what the baddies are supposed to think. But I will be neither a duck, nor sitting."

"What then?"

"I'm not sure yet. I will talk to Charlie, and we will sort it out. In the meantime, you need to pack. I will escort you ashore and drive you to Bangor where you will board the first plane south."

"Then you will play that movie guy on the mean streets of Scone."

"Hardly streets, and no, I won't be walking about hoping to draw them out. I will be holed up in one of several spots waiting for them to come to me."

"How is that any different than a sitting duck?"

"I won't be quacking, for one thing."

"Very funny." Ruth paced over to the window and stared at the pines across the gravel road to the east. "I still don't get it.

Why here and not back home or someplace where there can be all sorts of support?"

"That is a very good question, ma'am. Okay, here's why. Look around you. How big is this island? How does one get to it? What are the chances someone could get here unnoticed? Henry Potter sees all, knows all. It's a closed system, Ruth. Closed and therefore, easily controlled."

"But couldn't they be here already?"

"Not likely. Nobody knows we're here, remember? Even Charlie had no idea where we were. The director with all the technology at his disposal couldn't find us. Think about it. What are the chances I'd end up on the same island where Archie bought the farm, or in this case the bed-and-breakfast? They're not here—at least not yet."

"Then why don't we hunker down and wait until the director and his minions find the bastards?"

"Hunkering won't do. If that were the case, the director would have said to Charlie at the outset, 'Tell Ike to hunker down until I've found the bastards.' You see?"

"No, but I take your point. So, if the CIA couldn't locate you, how will the bad guys do it? Find you in this, the unlikeliest of all places?"

"When I'm ready, I will tell them."

"You're kidding." Ruth studied Ike's expression. "You're not kidding, are you?"

"Sorry, no. Once everything is in place, I will call Charlie on his open phone and have a casual conversation during which I will mention, but not actually say, where I am. They will take an hour, or a day, depending on how smart they are, to figure it out and be on their way north."

"So, why don't we lay low and not bother to call Charlie?"

"I told you, it's a matter of sooner or later, you see? Not if, but when, and as it is my rear end on the line, I want to determine the when. And as to doing it now, as much as I'd like to retire, spending the rest of my life on Scone Island isn't my idea of a place to grow old gracefully."

"But after a while—"

"By the look of it, Ruth, these are very professional killers. If they found the others, and especially Archie, who the CIA hid in a way that should have been foolproof, they will find me eventually. And because of that, I refuse to be looking over my shoulder and wondering for whatever time it takes them to track me down. They need to be stopped, and this is the ideal place to stop them."

"Pour me another slug of that bad whisky, Ike, and let me think."

"It is very good whiskey, and you do not need to think. You need to pack. I'll arrange for a ride to the mainland on one of the Gott brother's boats."

"I'm to leave you to the mercy of God knows how many homicidal maniacs and good old Charlie, who might or might not be able to help—that's right isn't it —might or might not?"

Ike shrugged. "He has assets he can bring into play."

"Bull. The director will send him on a mission to Katmandu. There will be no assets."

"As I said he has assets, and ones not necessarily controlled by the director."

"How's that work?"

"It's the nature of his job. You are better off not knowing why."

"If you tell me you'll have to kill me—isn't that the way it goes? Come on Ike, this is serious." She began pacing across the old-fashioned hook rug some ancestor had made or purchased many years ago. "If I drink anymore of this booze, I will lose all self-control. But you already knew that, you son of a—"

"Tut. Be careful. I am, after all, the one holding the gun."

"Yeah, right." Ruth returned to the center of the room and screwed up her face, either lost in her own world, Ike thought, or succumbing to the effects of the whiskey. She was on enough pain medication which, if it reacted with the booze, could easily have produced some kind of topical amnesia. It was neither.

"Okay, here's the deal, Schwartz. Listen carefully because I am not going to repeat myself. I am not going to leave you on this island alone." Ike started to protest, but she silenced him with a scowl. "Don't say a word. Please recall how you felt when the people with whom you used to play peek-a-boo back then killed Eloise, your first and as yet only wife. Do you want to put me through that?"

"I…"

"Listen, Captain America, I have thrown my lot in with you for whatever comes next. You want to know why?" Ike opened his mouth. "Shut up, I'm on a roll here. When I was lying in a comatose state, I had time to think—that is, in the occasional lucid moments given to me—and I came to understand one very important thing. You are the best offer I'm likely to get, now or ever. So, if you stay, I stay. I am not willing to go through life wondering what it would have been like if. Do you see? I'm staying. That's it, period."

Ike stared at the woman who was as different from him as night is from day. What a piece of work! He shook his head. He knew better than to argue. When Ruth made up her mind there would be no changing it.

"You are an idiot," he said.

"Yeah, but I'm great in bed."

Chapter Thirty

Charlie Garland felt sure the director's watchful eye and that of his aide were locked on him as he left the main building at Langley. He drove all the way to the other side of the Potomac before he retrieved the thumb drive from his pants' cuff. It took him nearly an hour in unusually heavy traffic to find the bar where he, Ike, and Ike's then girlfriend/fiancée, Eloise, had met years ago. How many years ago? He usually avoided thinking about it, but enough time had passed for the wounds to heal. Still, remembering what had happened to Eloise made him wince.

He parked and slipped his iPad II from under the car seat. He'd have a look at the files he'd pirated while he waited for Ike's call. Over the years Charlie had become a sometime regular, at least on those occasions when he was in Georgetown. The barkeep nodded a welcome and wiped the counter in front of an empty stool.

"I'm going to need a booth today, Solly" Charlie said and moved to one farthest from the door and in deep shadow. He sat facing the entrance so that he could keep an eye on who came and went.

"Booth it is. Say, I been meaning to ask you Mr. Garland, whatever happened to the big guy who used to come in here with you a couple of years back?"

"What big guy?"

"Jeez, I don't know who he was...the big guy, you know? Oh yeah, he was going to marry that redheaded Irish dame the last time he was in here. Did he?"

"You mean Ike. Yeah, he did. She was a blonde, by the way."

"Well that's good. Him getting married, I mean. I coulda swore she was a redhead."

"Good they married. Yeah, it was." And it was while it lasted. Not so good after that.

Ike and Eloise, how many summers ago? He'd told Ike then it would be his last great crab feast of the season and Ike had allowed himself to be talked into going, not because he wanted to crack crabs, which he did, or because he felt any particular need to be in the company of other people, which he did not, but because, Charlie had guessed, he was bored and restless, and an evening alone in his apartment was low on his list of things to do on a weekend.

Charlie had offered, and he accepted the obligatory gin and tonic. In those days, Ike only drank gin and tonic. Where others might relegate that mix as strictly a summer drink, only to be enjoyed between Memorial and Labor Day—like the wearing of white shoes—for Ike it was a year-round choice. That was Ike, safe, predictable, and careful. Especially careful. When an agency guy, from analysis or somewhere, had appeared with Eloise on his arm Ike's world had changed forever.

Eloise was tall, slim, and very blonde. She had inherited a set of wonderful green eyes and Ike told Charlie he thought she was the most beautiful woman he'd ever seen. She could have been anything from a supermodel to a plain Jane, but in Ike's eyes she was as he described her. The truth lay somewhere in between.

Ike had instructed Eloise how to use the little wooden mallet to crack the claws to get at the meat. She'd said something like she did not mind crabmeat but she thought eating one seemed more like eating a big bug. The two of them laughed, drank beer, and piled the shells up in the center of the table, oblivious of everyone else.

Sometime after midnight, Ike had taken her home. Charlie did not remember them leaving or how Ike managed to disengage her from whomever had brought her to the party in the first place. The next day the three of them met here in this very pub, and Ike announced they were going to be married. For the most careful man he'd ever known, Charlie thought that for Ike Schwartz to act this precipitously seemed completely out of character. Two days after that, they were married. Four days after their meeting, with some string pulling to get Eloise a passport, they were on a hastily arranged honeymoon in Europe. The first leg was London, then on to Paris, Zurich, and Rome. They'd never made it to Rome.

"The usual, Mr. Garland?"

"What? Oh, yeah, and can you fix me up with a corned beef on rye? Go easy on the mustard and for crying out loud, Solly, no mayo. Mayonnaise on corned beef *is* blasphemy."

"Maybe in a kosher deli it is, but not in Georgetown. In this end of town it's called aioli and is considered required eating. So, okay I got it, no mayo."

During this exchange, Solly had blocked his view of the door and Charlie nearly missed the man wearing dark aviator sunglasses and a black suit enter. Nice move on the guy's part, he thought. It had almost worked. He wondered if everybody could spot a tail from the agency as quickly as he could. If so, Langley was screwed. Someone should tell the young man that wearing a black suit, a white shirt, and conspicuous sunglasses do not do much if your aim is to blend in. Then again, perhaps that was the point. The director might have sent this obvious operative precisely to make sure Charlie knew the agency had him in their sights. So, okay.

He placed his folded newspaper in front of his iPad. Unless sunglasses sat next to him, he'd assume Charlie was eating corned beef, drinking a beer, and reading the sports pages. That is, he would unless he happened to know that Charlie never read the sports pages—couldn't tell you the difference between a squeeze play, a slam dunk, and a hail Mary. With the thumb drive plugged in, he began reading through the files. His sandwich arrived with his beer. The pub began to fill with lunchtime customers, at least half of whom ordered and then turned their attention to their smart phones. The pub soon filled with the tick-tick of texting, the murmur of one-sided conversations. Some silently browsed the Internet, burning off minutes and gray cells on one of the myriad mindless activities provided by an endless supply of apps designed to promote time-wasting to an art form. Good. Charlie had counted on that.

Eden Saint Clare happened to glance over at the precise moment the man's phone buzzed. She didn't really believe she'd heard the buzz all the way across the room, and it startled her. Coincidence surely—a common occurrence in her experience. Frequently, she'd have a thought and within minutes someone, usually her daughter, would say or have same thought. She and Ruth seemed to have been connected that way since her childhood. She'd seem to know what Ruth was up to, and, frequently, when it might end badly. But intuiting this man and his phone? Not likely. Still…if that call had something to do with Ruth, what then? Would that count? A ridiculous thought—how could it? She scrutinized him over the top of her luncheon menu. He'd turned away but not before she realized she'd seen that profile before—several times. That in itself didn't strike her as unusual. People who stayed in the same hotel were bound to run across each other often. But as she thought about it, every time they'd met he'd averted his eyes. She had a thing about people who refused to make eye contact—didn't trust them. Also, it seemed like this man turned up everywhere she went, the restaurant, Marshall-Fields…not Marshall-Fields, Macy's now. Why would anyone want to change an iconic Chicago department store name for an iconic New York one? No wonder they called Chicago the Second City—stupid New Yorkers! She hoped Macy's declared chapter eleven…or was it seven? She could never remember which was which. So, what was this bird up to? As much as she disliked doing it, she guessed she needed to call Charlie Garland

and find out. Without any compelling reason to believe it, she assumed he would know.

Charlie's sandwich had been reduced to crusts and crumbs and his second beer gone flat before he found what he'd been looking for. He'd read three of the files through twice and found nothing of interest. He had plowed his way well into the fourth when he realized that the visuals, the pictures, maps and so forth, were not displayed. He had to click on each title separately to bring them up. Once he discovered that, he started over. Not surprisingly he found images in all the files—too many, actually. How to sort through them all? There were the expected pictures of Jackson, Bernstein, Whitlock and a younger, gaunter Ike. And there were other faces. Dangerous Semitic faces shaded by keffiyehs in the Libyan Desert and broad Slavic ones from Bosnia. Some exhausted Navy SEALS and the four apparently bored agents in Puerto Rico on a training mission of some sort.

Something, or more accurately someone, in the Bosnia set drew him back. Another familiar figure stood off to one side, slightly out of focus but identifiable nonetheless—a United States Army colonel, ostensibly the military liaison to Archie's Bosnia operation, his face partially in the shadows cast by a fir tree. A face that blurred as it turned toward the camera the instant the shutter closed. Years had passed since the picture had been deposited into the file, but Charlie would recognize the director of the CIA anywhere. Another wrinkle added to the heavily creased conspiratorial fabric. The director had been involved in one of Archie's capers. Why hadn't he mentioned it? Charlie would have to mull over that. There had to be a reason the chief did not want these files in his possession. Now, he believed he knew.

In the last file, aside from the six or seven pictures of some nasty-looking tribesmen wearing camo uniforms from some country's army—not the US—he found a group picture of the four men standing on what appeared to be savanna in Nigeria. A fifth man, identified as Daniel Ostrofsky, stood with them.

Charlie read the file through again. It had been an arms sting, guns to antigovernment forces in exchange for conflict diamonds. Except for a few demo pieces, the rifles had no firing pins or recoil springs. The narrative identified Ostrofsky as the broker. His cover, according to the file, was a jungle doctor and a presumed freelance troublemaker, but not a big fish in the large and murky pond of international arms dealing at the time. As with too many of Archie's ops, this one had gone south in a hurry. Ostrofsky had been killed before he'd revealed the arms network or delivered the diamonds. The guns were lost but would resurface later in Somalia, repaired, operational, and involved in the Mogadishu fiasco. Charlie studied the blurry photo for several minutes. Ostrofsky? The face was familiar but the name…Charlie slid the iPad aside and this time he did read the newspaper. He didn't know what he'd find but he was sure he'd seen that face recently.

He stole a peek at Sunglasses. The young man had his hands folded in front of his face and his lips moved as if in prayer. Charlie assumed his hands held a smart phone and the director or his aide was getting an earful. He hoped the guy had it right. That is, not what Charlie had found in the report—there was no way he could know that—but that Charlie was in a bar behaving himself per the director's orders. Then again, who the hell cared what the director thought? In the middle of this thought he found the face that reminded him of Ostrofsky in the national news. Charlie let his gaze rest a second on another grainy picture. If he had to keep this up very much longer, he'd go blind. The man resembled the late Dr. Ostrofsky slightly—an older brother, perhaps? He compared the newsprint to the photo in the file. Years had yellowed the picture before the file had been digitalized and stored on the Company's storage server. And the photos were not good to begin with. If the two were related, which seemed unlikely, the name seemed to have morphed to Osborn. He studied the picture. This Osborn stood next to the Secretary of State, the President of the United States, and a fourth man identified only as Martin Pangborn. The latter must have been important to be included in a photo op with the Leader of the Free World. Somewhere, Charlie was sure, he'd heard that name before.

What did he have now? Names without clear connections to the killings. A dead man who looked vaguely like a possibly important live one, and too many corpses scattered across the continent—from Maine to Colorado. He waited for a flash of inspiration. None came.

His phone rang. Sunglasses sat up.

Not Ike, Eden Saint Clare. "Mister Garland," she said testily, "what are you playing at?"

"You have the advantage of me, Ms. Saint Clare." Sunglasses turned his back and was speaking rapidly into his phone. "Playing at what?"

"There is a man here who has been following me ever since I arrived in Chicago. He has your imprimatur stamped on his forehead. Why is that?"

"I am at a loss, Eden. Are you're sure he's one of mine?"

"Yours generically or yours actually, yes. Either way I need to know why I am being stalked by a man in a cheap suit and bad haircut."

"I see. What is he doing now?"

"He's…wait. He left. He received a phone call and then hot-footed it out the door. He didn't even finish his lunch."

"Ah."

"Ah? That's all you have to say to me? Ah?"

"I am guessing, understand, but I am reasonably sure you may have seen the last of him."

"I have? Why?"

"He's been called off."

"Called off? Well then, who called him on?"

"I did."

"Why?"

"Not at liberty to say now. Let's just say I had a concern for you, for Ike, and for Ruth. Will that do?"

"Will it do? You've told me nothing. I have a very smarmy spy hot on my trail, put there by you, and you tell me, and I paraphrase, it's for my own good? I haven't heard that line since I was seventeen, and it turned out not to be true then, either."

"Eden, take some advice from one who, believe it or not, really does care. Book a flight somewhere and go hide for a while or, better yet, go back to Picketsville and ask for a twenty-four-seven watch by one of Ike's people."

"Now you're scaring me."

"Good. That was the general idea."

Charlie hung up. What was holding up Ike?

Chapter Thirty-one

"We need a plan," Ruth said. She had a note book and pencil in her hand, waiting for Ike to speak. "Look, I am Effie Perrine and naturally you are Sam Spade. What's next boss?"

"I think, Effie, we reconsider your decision to put yourself in harm's way, which you made out of a misguided sense of sentimentality. You need to get off the island, now."

"You are being deliberately block-headed with me. I know that, and I appreciate it for a many reasons, not the least of which is because I think you cannot bear to contemplate what life would be like if I, like Eloise, were killed as a result of a CIA screw-up. And as screw-ups go, this seems to be shaping up as a real doozy. I take your point. Therefore, I will not be angry with you. I do understand. What does make me angry is the notion that you cannot see the reverse. How will it be if I lose you in a CIA screw-up, huh? How will I cope, do you suppose? Have you even thought of that? No, and who appointed you Horatius at the bridge anyway?"

"Once a history maven, always a history maven. Okay, you have a point. About the bridge I mean, not me as Horatius, and you are right, I cannot bear the thought of nasty men—I assume the people who are coming after me are men—I cannot bear the thought of them taking you with me, excuse the cliché, in a hail of bullets. Worse, you are right. I cannot imagine how I would manage if I survived and you didn't. Please leave now." Ruth opened her mouth to speak but Ike waved her off. "Listen, you are still recovering from serious trauma. You have bones that as yet are not completely knit. You lay in a coma for…too long. If we have to run any distance, you couldn't do it. It will be dangerous enough with me able to move around. The fact you cannot follow makes what I have to do ten times more difficult."

"Point taken. Now you listen. I will not hold you back. I limp because I prefer it to the pain caused by not doing so. But then I prefer staying by your side to the pain, you see? I can, if I have to, run, jump and, more importantly, and you probably didn't know this about me considering my public stand on firearms generally, I can shoot the eye out of a gnat at thirty feet."

"Bullshit."

"It is true. My father, who you may remember from your other life, did not share my views on the idiocy of having an armed citizenry. When I was at that age when daughters dote on their fathers, he taught me how to shoot. So, now you know the last dark secret that I have kept from you. All is revealed and the mystery in our relationship forever gone. I hope you're satisfied."

"Ruth—"

"Ike, if I can walk, jog, and shoot, I should be considered an asset, as you spooks say, not the liability you make me out to be. I don't know how much help you can expect from Charlie. And the director, if I understand the situation correctly, isn't going to offer up anything more substantial than a sympathy card and that after the fact. Damn it, Ike, you need me. Do not try to do this alone. Do not shut me out."

"I just—"

"Hush, no more noble sacrifice and chivalry. Here's the deal, Schwartz. You say you want to get married, right? That being the case, if I stay you name the day and time. If you shove me off this island, you get your ring back in the mail. I'm serious about this. Tell me I'm staying."

"You are a hard woman, Harris. You can shoot? Really?"

"Close your eyes and think of all the things I do physically, if you follow my meaning. Of that array, which I can see has already started you drooling, which do you think I do best? Don't answer, hold that thought. Now, I promise you I shoot better than I can do that. Good, you are smiling. To keep that grin on your face, I will demonstrate both of these skills after dinner."

"Okay, okay, I surrender, but when we're both standing in line at the Pearly Gates, remember, it was your idea."

"You really think we are destined for the Pearly Gates? I'm thinking a better investment would be in asbestos underwear, considering where we're likely to end up. What did you mean about my being right about the bridge?"

"The brave Horatius, if you remember, stood on the bridge to defend Rome more or less by himself as the army behind him tore the stones away. Then—"

"I know the rest. What are you driving at?"

"Horatius had the bridge torn away behind him so the invading army could not cross the river into Rome. Scone Island is difficult to reach in the same way. To get to us—note please, I did say us—they have to cross four nautical miles of angry ocean."

"Angry?"

"Pray for a Nor'easter. And when they get here, they have limited choices as to where they can come ashore, especially if they want to arrive unobserved."

"How so?"

"Look at the map. The east side of the island is a cliff that extends from Archie's place in the north almost to Southport. There is no appreciable beach on which to land, even at low tide, and then they'd still have to scale anywhere from ten to thirty feet of rocks. That leaves the west shore, and it's only marginally better. The shore flattens out on the west side, and you can see in the past where residents have attempted to build piers out into the strait, only to have winter storms tear them out. The pilings for some of them are still there, which creates a hazard to the amateur sailor. Landing, for example, on the gravel beach opposite this house is possible. However, to arrive without being seen means sailing in at night, and that could be tricky, what with your twelve-foot tides."

"Tides?'

"If they arrive at the ebb and beach their boats, they might discover them washed away in the flood if they didn't time their departure correctly."

"And the reverse, if they come in at high tide?"

"Right. They might not be able to launch them across thirty feet of rocks and gravel."

"So what will they do?"

"I don't know, but if it were me, I would either arrive pretending to be a summer renter or I'd come in from the east."

"I thought you said the east is no good."

"I did. I left one thing out. You know where Archie took his nose dive? Well, there are steps chiseled into the rock face near that point. At some time in the past the owners of Cliffside had a small beach and pier down there. The pier is long gone and the steps are worn and potentially dangerous to scale, but they could be the entry of choice, because they think we will not expect them to come that way."

"Henry Potter would spot a phony renter in a minute. You should talk to him. He could arrange a signal or something."

"Excellent. That will be your first assignment, Effie."

"Who?"

"You said you were Effie Perrine."

"Right. I'm on it. What will you do?"

"Set some alarms and traps, I think. If we were playing paint ball, this would be a great way to spend a couple of days."

"But it's not. I'm off to con Henry Potter. How much do I tell him?"

"As little as possible. Make up some cock-and-bull story about what's-his-name renting property he didn't own to folks down east."

"What's his name? Could you possibly be a bit more specific?"

"Barstow. He was the guy looking to buy properties on the island, remember. He managed to annoy a lot of people while he was here. Henry will believe you. Tell him I'm here on special undercover assignment to catch him and expose him. I'll probably have to modify the story later, but we need to start somewhere."

"That's very original. You should give up the police business and go into writing fiction."

"I'll leave that to politicians. Now hustle on down to the store. Talk to Henry Potter. Set a password, on the off-chance Charlie can drum up some help, and stock up on anything that looks edible. We're about out of comestibles and I don't want to miss dinner."

"You're hungry?'

"Yes, but that's not why. After dinner, you said you promised a demonstration of two of your more impressive skills. I don't want you begging off because the antecedent dinner did not occur."

"Spade, you sly dog. No wonder Brigid O'Shaughnessy fell for you."

"That's not how the story goes, but thanks anyway. Now go find Potter, and I will call Charlie. It's time to find out how deep this hole we're about to jump into is."

Chapter Thirty-two

Charlie had a small Swiss Army knife with the logo of a corporate airport located in Savannah embossed on it. He fished it out of his pants pocket and cut out the newspaper article with the picture of the Presidential party. He folded it and stowed it in his jacket pocket. The rest he pushed aside with his plate and half empty beer glass. Sunglasses maintained his studied indifference to Charlie and anything else within ten feet of him. The kid needed some training if he wanted a long-term career in the agency. On reflection, Charlie realized that try as he might, he did not recognize this man. The agency employed a large number of people, many, perhaps even most of whom, agents in particular, didn't work in the Langley compound. Failure to recognize one in particular should not surprise him. But, since the director's fingerprints were all over this operation, it seemed logical that the kid should come from the Big House. Charlie was not one to panic, but at that moment the thought occurred to him that the director might not be the only one tracking his phone calls. Indeed, the director might well have been tracking the trackers, so to speak. That would explain some, but not all of his recent behavior. He raised his beer glass and scanned the distorted image of the man at the bar through its thick bottom. This guy could represent a threat from a totally different quarter.

Either way, he thought, someone had him on his or her radar. He let his gaze slide across the rest of the bar, looking for any other semi-familiar faces or maybe stereotypical ones. He didn't find either. If a fellow spook occupied any of the remaining tables and booths, he wasn't going to locate him today, which meant that they were very good or not present. It had been a long time since Charlie had worked in the field, and the disconcerting idea crossed his mind that he might have lost a step.

The pub filled up with lunch seekers all, or nearly all, of whom were busily engaged with their smart phones, e-readers, and PDAs, texting, checking the Internet for e-mail, stock quotes, playing Angry Birds, or God only knew what else. The conversational noise, which a decade ago would have approached raucous, amounted only to a communal murmur as luncheon companions occasionally looked up from their devices to report some tidbit of news gleaned from cyberspace to their companion and then only to refocus, cross-eyed, on the tiny screens that now defined their existence.

As much as he disliked this pervasive noncommunication, it did serve his purpose at the moment. There would be so much traffic jamming the several wireless networks servicing the immediate area that if anyone were fishing in the cyber-pool in an attempt to locate and then monitor any specific phone, they would have to sort through more than two dozen sending/receiving modules concentrated in this single quarter acre of Georgetown. And since his was neither registered in anyone's name nor on any particular network, and because Ike would be using a satphone, he felt confident that when Ike finally called, it would go untracked. Charlie had put his second cell phone on vibrate. At that moment it danced across the table and he managed to grab it before it slipped off the edge and onto the floor.

He flipped it open all the while keeping an eye on his watcher. His sunglasses glinted and the expression on Charlie's watcher twitched. He turned away and judging by his body language, began talking into his own phone. For the people he represented, Charlie's boss or someone else, the hunt was on. Good luck with that.

"Ike, we'd better keep this short. What can you tell me?"

"That would be my question to you. Here's all I have. I am in position to meet an assassin or two with, I think success. More than two and I have a problem. My main concern is marking their approach. The island is a closed system. Once they're landed, I have the advantage. But for me to survive, I have to know when and where they hit the beach. Can you spring anybody to help me?"

"I can try. My problem is I have been condemned to purgatory or more accurately, Barratt, Colorado, to investigate Neil Bernstein's disappearance and probable death. The director made it clear I am to stay away for at least a week. That is the preamble, by the way. The immediate answer is, probably not. I would come myself in a New York minute, you know, but the use of CIA personnel in a domestic situation is not only against the law…I know, yadda, yadda…but it would be a career-ender for anyone who's caught doing it. Our peerless leader will be very unforgiving if the malefactor were found out. The best I can do is to ask for volunteers. I have access to some assets, as you may know but had better keep pretending you don't, that, under normal circumstances, the director cannot keep from doing their job if I require them. It assumes, of course, their deployment has something to do with my job description and this hardly qualifies as normal. I will try but…"

"Don't compromise either yourself or them, but if they were able to monitor the possible entry points to the island, I could probably do the rest. There is a local cop up here who is green enough to be schmoozed into helping me without involving the rest of the locals."

"I might be able to manage something. Then, if they get careless with their government issued equipment after that, well, that would be a shame but…"

"Listen, Charlie, I do have another big problem, Ruth refuses to leave the island. She has it in mind we should go out back to back, guns blazing."

"Archie's stuff should have included some choral hydrate. Knock her out and tuck her away in the basement until it's over."

"It's a thought. Thanks."

"Okay. One last thing and then we'd better drop this. I've been scouring the files that describe ops the four of you worked. I think the thing traces back to one of three operations the four of you ran in Nigeria, Libya, or Bosnia. Do you remember them?"

"I think the Nigeria business was a sting. We provided guns in exchange for conflict diamonds, only the guns were bogus. I'm a little vague on the Bosnia one. It was connected somehow to a United Nations thing—or not. Libya had to do with Lockerbie."

"In Nigeria, you're right, the sting went south. The diamonds were never delivered."

"Okay, yes. We were to work with a local doctor. He had a hospital or clinic near the beach, and he brokered the deal. We dropped the guns—they didn't have firing pins and something else, right? We stacked them in the clinic and then Archie and the doc got into a pissing match. You know Archie. He tried to bluff everybody for one thing or another. He would imply he knew a whole lot more about the person he was dealing with than he really did. It must have backfired because the next thing I remember the place was crawling with guys in uniforms carrying Uzis and machetes. We were lucky to get out of there alive."

"Do you remember the doctor's name?"

"I'd have to think about that."

"Was it Ostrofsky?"

"Sounds right. Sneaky little bastard, if I remember correctly. As I said, he ran a clinic of some sort. Weird sort of place. It had a fence like a prison around it, you know, topped with razor wire? There were all kinds of crazies running loose on the continent then. He told us he put up the fence to keep them out, or if they came in, they did so only at his invitation. Still, a razor wire fence seemed a little over the top. Oh, and armed guards in the compound, too."

"That's all?"

"All? I'd have to think on it a while, but yeah, the patients didn't look all that sick. I wondered about that at the time. I expected to see people in beds and those hospital gowns that don't cover your butt and tubes running in their arms and other miscellaneous orifices, but most of them were walking around. They looked beat up, like they'd been in a fight lately, pistol whipped maybe, but only a few were in beds and bandaged."

"They had been in a fight? Maybe they were fleeing the Congo."

"Possible, but they looked like civilians, you know. I would have sworn that some of their bruises were rifle butt strikes. I don't know, Charlie. It was long ago and another life."

"I understand. Do you think the doctor might be a link to what is going down now?"

"Ostrofsky? Like I said, I don't know, Charlie, Besides, I thought he was dead, so how would that work?"

"It wouldn't, I guess. Call it a hunch. Do you think it's possible he might have double crossed you and kept the diamonds?"

"Anything is possible. Those were crazy times. Maybe someone on the other side tipped off the gun buyers and that's when we had to boogie out of there. What about Bosnia?"

"Nothing solid, but the director served as military liaison on that one. Do you remember him?"

"You're kidding. He did? Hell, Charlie, I must be getting old, you'd think I'd remember that, wouldn't you. He was there?"

"I have a picture that says he was. I don't know what that means. You should try to remember if there was anything that happened that would not have made its way into the file."

"Okay, first, I do not remember the Army guy being the director. He wasn't on the scene often enough to make an impression. What would he have been doing there anyway? The operation had to do with supporting a local partisan group that the Company believed was composed of true blue democracy lovers. They weren't, by the way. Red as a fireman's BVD's. I have no idea what interest the DoD might have had in that beyond coordinating some air strikes. We were doing a lot of that back then."

"Nothing new there. Okay, can you tell me anything about Libya? This file is a little vague as well."

"It was a recruiting mission. Remember, we had a sea change in the country's position regarding Colonel Qadaffi about that time. The agency had him pegged as all show and no-go. After Lockerbie, we had to reconsider. The pooh-bahs in State thought we needed better eyes in Libya. We went in to find some."

"Names?"

"Come on, Charlie. They were hard enough to keep straight at the time. You think I remember now? No way. Archie would know, but he's dead. Aren't they in the file?"

"Blacked out. Since the Little Colonel's ouster, who knows what's up in that country? It'll be years before it all shakes out. The fact that some of the folks now moving into power positions may have at one time been on our payroll could play hell with their ability to move upward in the new order. It looks like someone with the clout to make the names disappear did not want to that to happen."

"If the names are blacked out, that's probably why, that or someone is looking for something else—deniability maybe."

"Or special and therefore useful knowledge to be trotted out on some future occasion. Okay, here's the big question, is the possibility that the four of you could remember any of those names a threat serious enough for someone to want to kill you?"

"There's no way to know. Possibly, but even if it is, would they have the capacity to pull something like what happened here and in Baltimore from Libya?"

"If they had help, they could. Who would be interested enough and in a position to do it? To answer that question and others like the doctor, for example, I'll need to dig deeper into files, and I can't do that at present. I have been sent to my room, or rather to Colorado."

"At the moment, none of this is important to me. The killers are in the hunt, and that's the only thing that matters, not the why."

"Exactly...but if it is an inside job..." Charlie let the words hang.

"For this to end, Charlie, you will have to figure that out. In the meantime, if you do manage to send help, there is an old down-easter here named Henry Potter. He is our watchdog. He will be expecting a password. They should say, 'I'm a friend of the VanDeVeers.' He will be logging in any and all strangers to the island. If your people say that, he'll send them to Ruth and me. If they don't, he'll flag them."

"'I'm a friend of the VanDeVeers.' Got it. Be talking later, when you're ready to be found."

Chapter Thirty-three

Before he left Washington, Charlie booked his motel in Barratt through the agency's travel service being careful to follow regulations to the letter. Once in Denver, he picked up his rental car and set out for Barratt. But before he'd cleared Denver metro, he'd pulled in at a Salvation Army store and made a few purchases: a suitcase and a job-lot of clothes. After he'd arrived in Barratt at his officially sanctioned motel room, he opened the case and removed a few pieces at random. He hung jackets in the closet, stuffed shirts and socks into drawers, and scattered laundry on the floor. In the bathroom he removed the wrappers from the little bars of soap, dumped half of the shampoo down the drain, ran the shower, left a damp towel on the floor, and returned to the room and rumpled the bedclothes. It wouldn't fool an experienced eye, but he guessed or hoped the director wouldn't waste an experienced team on the Barratt end of the business. He wasn't sure about the other party, if there was one. He glanced around and satisfied that, to the less perceptive, he was in residence; he drove away and paid cash for another room in a non-chain motel a few miles away from Barratt. He really did not want an agency babysitter. After checking in with a false ID, he drove on to Barratt. It was time to find out what happened to Bernstein.

If he tried hard enough, Charlie thought he could make out the scent of mountain pine and spruce. The Rockies were certainly well within sight. He smiled at the thought. Except for the Rocky Mountains looming on its near horizon, Barratt, Colorado could have been any small town in any state in the union. There was little else to smile at in Barratt. An east-west street ran straight through the town, intersected at its midpoint by the predictable cross street, guarded only by four-way stop signs. It, in turn, shot north and south. Both thoroughfares came from, or went to someplace important. Like dozens of forgotten towns across the country, Barratt looked tired and down on its luck, another victim of the Eisenhower administration's decision to build an enormous interstate highway system in the mid-twentieth century. Countless towns and villages that dotted the old historical routes north and south, east and west—Route 1, the storied Route 66—were now all gone to seed or well on their way, left behind, bypassed, and forgotten. They either changed or died. Most, like Barratt, died.

He found the police station a block south of the main drag, located in a forlorn two-story brick building that might once have been a bus station. It was a municipal building typical to small, economically depressed towns everywhere. Of course, that assumed at one time Barratt might have been an important enough venue to warrant a bus station. The evidence that it was not could be seen in the badly patched potholes and nearly invisible lane markers in its streets.

He pushed his way through the station's double glass doors. Painted in semigloss institutional green, the entry boasted a counter running its length and an old cop behind it. The area reeked of stale cigarette smoke. So much for a smoke-free environment. That bit of progressive doctrine had not survived the trip west, it seemed. The cop behind the counter had to be double-dipping—Social Security and this job. He was grizzled in the way of old men who've skipped their morning shave for a day or two. It wasn't the neo-stylish grunge look affected by male celebrities, clothing models, and their wannabes, but rather the carelessness of old age or a throwback to an era when men bathed and shaved once a week—on Saturday night. It was rural Colorado, after all.

Charlie flashed an ID that declared him to be a Special Investigator from the Colorado state police. He felt sure that these folks would have had little to do with the state cops if possible, so he should get an entrée without much in the way of verification. It was the best cover he could think of in his haste to leave D.C.

The old guy peered at his card and badge through reading glasses with lenses that resembled a fingerprint array more than an aid to vision.

"Bit out of your jurisdiction ain't you, Inspector?" the old cop said.

"Well, that depends, Sergeant. It is sergeant isn't it?" The old man nodded and puffed up a bit—as much as he could, given his advanced years and obvious tobacco-induced emphysema. "Not an official visit, you know. My chief sent me down here to ask one or two questions about a reported accident out this way a week or so ago. It seems the family isn't satisfied or something. You know how that goes."

The old cop nodded and gave Charlie a knowing look.

"So, I thought I'd just pop in and see iff'n y'all might have a thing or two to tell me." Charlie, when called on, could speak country cracker as well as the next man.

"Well, sir, I can sure appreciate that, I can, but I ain't so sure it's up to me. I'll have to check with the chief."

"How about you do that, Sarge."

"Yep…well, sir, here's the problem. He ain't here."

"When will he be back?"

"No telling. The trout are running real good up-country and the chief, well, he don't miss getting him his rainbows when they're running, no sir."

"He's fishing for rainbow trout? So, who is here that can help me?"

"Jack Morris, that's Lieutenant Morris, is the second-in-command, you could say, but he ain't here either. He was called out to a ruckus over to the Bailey's Motel."

"That's the motel on the other end of town, right? Can you raise him on the radio? All I need is his okay to read through a file."

"I can try. What file would that be?"

"A climbing accident involving Neil Bernstein."

The desk officer's expression shifted from ingenuous affability to poorly concealed cunning. "I believe that there file is sealed or something."

"Sealed? What do you mean it's sealed?"

"I believe there is this court order that's done been slapped on it. Something to do with the…" The old man seemed to search his limited imagination for an appropriate reason. Charlie could almost hear the wheels spinning. "Homeland Security," he blurted.

"Homeland Security had a court order placed on a file to seal the accidental death of a young rock climber? Sergeant, I don't think so. Really?"

"Yep. It were something like that. So, I don't have to call the lieutenant on account of it's all hush-hush."

Charlie noticed a young officer doing his paper work at a steel desk that had seen its best days well before it turned up at the federal surplus property center to be claimed by this back-country outfit. He did not look happy. Whether his unhappiness had anything to do with the conversation at the desk or what lay on his desk, he couldn't tell, but Charlie felt sure the cop had overheard the conversation and knew something. Would he share?

"Well, okay," Charlie said loudly enough so the cop in the corner could hear. "I expect I'll pick me up some dinner over at that diner on Main Street. If the chief or the lieutenant can help me out, maybe they could drop by or give me a call."

"I'll tell them, but don't hold your breath, Inspector," the old cop said and grinned revealing a set of tobacco-stained dentures. That would explain the clicking that followed his every sibilant.

Charlie nodded, dropped his bogus business card on the counter, and shot the young cop a look. He pushed back through the glass doors and out to the street. Did he want to call Ike yet? His cell phone indicated enough signal strength to make the call. He shrugged and made for the diner. Diners are an American institution, and Charlie began to relax in the mixed aromas of frying bacon, coffee, and canned gravy. He found an empty booth, ordered coffee, the Salisbury steak dinner, and a slice of apple pie. The pie had been billed as homemade. The menu, like the old cop, lied. The place that pie had called home was more likely a factory in Denver than the diner's attached kitchen. He shoved it aside and ate his dinner…and waited. Whether his wait would be for Ike, the young cop from the station, or perhaps another, more important local cop, he couldn't say. But he didn't have to wait long. The young officer from the station stepped in and sat down at the counter.

Sandy Ansona settled onto a stool and ordered a burger, fries, and coffee. He scanned the mirror opposite and found the state inspector sitting in a booth in the corner and watching him. He looked away. He had a decision to make; one that could, if he had it wrong, end his career. Did he dare talk to this guy? Would he do any more than his brother could, or would this guy cover the "thin blue line" and their respective rear ends? The town needed a deep cleaning, as his dentist would say. What were the chances this man from Denver would be the means of getting it done? He chewed his burger and drank his coffee. Then, his mind made up, scribbled a message on his napkin and headed to the restrooms. As he passed the inspector, he staggered slightly and bumped his table. He apologized, stooped and retrieved a napkin which apparently had dropped to the floor and placed it on the table. He proceeded to the restroom.

Chapter Thirty-four

The days grow longer in Maine as May makes its transit to June and the earth tilts toward the summer solstice. If it were not so, Ike and Ruth would have been stumbling around in the dark on the footpath that crossed the island while lugging Archie Whitlock's duffle and satphone.

"What are we doing?" Ruth struggled to keep up with Ike. She'd been recklessly nonchalant when describing her tolerance to pain, but she could not pull back now or Ike would surely pack her off to Picketsville, threats of a marital breakup notwithstanding. In fact, she wondered why he hadn't done so already. He knew her threat was merely rhetorical. She preferred not to think about it even as she acknowledged she had no power to refuse were he to insist, so she grunted along in his wake trying, but failing, to ignore the painful jolts that shot up her barely healed broken leg.

"We're looking for lurks." Ike slowed his pace, either in response to her grunting or because he had seen something.

"Looking for what? What did you say we're looking for? A lurk? What's a lurk?"

"You've seen leopards in trees?"

"Not lately, Schwartz. Very few big cats make it to Picketsville. Or are you suggesting that African fauna have taken up residence on this island? They're after the deer perhaps?"

"Don't go all smarty-pants with me, kiddo. Leopards lurk in trees to avoid danger and to wait for prey. We need places to do the same thing if a massacre is to be avoided. We will find cover and good lines of fire in a variety of spots here and there. We will stock those spots with some of Archie's stuff. Then as the scenario unfolds we will have places we either can retreat to that are defensible and stocked with the things we need to hold out, or where we lie in wait for the nasties to come to us."

"That's a lurk? Are you speaking spook talk or did you make that up?"

"The latter. Look there." Ike pointed to a shallow defilade next to the path. "That depression can be made secure. Go gather some brush. I saw a good-sized log back along the path. If we put it across the front here, then…" He didn't finish his sentence but jogged down the path in the direction they'd come. Ruth wasn't sure why, but she gathered armfuls of brush and piled them up next to the soon-to-be lurk. A moment later Ike hove into view dragging a sizable tree trunk.

"Holy cow, Ike, that thing is as big around as me."

"Bigger, actually. You have not kept up with your wasted shape since your holiday in the hospital."

"Wasted? Is that spelled with an *i* in the middle or do you mean the other one? Be careful how you answer."

"Whatever. Here, help me slide this parallel to the path."

They pulled and tugged and managed to build a passable fortress at the spot. Ike removed several items and placed them out of sight under the tree's trunk. Ruth arranged the brush around the sides and front. She stepped back to inspect her work and then leaned in to reposition several branches.

"It's fine, Ruth. This is not an Ikebana show. The brush only has to provide cover. Aesthetics can wait for another day."

"Philistine."

"Yeah, yeah. Okay, let's move on and find another." They headed east toward the road leading to Cliffside.

"How about the old watch tower for a lurk?"

"Good idea, except for the stairs, or more accurately the ladder. Getting up and down could be a problem for you." Ruth wanted to object, to declare her toughness and her unwillingness to admit that she really did hurt. Instead, she shrugged, relieved.

"Anyway, it could easily end up being a trap," Ike went on. "If we were caught up in it, getting out alive would be next to impossible. If we use it at all, it will be to track them in, assuming they come in from the ocean side."

"You think they will?"

"At the moment it seems the most likely spot, but I'm taking no chances I'm wrong. We will need to set up some sort of watch on the beaches on the west side."

"How? There are only two of us."

"I am hoping Charlie finds us some volunteers. His people would be sacked if they were caught in a domestic, that is, continental US operation, but I'm hoping he'll find something. In the meantime I plan to call Stone. If I can pry him loose from his boss, he could watch the beach. And he'd have his own night vision goggles."

"His own? We have them?"

"We do. Archie was very thorough. We have the goggles, plenty of ammunition, a variety of firearms, and some exotic stuff I'm trying to remember how to deploy."

"Do I want to know what the exotic stuff is?"

"Given your sense of outrage at all things that discharge lethal or dangerous projectiles, no, you do not."

"I must have been crazy to throw in with you. What was I thinking?"

"Don't beat yourself up. It was animal magnetism. You couldn't help yourself."

"Right, I keep forgetting. Where will we place the next lurk?"

"I think we need at least two more. If they come in at the stone steps, we start this game at Cliffside. After the first skirmish, assuming we don't win on the first go-round, we will pull back. If one of the roads south is blocked, say West Road, we need to be able to use North Road. So, we put one north of the watch tower on West and one up from your house on North."

"Why don't we hole up in the house and make them come to us."

"It's a thought, but one of the exotic things in Archie's bag was incendiaries. I have to assume they will be carrying something similar, and you do not want to be in one of these stick-and-shingle cottages if it catches fire."

"Good Lord, Ike. Is that for real? Do people really have stuff like that?"

"We do. They might."

"Shit. We better have dinner soon, I'm thinking. 'The condemned man ate a hearty meal.' I am so glad you don't do this every day. Listen, I'm putting another condition on this deal."

"Another? What was the first?"

"Jeez, they forget so soon. Marriage, donkey brain. I said—"

"I remember. I wanted to make sure you did, too. And exactly what are you adding to your original bit of extortion?"

"If we get out of this alive—"

"An outcome sincerely to be hoped."

"Shut up for a minute. If we survive this, you will never, not ever, allow Charlie Garland into our lives again nor will you allow yourself to be put in this kind of outhouse again ever."

"That is a lot of 'evers,' but okay. It will break Charlie's heart; besides, this is not his doing, as you well know. This particular creature crawled up out of the black lagoon that is my past. Charlie only wanted to give me a heads-up."

"Yeah, I know. Bully for him. Nevertheless, I'm not willing to live like the heroine in a Bruce Willis movie. When we return to the wilds of Virginia, no guns, no men intent on dispatching you and yours, no incendiaries, rocket launchers, or weapons of mass destruction, got it?"

"Got it. Let's have a quick look at that watch tower."

They walked the hundred yards further along the path that veered north and then turned right to the old military site. Two long buildings sat side by side, and a smaller one at right angles formed a rough quadrangle to the west of the watchtower. Ike imagined young men in army brown—the brown shoe army, they called themselves—assembled in squads and platoons. Morning roll call. He guessed the smaller building served as the mess hall, the larger ones as barracks.

"The buildings look in pretty good shape, considering."

"I think the island's Residents Council, or whatever it's called, has permission to use them and they have cookouts and picnics here in the summer. They maintain them, anyway."

They passed a playground which featured a very old, brightly painted Jeep as its focal point.

"What is an orange jeep doing on the island?"

"I guess the military left it after the war. It would cost a fortune to ship it back to the mainland. When the residents built the playground, they incorporated it. The artillery pieces were still in place for a while, too. I think they just spiked them and left. The barrels were filled with cement."

"Were? I don't see any cannons."

"They're gone. In the early seventies, when the antiwar protests were in full swing, some of the island's more liberal-minded and anti-military residents shoved them over the cliff into the ocean. If you look over the side at low tide you can still see them. All rusted and falling apart, though."

Ike shook his head. "Those were sad days, a nation divided and its young men and women, reluctant soldiers for the most part, forgotten, disparaged, and lost in the din of rhetoric and recrimination from people who should have known better."

He walked to the tower and stood staring at its door, secured with a cheap combination lock.

"Looks like you're out of luck if you want to climb up to the top, Ike. That is unless you can crack the combination."

"Not necessary. All I need is a soda can, a pair of scissors and five minutes."

"More spycraft?"

"Nope, only what every kid who regularly checks out U-tube knows. Watch and learn."

He found an aluminum can in the grass and using his pocket knife, cut a rectangle from its side. He made four more quick cuts, folded the metal, and wrapped the result around the shackle and pressed it down. The lock popped open.

"That's amazing. You learned that from the Internet?"

"Yep. When we do a drug search at a school, that's why we are reluctant to accuse a kid of possession just because the weed is in his locker. Anybody who knows this trick could have put it there."

"I need to talk to my security people when I go back to work. Oops, I mean *if* I go back to work."

"I admire your confidence in our chances of survival. Okay, look, it's getting too dark to do anything else today. First thing in the morning, we'll finish up and then set the dogs loose. It's time to call Charlie and then have some dinner, such as it is. Then you will see to it that 'the condemned man' has his demonstration, as promised."

"You never give up, do you?"

"Never."

"And you promise, no more living on the edge?"

"Cross my heart—"

"And hope to die…not the sort of reassurance I was hoping to hear. What now?"

"Well, while we are sitting around wondering if there will be a wedding to buy me a gift for, crank up your computer and find out how you purchase Pine Tree Island."

"You're kidding. You were serious about that?"

"Absolutely."

"And you want it, why?"

"Thinking about a comfortable retirement."

"On Pine Tree Island?"

"In a manner of speaking, yes."

"You're the idiot this time…and don't even say it."

Chapter Thirty-five

Charlie glanced at the square of rumpled tissue paper in front of him. It seemed a simple enough message. He was to wait five minutes and then drive north out of town. It would be best if he went over the speed limit a little. That was all.

He nodded to the cop as he walked by on his way to the parking lot. Five minutes it would be. His phone buzzed—Ike, bad timing.

"Ike, I can't talk very long. I may be on to something. The investigation into Bernstein's death is beginning to smell. I'll know if there is anything useful to report in about five."

"Good, but understand, at the moment I am far more concerned with what's happening here. Can Santa find me some elves? I need help. There is too much shore line for me to watch, especially at night. Anything would help. Oh, and tell me about Frank Barstow."

"Sorry, who?"

"Last fall, you used that name to flim-flam some Chicago lawyers. I want to know if you'd been busy up here."

"Me? On that island?"

"That is the question, yes."

"Then the answer is, no. Why?"

"I'm having a hard time getting my mind around the possibility that the agency allowed a rogue and rambler like Archie to wander around loose with no adult supervision, if you follow me."

"And?"

"And that means, if I'm correct, someone is already on the island assigned to watch our boy and make sure he stayed out of trouble."

"And you're guessing it was Barstow, and because that was a moniker I once used you thought that I might have…what were you thinking?"

"That the name is too much of a coincidence, so I was hoping you could tell me."

"I would if I could. Like it or not, coincidence wins in this case and beyond that I cannot say. The boss is playing this one very close to his chest. At least he's not letting me see his hand, so I don't know if there is someone from our shop up there or not. But, it's hard to believe the director didn't have someone on the island."

"Can you find out?"

"As you know, I am in the doghouse so, no. But if there is someone, wouldn't he have deployed him or her by now?"

"How would he do that, since he doesn't know I'm here and I am not about to tell him—not yet, anyway."

"Then as far as local help goes, you're screwed." Ike remained silent for a moment. "Ike? Are you still there?"

"The director came to the CIA from the Pentagon, didn't he?"

"Yes. He had a background in intel. Did you remember something about any of the ops he shared with you?"

"Nothing beyond what you told me, but at the moment I'm more interested in his subsequent life in the E Ring."

"Again, right now I can't help you with that either. Ike, I have to go,"

"I understand. Go chase your lead. Ruth and I are done for the night. When we're ready, I will call you on the open phone and we will discuss the fact that I can't tell you where I am, but that I'm on special assignment investigating Archie's death. That will get our bad boys on a plane to Maine within the hour."

"Very neat. Let them believe they are smart. Okay, I'm off to play state investigator. Good luck."

Charlie hung up and left the diner. He had to stop for a second to get his bearings. Which way was north? It would be very embarrassing to tear off south or west, receive a speeding ticket from some other cop, and miss his chance to gather the information the young man wanted to give him. His rental had a compass built into its navigating system. A mile and a half out of town, cruising along at five miles an hour over the limit, he saw the red and blue flashing lights in his rear view mirror. He pulled over and waited.

"This had better be good," he muttered and waited for the young cop to reach his rolled down window.

"You know you were exceeding the limit," the cop said.

"Yes. I'm afraid I must have been thinking about something else. You know how it is. I had made an inquiry at your police station and received some curious news about a friend of mine."

"Curious?" The cop had his citation book out and started to write. "You do know I will have to write this up."

"Of course. The law is the law. Is there anything else you might have to tell me? Caution me, perhaps?"

"You were asking about a climber named Bernstein. License and registration, please." Charlie handed him the rental car's papers and the license he'd had made up for the occasion.

"So what is your interest—the state's interest in a climbing accident?"

Charlie decided to take a chance. This cop desperately wanted to tell him something and needed a nudge. "We're not sure he fell."

The cop started. "No? You think he had help off the cliff?"

"Corporal, we are in the middle of nowhere because you asked me to meet you out here. You want to tell me something but are hesitating. Why is that?"

"I wondered, but the chief said accident and the ME's office didn't object, so I didn't know for sure, but like I said, I had some doubts, is all."

"Why?"

"Two reasons. First, your climber was wearing a gold and steel Rolex watch. What kind of idiot scales a stone wall wearing a watch that is worth a down payment on a house?"

"Point taken. From what we know about the man, he was not an idiot. He was an experienced climber."

"Right, that's the second thing. He had on slacks and a sweater. You don't climb in picnic togs. Also no boots, no pitons or bashies in a bag, no rope, nothing."

"Certainly that is suspicious, but don't some climbers like to climb solo? Crack climbing I think it's called?"

"Maybe, but if he were going up that particular face free solo he'd have had a bummer at least. I mean, who makes it up near to the top, high enough so the fall kills him, and still has clean slacks and no scrapes or damage to his nails much less to his hands and, oh yeah, he was wearing a ring. Climbers, free climbers especially, would never start up with a class ring on their finger."

"No. So, what do you think happened?"

"No clue. That's all I know, but that's not why I wanted to meet you."

"No? Why then?" The air had turned cold and now Charlie was sure he smelled the conifers as well as the possibility of snow. The cop had a jacket with fake fur collar. Charlie had on a sports coat and tie. If they didn't finish their interview soon, one of them would soon freeze to death, and the cop didn't look like the one.

"Like I said, the man wore a Rolex and had a pistol in his duffel."

"A pistol? What sort?"

"Look, I spent a tour or two in the desert, you know, MPs. I'd swear it was government issue."

"And?"

"Well, the Rolex is now on the chief's wrist and the M-11, that's a 9 mm Sig Sauer—"

"I know what it is. You didn't happen to get the serial number by any chance?"

The cop reached in the window and retrieved Charlie's citation. He turned it over, wrote on the back, and returned it to Charlie. "What happens now?"

"Where is the gun?"

"Lieutenant's got it."

"You have a very dysfunctional police department."

"You could say that."

"Okay, here's what happens now. You hop back in your cruiser and forget we ever had this conversation. Rolexes are registered by number. Your chief is in possession of stolen property. Unless he can produce a bill of sale with Neil Bernstein's signature on it, he is done as a cop. Your lieutenant is packing an unauthorized bit of government property. He will not be able to explain that away and will be looking for a new career as well."

"You're from the state. How do I know the big shots back in the attorney general's office won't sweep this under the rug like they do everything else that goes on out here?"

"Listen carefully. Under the rubric that we never had this conversation, I am not from the state, I am federal. The murdered man was a colleague. He died in a federal park. Your two bozo cops interfered with an investigation of a felony on federal property, as it happens. That makes it a federal case all round. We done here? I'm freezing."

"Yeah…no, wait. There's one more thing. I don't know if it's important, but I saw evidence that a chopper, a big one, had been in the mountain meadow about that time. Does that mean anything to you?"

Charlie's teeth had begun to chatter. "It means, if you were to fall out of a helicopter rather than off a cliff face, you wouldn't scrape your knees, muss up your slacks, and you'd still be in possession of your Rolex and class ring. That's good work, corporal. Thank you. You will not be hearing from me again, but you can expect a few stony-faced federal types in your neighborhood in the very near future."

Charlie rolled up the window and put the heater on high. He was almost warm by the time he arrived back at his off-the-books motel.

Eden Saint Clare decided she'd had it. It was one thing to have to put up with lawyers and a disingenuous sister-in law, quite another to sit twiddling her thumbs in Chicago wondering what the hell her daughter was up to in Aunt Margaret's cottage. And then, to top it off, that bit of bizarre advice from Charlie Garland? What was that all about? She should go hide or ask for twenty-four-seven protection back home? Why? Someone must have stepped into a pile of you-know-what, but who and where? Well, she'd find out, and the hell with Garland and his pals who played hide-and-seek on the taxpayer's dime. After all she'd spotted the jerk who'd been shadowing her. Okay, not right away, but eventually. The idiot probably thought because she was a woman she wouldn't notice and became careless. Now he'd gone.

She wanted some answers. If she flew to Maine, she'd be following Garland's advice to hide, wouldn't she? Nobody knew about that remote place. And if Ike knew anything, she'd get answers. He was connected, and he owed her that much. Besides, Maine might be very nice this time of year; chilly, but nice. She'd make a quick run to the Magnificent Mile and shop for a nice ski jacket and some slacks, something in taupe with a fur trim. No, probably not fur. Too not-PC.

Chapter Thirty-six

A fire crackled in the living room—the front parlor in earlier times. It snapped and shot sparks like tiny missiles into the fire screen as the soft pine Ike used to create the heat needed to set the hardwoods to burning did its job. The Coleman lantern sat unlit in the corner, its white light absent and the room cozier for it. Ike put his feet up on the coffee table in front of the sofa on which he and Ruth were now seated. They had come in to the comfort of fire and hearth after they'd finished their meager dinner and after Ruth, as promised, had demonstrated her skill with a hand gun. Shooting "the eye out of a gnat" grossly overstated Ruth's abilities, but she did manage to hit one of the four Spam cans he's set up and two other shots came near enough, judging by the damage done to the piece of drift wood on which the cans had been placed. It would do. In a gun battle, he'd explained to a chagrined Ruth, if there was to be one, the best you could hope for was an intense field of fire—lots of bullets flying in the general area of the enemy. It seemed counterintuitive to Ruth and she said so, to which Ike had replied that obviously she watched too much television.

"I rarely watch the tube except with you when you stream old movies and English mysteries with that Internet streaming thingy."

"The obvious source of your misinformation in either case."

"Okay, I give up. You are the expert in mayhem."

"I am. At least in the present company, I am. Not saying much, though."

They had settled into silence, each studying the dancing pattern the flames made as the logs hissed and popped.

Ruth shivered. "Woo," she said.

"Woo? Sorry not following you."

"Nothing."

"Woo, as in nothing? Come on what's with woo?"

"Okay, it's silly. When I was growing up and in a jam, or trouble, or more often about to do something my parents would surely disapprove, I'd get this shivery feeling before my mother popped around the corner and caught me red-handed, that's all."

"You're expecting the newly lithesome Eden Saint Clare to pop in on us now?"

"No, of course not, I had a feeling like that is all. Enough for a small woo."

"Right. Shivery feeling and a 'woo.' Have I got it?"

"Don't get smart. You told me yourself you get hunches and premonitions and they kept you out of trouble in the past."

"I did indeed." Ike's expression slipped into something resembling a trance.

"So, what are you thinking? Having a 'woo' yourself?"

"No wooing here. I was wondering more than thinking. There are a few things I need to work through, that's all."

"What kind of things? Besides the rest of the demonstration I promised you. I haven't forgotten, so you don't have to make your usual unseemly fuss."

"I wasn't planning to. I trust you to keep your word, now or eventually. No, several things have been crawling around in my cerebral cortex. For instance, how likely is it Archie Whitlock came to the island without the agency knowing? And as a corollary, and assuming they did, isn't it equally likely that they have placed someone on the island whose job it is, or was, to keep track of him?"

"On that score, I confess cluelessness. I think the world of spies is a sea of lies. Did I make that up or am I quoting someone else and I've forgotten who? It sounds like Ogden Nash. Anyway, why is that important?"

"It is important because if I am right, it means there is either help nearby or it creates another problem for us."

"I'm going with help. Of course, I do not know what I'm talking about, but I like help better than another problem."

"As do I. We will have to see what turns up. The next thing I would like to know is that little walkway on the roof—"

"The widow's walk?"

"Exactly. Is it merely decorative, or is there access to it and can one actually walk on it?"

"I am not sure."

"You never went up there?"

"The few times I visited my great-aunt Margaret, the attic door was kept locked and I had strict instructions not to try to open it."

"And you, being the perfect angel you were back then, did not try."

"I did not, but it had nothing to do with being angelic. My great-uncle Oscar had mysteriously disappeared some years before and I got it in my head that he was locked up in the attic, doubtless dead and moldering."

"Vivid imagination?"

"More like the only explanation I could dream up for a missing Uncle Oscar. The grown-ups were not going to say anything. I think old Oscar ran off with a chambermaid. They still had them back then, and no one wanted to try to explain what that involved to a nine-year old."

"Ah, the age of innocence. Nowadays kids are exposed to so much sex and violence on television, a missing uncle and chambermaid would seem pretty small potatoes. So, anyway, the widow's walk, is it a functioning walk or an architectural frew-fraw?"

"We'll have to go see. I really don't know. Not tonight, though. It's cold and dark, and I'll have to find the key to the attic door if it's locked."

"Tomorrow morning would be fine."

"Do I want to know why you need to use the walkway?"

"If it's accessible, I imagine it has a view of the west shoreline all the way to The Bite. I'm also guessing it has a line of sight to the watch tower on the other side of the island as well. If that is the case, we can watch both and have a means of signaling to each other if we see anyone coming ashore."

"Signaling? How?"

"Flash light."

"One if by land, two if by sea?"

"Several quick blinks which will mean 'here they come, get a move on.'"

"I see. Yes, we could. I have an ancillary question. When the bugle blows and all this craziness begins, when do we sleep?"

"In the absence of any help from the outside, we don't."

"Then I'm going to bed right now and get in some serious REMs while I still can. Sorry about the second part of the promise, but I need sleep more than you need that. You can have your fun later, if we survive."

"Good thinking. Only you will not mind if, after we have buried ourselves in the duvet, I try to change your mind?"

"There is no mercy with you is there, Schwartz?"

"Who ever heard of a merciful cop?"

The next morning Ike stood on the widow's walk with the wind whipping at his parka. The air held the tang of salt and sea and on any other occasion he'd have noticed and remarked on it, but not now, not under the circumstances.

He'd been correct. From the top of Ruth's roof he could see north to the cliff that bounded Cliffside on the west, and south as far as the old Coast Guard building and The Bite. With Archie's night vision goggles they could easily monitor this stretch of coast. To the east he could make out the top of the watch tower peeking over the treetops. If he was stationed there and Ruth here on the top of her house, they would not be surprised by anyone coming ashore. But, as Ruth had reminded him, how were they going to stay awake for the hours that could elapse before his attackers decided to move? They would need some help. He directed his gaze southward again and caught sight of a launch headed toward the island. He trained his binoculars on the boat and made out the logo of the Sheriff's office on the side. Stone?

He climbed down from his aerie and told Ruth of their good luck. He then set her to sorting the remainder of their supplies, the items not to be squirreled away in one of the lurks.

"I am off to tackle Deputy Stone and Henry Potter. When I get back, we will finish the preparations on the various escape routes and then…" He didn't finish the sentence. He didn't have to.

"While you are at the store, buy out Potter's stock of booze. I have a sinking feeling we will need it pretty soon."

"Last thing we need, but I will empty his bandages and first aid supplies."

Ruth covered her ears. "Not listening…la, la, la, la, la…"

"Right. As long as you understand and remember, it is not too late to leave the island."

"La, la, la, la."

Chapter Thirty-seven

Charlie didn't get a good read on the director's reaction when he reported Neil Bernstein's death and the response to it by the Barratt police. The director did make it clear that the penalty for abusing the system, particularly as it affected one of his agents, would be quick and uncompromising. That said, Charlie was to stand down until the FBI arrived and then tell them what he knew. Charlie said he would. He returned to his official motel long enough to ruin the housekeeping crew's hard work once again, this time adding trash to the wastepaper baskets and a supply of fast food paper bags and empty Starbucks cups to the general disorder. Then he retreated to his unofficial residence to relax and think. He wondered if, by booking the double rooms, he wasn't being overly cautious, paranoid even. He dismissed the thought. After all, he drew his paycheck from the CIA. Of course he was paranoid. It was in his job description.

With little else to do, he began to call around the country for volunteers to provide backup for Ike. He had made less than a half dozen when his phone chirped and the director's aide, Mark, informed him that under no circumstances was he to drag anyone else in on the Archie Whitlock business, and his access to his draw-down agents had been blocked. Bingo. As the old joke goes, you're not paranoid if they really are after you. Archie, Ike, Neil, Al, and a younger director in Bosnia… connected? And if so, how?

Now he had nothing to do but wait until he heard from Ike and to deal with the Feds sent to clean up Barratt's dirty cops when they arrived. If they didn't come in the next few days, he'd miss that show, too. Either way, since the agency had cut off all other avenues of support for Ike, he would need to move in himself. To do that, he'd have to be in two places at once and that meant, in turn, he would need to dust off his *doppelganger* routine— a ploy he'd managed a few times in the past. It was a tricky move under the best of conditions, and the current ones were a long way from the best of anything. But, no way would he leave Ike hanging out to dry. Besides, he liked Ruth Harris and owed her something for saving Ike from himself back when his life seemed dark indeed. The thought of the two of them knocking heads with the kind of people who could access the kind of resources that allowed them to drop a CIA operative from a helicopter in the middle of a federal park clinched his determination to proceed with his plans even if it could be construed as an attempt to flip off the boss who, the more he thought about it, genuinely deserved a flipping at a minimum.

The double switch required that he find someone who shared his stature and was willing to do something off the wall, but not, strictly speaking, illegal for money. He decided to drive to Aspen. He would have no difficulty finding a suitable double among what he guessed would be a more than ample supply of financially strapped ski bums stuck in town as the tourist season melted away with the snow. With tourists bailing, their chances to cadge meals and lodging with compliant, would-be celebrities and snow bunnies would have shrunk significantly. He felt certain he could find someone near enough to his size who'd jump at a chance to exchange some small inconvenience for cash and a plane ticket to the next free lunch venue. And if his man was not in Aspen, he'd try Vail and, if necessary, the whole string of ski resorts and tourist towns that dotted the general area. He'd have his man, or woman for that matter, in a day—two at the latest. What broke drifter wouldn't be happy to spend a short week in a motel with room service and three fifths of double-malt scotch for an opportunity to move on to greener pastures for free?

◇◇◇

Ike arrived at Potter's store a few minutes after the police launch discharged its occupants. He recognized the broad back of Deputy Tom Stone entering the store lugging an official-looking satchel and an armful of packages. Apparently the launch skipper had been persuaded to serve as the mail boat as well. He hoped to corral both Stone and Potter. Explaining what he needed from them would require a carefully crafted and creative story. That is to say he'd have to lie convincingly while making the improbable plausible to two men who, he had no doubts, were no fools. But, before he did that, he needed to pump them both for more information.

During his first minutes with Henry Potter, he caught sight of a woman making a quick exit from the side door. It had been out of the corner of his eye, to be sure, but it triggered something—another one of those moments, not unlike the one he'd experienced when he'd seen Archie's weather tower go up. Only later did he figure that one out. Archie had one like it when he lived in Louisiana with his third or his fourth wife. Difficult at the remove of nearly ten years to keep Archie's wives straight, or his weather stations, for that matter. He remembered thinking at the time that her name sounded phony, like she'd made it up somewhere along the way. Cora something…Cora Sharpe she called herself. He had toyed with the idea of tapping into the agency's system and tracing her, but by the time he'd gotten around to it, Archie had moved on, this time to a stewardess—that's what they were called back then, not flight attendants. So what was it about the fleeting figure in the door that made him miss a beat?

"What say?" Potter leaned in to study Ike.

"Sorry. Something distracted me for a moment. Can you tell me who that woman was who ducked out the door?"

"Miz Smithwick, I reckon." He lowered his glasses which were perched on the top of his head and peered in the direction Ike had indicated. "Yep, she's one of the island's regulars. Been coming to the island since she were a kid back in the fifties, maybe earlier. Before my time, for sure."

"It's a little early for the summer people to arrive isn't it?"

"Well, it is that. They mostly show up here after Memorial Day, which is next week, of course. I reckon they'll start turning up in the days after that. It'll mostly be residents to clean up their properties, stock the larder and such, but yep, they're on the way, you could say."

"Does Mrs. Smithwick usually arrive this early?"

"Well, no sir, she told me she heard it were going to be a soft spring up here and she up and decided to come a month early this year."

"People do, you know. There was this lady come up about that time too. Writer or something. She said she needed to find her muse, whatever that is. Ain't seen much of her since though. Now, that there Miz Smithwick, she were married to some fella in Washington, D.C. 'Course, he went and died some years back. There was talk then but…"

"What kind of talk?"

"Didn't amount to much. You probably remember when the Congress was on a witch hunt back then about them Savings and Loans. I think he had to testify or something. It didn't help none that he came to the country after World War II as some kind of refugee. Had that thick accent."

"Accent? With a name like Smithwick? What kind of accent?"

"Couldn't say. Somebody allowed as how he was from Africa, somewhere, but that don't seem likely, unless it were South Africa. The man was as white as you and me."

"You said they came a month ago?" Potter waggled his bushy eyebrows and shrugged. "Tell me, the man who fell off the cliff, he was on the island then, too?"

"Well, now that you mention it, Mister Staley did come the same time them two did."

Ike grilled him for another fifteen minutes and then told him "the story." Potter's eyes widened, squinted tight, and then he gave Ike a knowing wink. One down. One to go.

Stone turned out to be a harder sell. The tricky part involved distancing the deputy from his boss. He needed Stone on the ground but he definitely did not want to have to explain to the county sheriff why he, Ike, had been sent "on special assignment" to investigate the alleged murder of an anonymous old man. Ike implied, but was careful not to say so directly, that he was a federal agent, undercover, and the dead man had connections to organized crime. Fortunately Stone was still young and green and not conscious of the fact that cops sometimes lied. Most of the time they did so in the pursuit of the greater good, but occasionally they did it to cover their rear ends, and, once in a great while because they were dirty. The kid would learn in time. Ike felt a momentary pang of guilt for using the kid, but his choices were limited and the twinge did not last very long. When he felt sure Stone understood what he needed from him and Potter had assured him he understood the key words needed from strangers who arrived pretending to be renters, he set off for the cottage. He had to pass the Coast Guard Station on the way. He had paid little or no attention to it the several times he'd passed it before, but at this particular moment he felt drawn to its padlocked door. As much as he wanted to get back to Ruth, he veered away from the road and made his way down the slight incline that led to the building.

The door's lock hung from a rusty hasp and matched the two he'd seen on Pine Tree Island when he'd discovered the concrete construction. He guessed this lock would succumb to a rock as well. It would be interesting to know what Captain Gustave Staehle had left behind when he and his charges had vacated the island. It seemed odd that no one had broken in to the building after all this time. World War II ended before most of the people on the island were born. You'd have thought curiosity would have piqued someone enough to have a quick look inside at least. He walked north along the length of the building and turned the corner. At this point, he figured he would be out of sight. He found another door, this one secured not with the presumed standard Coast Guard issue padlock but a brand new combination lock, the twin of the one securing the Watch Tower door.

Somebody had a secret. But did it have anything to do with his current predicament? Probably not, but then again, perhaps it did. He would make a visit to the building after dark.

He'd been staring at the door and its lock for several minutes when he felt the hair on the back of his neck prickle. He couldn't be sure, but this sixth sense had served him well in the old days and now suggested he was being watched. A quick three-sixty sweep of his surroundings revealed nothing. Potter had his back to him at the store. Stone had wandered off somewhere. His eyes weren't what they used to be, of course, and he might have missed someone in the shrubbery. The feeling did not go away. Someone had him in sight, of that he was sure. He guessed it was time to start packing his hand gun.

Chapter Thirty-eight

Ike found Ruth sitting on the porch chin in hand and deep in thought, or so he assumed. He didn't know whether he dared disturb her or not. The ancient wicker creaked and groaned as he took a seat next to her. He waited.

"Schwartz, are you absolutely sure there are no alternatives, more attractive alternatives, available other than a shoot-out at the Not So OK Corral? I want to know that if I am about to cash in my chips early, I am exercising the best possible option."

"You know full well that there is a better scenario with respect to your chip cashing—you leave the island right now."

"And you would tackle the assassins or whatever they are alone. Yes, I know about that one. I have rejected it out of hand. Or, more accurately, I have put you on the famous horns of a dilemma. And, in case you're approaching dotage and have forgotten, I gave you my reasons for rejecting it. I'm asking if, other than me bailing out, there might not be a safer course."

Ike let his gaze shift across the roadway and then south toward The Bite. Was there? None he could think of. "Nope, but I'm open to suggestions."

"This is not my game, but it occurs to me that we have an advantage we need to exploit."

"And that is?"

"They have no idea where they must look to find us. We, on the other hand, once they have landed will know exactly where they are all the time. That being the case, and you being the cool hand that you are, why don't we lure them into the open say over there where the path meets the road and, using Mister Whitlock's very sophisticated rifle, snipe them."

"Snipe them?"

"We set up the widow's walk as one of our lurks and shoot them from it. Isn't that what a sniper does? We'll have our own grown-up version of a snipe hunt."

"I don't think sniper comes from snipe hunt…wait, you know, maybe it does. I never really thought about it."

"I looked it up while you were bamboozling Potter and Stone. It refers to the ability of soldiers in colonial India to shoot the snipe which is 'any of about twenty-five wading bird species in three genera in the family *Scolopacidae*.' Apparently the little critters were difficult to bring down. Can't think why."

"Bamboozling? Ah, that would be from the act of hunting the Great Crested Bamboozle of Tasmania which is said to paint its eggs gold so that greedy farmers will hatch them in the hopes of obtaining a goose which lays—"

"Knock it off. I asked you a question, which you have avoided by punting it back to me. So, okay, you have my suggestion. What do you think?"

"It is a fine idea. My concern is that if they represent more than two or three, there is a very good possibility the sniper, and that would be me I take it, could end up trapped forty feet above ground with no means of escape."

"What if there were two snipe shooters, one up top and one below. If the first volley doesn't get them all, well, then when they go for the house, number two shoots them from the side."

"Possible. We'll call that plan R."

"R? Isn't it usual to start with A?"

"It is, but we are on a short string here and R for Ruth seemed more appropriate. The next will be S, you see?"

"For Schwartz?"

"Exactly."

"I must say, for a couple facing probable extinction, we are taking this with great good humor. Do you mind if I break the mood here and tell you I am scared spitless?"

"You and me both, kiddo. It's called gallows humor."

"Ah, we agree on that at least. So what is plan S?"

"Whatever we do, Ruth, will depend on three things at least. How many there are, where and when they come ashore, and what they bring with them. If we can catch them on the steps on the cliff, for example, it will be like shooting fish in a barrel."

"Stop! A question for you that requires an answer before we shoot fish, snipe, or anything real or metaphorical. If these bad people are eliminated, and if whoever is behind this, assuming someone is, really wants you dead, won't he or they simply send another crew? This could go on forever."

Ike smiled. No dummy, this woman. "Of course. If shooting occurs, it must be less than lethal for at least one victim, hopefully several. We need to know who or what brought this on. We find that out by taking them alive and asking the right questions."

"I see. So, not only must you shoot the snipe or the Greater Crested Bamboozle, but you must also not kill him, it, or her?"

"That would be best."

"Ike, this has gone from being merely difficult to damned near impossible. There are only the two of us. As much as I thought I could shoot straight, you saw for yourself I am a mediocre shot at best."

"You're good enough, and as you noted, played right, we have the advantage of knowing."

"Why am I not encouraged?"

"Because, for all your fantasizing, you are at heart a realist. It will serve us well, I think."

"Fantasizing? Who's fantasizing? You are if you think the two of us are going to pull this off."

"Perhaps. But think of what we can tell our grandchildren if we do."

"Grandchildren? Now you are in fantasy land."

"Okay, so much for support and encouragement. It's time to call Charlie and get this game started. Once the call is made, we will have eight hours at the outside to get ready. If praying is in your playbook, now is the time to start."

"One last thing...This is really silly, and I don't know why I even bothered except, for all your obvious faults, you usually know what you're doing. I searched the Internet and I know how to buy Pine Tree Island. You fill out forms in quadruplicate, put in a bid or an offer, etc. etc. Will you please tell me why I am doing this in light of our probable demise?"

"Because I believe in the two of us. See, if I were to buy into the dying thing, it would be like a...you know..."

"A self-fulfilling prophesy?"

"Yes, maybe. Anything else?"

"That was it. Oh, and before we find out what it's like to experience rigor mortis, one last goodbye. You think we could manage that?"

"Done. Okay, here we go." Ike flipped open the satphone and punched in Charlie's open number.

◇◇◇

The FBI wasted no time in storming the Barratt Police department. They operated on the assumption that small towns have highly tuned grapevines and once it became public knowledge they had arrived, every bit of evidence of wrong doing would be shredded, hidden, or disposed of before they got through the front door. They were very nearly right.

Charlie watched with some satisfaction as the chief and his lieutenant were hauled away and Sandy Ansona installed as Acting Chief. The appointment would likely not last long, but at least for a while the young man would have the satisfaction of having done the right thing.

He'd installed his erstwhile twin in his official motel only moments before the bureau arrived. He made sure the man who, as it happened did bear a striking resemblance to him, had his instructions about check-out and the return of the rental at Denver International Airport. Once assured he was set, he checked back with the FBI special agent-in-charge, signed off on his end of the operation, and took off for Laramie, Wyoming. From there he planned to take a twin engine to Helena, Montana, thence to Boise, Idaho, and, his trail by then sufficiently muddled, hop a flight to Manchester-Boston Regional Airport. The least likely place someone would expect him to use if he were headed to Maine. He figured he'd be in Mount Desert Island in less than twenty-four hours. Sometime during that transit he should hear from Ike and the operation would be in play. He only hoped he'd get to the island before it all went down.

Chapter Thirty-nine

Twenty miles south of Laramie Regional Airport, Charlie's cold phone chirped. He pulled off in a lay-by and answered. Ike.

"Is it that time?" he asked and checked his watch.

"Not yet. Something's come up. I need to check it out first."

"Something? What sort of something?"

"You sound like my mother when I came home late after a date."

"I like to think of myself as the mother you never had."

"Unfortunately for you, Charlie, I had a very nice mother whose only flaw was to say things like 'what sort of something.' It may not be important, but I have an uneasy feeling that we are not alone on this rock."

"Not following you, sorry."

"No need. I wanted to give you a quick heads-up. I have a job to do tonight. Then I'll call."

"Okay by me. I'm on my way, and a delay will give me an extra twelve hours to get to you."

"Charlie, you don't want to get the sack for me."

"If you mean by coming to your aid I will upset the director by refusing to follow orders, I don't care. If he's behind this, if he's the one who ordered a wet squad to eliminate the four of you, then I can't work for him, and won't. But if he wasn't, well, I believe that there are circumstances when it is, as they say, better to seek forgiveness than permission. Besides, there is something else you should know. The bad guys have access to helicopters, or at least one. That changes the odds significantly. I need to be there."

"Jesus, Charlie, who are these guys?"

"I haven't a clue beyond what we discussed earlier. I was hoping you would remember something."

"Sorry, been busy."

"Yes. Well, for what it's worth, we still have our three possibilities. The agency, that is to say the director, for reasons known only to him, has ordered the hit. Libyans who desperately need to stay anonymous are after you, or something happened in Africa that needs to stay buried. In each case, these guys believe that the four of you saw, heard, or know something that can cause them trouble big time."

"Or they think we might have and can't take any chances. I have turned over what you told me, and I am at a loss. I don't remember squat about those ops. I did have a brief mental jog when you said Africa, though."

"What?"

"Can't say. It came and went. I'll call you later. Where are you, anyway?"

"Outside Laramie, on my way to their airport. I think I will change my itinerary a bit, now that I think of it. I can get a Great Lakes flight from here to Denver, change planes and fly to Chicago and then take Southwest to Manchester. I'll drive up to you from New Hampshire. I'd planned to take a more circuitous route to keep the bloodhounds confused, but I think we are running out of time, and now I don't care if they know where I'm headed."

Eden Saint Clare tried Ruth's cell phone five times before she remembered there was no phone service on Scone Island and Ruth hadn't taken it with her anyway. A cab drove her to Midway airport where she shopped for a flight east, not the most economical way to book a trip, but she didn't care. She thought of herself as on a mission of mercy, sort of. Southwest had a flight to Boston only it didn't really go to Boston. It went to Manchester, New Hampshire. How does that work? Boston was in Massachusetts the last time she looked. The woman at the desk mentioned something about travel time to downtown Boston but Eden cut her off. Boston wasn't in New Hampshire, period.

After twenty minutes of haggling with a desk agent she finally purchased a fistful of tickets which, after several changes, would land her in Bangor, Maine at five AM the next morning. Another twenty minutes with another desk agent and she had exchanged them all for a new set that departed later, had an overnight in Boston, where she could get a decent night's sleep and a bath and then on to Bangor arriving at noon. She found a table in the airport bar, ordered two martinis, an early dinner, and settled in to wait for her flight to be called.

The office door cracked open an inch. The director of the CIA stared at it. It would not be good news. Good news burst through his door with a blast of Jeremiah Clarke's *Trumpet Voluntary,* figuratively speaking. Bad news entered an inch at a time like a rat seeking a piece of cheese.

"Come on in, Mark. You can tell me."

His rat-seeking-cheese aide sidled in. "Sir, we've lost Garland."

"You lost him. How, lost him? I was under the impression you had a team assigned to keep round-the-clock surveillance on him, binoculars, listening devices, the best goddam equipment available. How's it possible he slipped away?"

"Um…oldest trick in the book, I'm afraid. He hired someone to take his place. The double has been sitting in Garland's motel room living on room service and pay per view movies since the FBI cleared out of Barratt. I'm sorry, sir. I guess we trusted the gadgets to do the work for us, and somehow he figured it out."

"Like before when he knew that if he sat in a busy restaurant at lunchtime the wireless traffic would be so heavy we couldn't find and trace his store-bought phone. How, exactly, did your people finally figure out he'd run?"

"They saw a woman, girl actually, go to the motel door and knock. Garland isn't in the habit of having…Well, when the door opened to let her in, our people saw that it wasn't Garland."

"Who was it? Who'd he hire to sit in his room?"

"A professional ski instructor. That's what he called himself."

"So, if he hadn't gotten lonely and called his girlfriend, we might still be camped out across the street?"

"Yes, sir…"

"Okay, okay. Maybe we can make this work for us. Garland's on the move. He's going to Schwartz—"

"Sir, we don't know that."

"The hell we don't. Think about it. Why else would he bolt? If he's out, he has to use public transportation to get to Schwartz. Slap a full screen on every airport, train station and rental car facility between Denver and DC."

"DC? Sir, why DC? Do you think he's coming back here? Why would he do that?"

"Where else would he go? He needs to get the files we took from him. Without the files he won't know where to begin. He'll be here."

"Sir, I—"

"I want you to set up a back door he can find his way into the files if he wants. Fix that up with electronic security. Just him, mind you, and when he hacks in, we'll have him. We need him out of the game. Got it?"

"Yes, sir. In the meantime what if someone else tries to hack in? We could be seriously compromised."

"That's a risk we will have to take. Make sure that doesn't happen, okay? Damn, where the hell is Schwartz? We need to clean up this mess ASAP."

"Yes, sir, I'm on it. There's one more thing."

"Something else. What?"

"The President's man called."

"What did he want?"

"He said the President wanted to know if we'd made any progress."

"Tell him we're exploring 'alternate scenarios' or some crap like that. Never mind, I'll call Brattan myself. He was a good man once. He used to work for me in the DIA, did you know that?"

"No, sir."

"He did. Colonel Brattan was a damned fine officer back when he still had a backbone, but he went to the dark side and became a politician. I tell you, Mark, you put a man in an expensive suit and give him a driver and car paid for by the taxpayers and he'll turn soft and mushy and yellow like an over ripe banana. Too bad about him. Past redeeming by now. Okay, get on with it. I'll deal with the CinC and his groupies; you find Garland."

Chapter Forty

Ike waited until the sun set and then, over Ruth's objections, set out for the abandoned Coast Guard Station. He had no clear idea what he would be looking for, but a shiny new combination lock on the door could not be ignored. In their haste to demobilize in the mid-40s, the Coast Guard may or may not have left something useful behind. He doubted it, but, since someone had recently been in the building, his instinct told him he needed to know why and perhaps who. He had no real use for any materiel left over from the World War II, although a small antitank gun might come in handy if the bastards arrived in a helicopter. What were the odds the Coast Guard would have had an antitank gun? Ike's experience with government planners suggested that anything, even an antitank gun on an island in Maine, should not be ruled out.

In spite of the passage of time and the ravages of salty air, the station's dull olive exterior, though faded and chipped in places, remained intact. The paint scheme had been an attempt at camouflage, doubtless to conceal it from scout planes sent from the Third Reich. How a German plane would manage to cross thousands of ocean miles without refueling did not alter the decision to hide the station. After all, hadn't Lucky Lindy made it nonstop? Why not some plucky Nazi with murder in his heart and a bomb in the plane's belly? In 1942, going to war involved everyone. The apparent absurdity of the of the paint scheme had more to do with confirming they were at war than with any real threat from the air. For Ike, the badly peeling paint offered a convenient nonreflective surface. If he were being watched, he would soon disappear against the dark siding.

At the side door, Ike reached into his pocket and pulled out the scrap of soda can he'd cut and bent at the watch tower. He had the lock off and door open in under a minute. Once inside, he eased the door shut and lighted his flash. The building had only a few windows, but he shielded its beam anyway. The last thing he wanted to do was explain to Henry Potter or one of the permanent denizens of Southport what he was doing snooping around in the abandoned station. For all he knew, one of them might have replaced the government's big brass lock with the cheap one he'd breeched.

Three yards inside the foyer he discovered a small office, a roll top desk with papers and charts scattered across its surface. A small Coleman lantern sat on its top. Ike shook it. Empty, no fuel. He edged into the darkness. The wall that faced The Bite had multiple garage-like doors which were probably used to launch boats of some sort. In one corner, to the right of the first set of doors, the wall had been built out with what appeared to be a mount. At one time equipment of some sort must have been bolted to it. A trap door had been let into the floor immediately below. Perhaps tide and temperature gauges or some form of sonar to track German subs had been lowered through it into the sea.

The building extended out onto the scree well past the high tide line. He could hear water lapping against pilings. The tide must be at flood. Lifting the trap door took less effort than he'd expected. He aimed his flash down. Seaweed streamers festooned the pilings and almost hid the body wedged between one of them and its cross beam.

Ike stood and scratched his head. He would like to know who lay head down in the tide. He did not need another distraction. On the other hand, another death might be useful. He retreated to the desk and using a pencil, he didn't want to leave any finger prints, pushed the papers aside. There were maps and studies of the island—hydrological, geological. This must have been Barstow's hidey-hole. And that meant that the body in the water must be he.

Did he have an appointment with Staley/Archie that night? If he did, might he have witnessed what happened? And if so, mightn't he have high-tailed it to the one place he considered safe? Ike tried to visualize Barstow crouched in this dismal office. He must have been followed. Ike shook the lantern again. Barstow must have lighted the lantern and given himself away. They, whoever they were, found him, and…they must have left the lantern lit and it burned off all its fuel.

Ike called Tom Stone on the sat-phone.

"Deputy Stone?"

"Is that you, Mister Schwartz?"

"No, it is not me. It is an anonymous caller. An anonymous caller reporting a body jammed in the pilings under the old Coast Guard Station on Scone Island. This anonymous caller might speculate it is the missing Frank Barlow, were he available to be asked, which unfortunately, he is not."

"I don't understand."

"In the next twenty-four to forty-eight hours, son, this island is going to play host to some very nasty people. They are coming to kill me and anyone else who gets in their way. They have already done in Staley and Barstow and two other people you do not know or need to. You will do me and yourself a favor if you will get your forensic people out here investigating this new killing and stay here in The Bite for a few days. A police presence would be a great help to me."

"Wait, you say Staley's killers also killed Barstow and are coming back to the island for you?"

"They are."

"But wouldn't the fact we are in The Bite keep them away?"

"Possibly, but not for long. What it will do is limit their points of entry. If I'm to take them down, I need all the help I can get."

"You? Why you? It's our murder—"

"Murders."

"Okay, murders. They're ours. You are way out of your jurisdiction, Sheriff. This is our job."

"So, you will go to your boss and say, 'You know that dead guy out on the island? Well there's another dead guy out there and that visiting copper says bad guys from who knows where are on their way to up the body count.' And he will say what?"

"He'd want to know why the killers are coming and why you."

"Exactly. And do you know what I can tell him?"

"Well, no, how could I?"

"You couldn't and I can't. I have no idea why they are coming. All I know is they are. Do you think you can sell that to your boss?"

"It wouldn't be easy, but..."

"I don't want you to try, Stone. If you did, and if the Hancock County Sheriff's Department shows up, they will not come."

"That's good, isn't it?"

"No, that's bad. It only delays the inevitable. And for reasons I do not understand, there is an urgency to get this job done; that is to catch the guys. So, I am going to catch them. You can help by being here, but not being here, if you follow me. Make their job more difficult but not impossible."

"You don't want help?"

"Oh, but I do. But the kind of help I need has to have a particular skill set, which you do not have, and freedom to act in certain, shall we say unorthodox ways, which you definitely do not possess."

"I still don't understand."

"Don't try. Trust me. You can help me best by responding to this anonymous tip about a body in the water and making more of it than necessary and while you are at it, keep watch on the west beaches during the night."

"Watch the beach? Why?"

"In case whoever is out there tries to land there. I'd like to know."

"I can do that, but...you're sure that's all?"

"Positive. When the fireworks start, however, I would appreciate a little back-up by limiting the island's exit points." Ike thought a moment. "One more thing, watch for helicopter flights headed this way. If you see one, find out who it is. Legitimate flights, even hush-hush ones, will give any requesting authority a clearance code. If one is headed here and doesn't, give me a holler."

"I'll try, but I'm not sure I know how to do that."

"First time for everything, Deputy."

Ike punched off and headed for the door. At the desk, he paused and picked up a better hydrological survey than Archie's, folded it and shoved it into a pocket. He relocked the door and headed back to the cottage. Whatever he'd hoped to find in the station did not include a dead Frank Barstow. But even in death, the poor man could serve a higher purpose. Assuming, of course, that keeping the sheriff from Picketsville, Virginia, alive qualified as a higher purpose.

Chapter Forty-one

Ike slipped through the front door. Ruth started up in her chair and reached for the pistol Ike had given her "for familiarization." It wasn't loaded.

"It's only me. No problem," he said.

"No problem? I'm sitting here attempting to digest fried Spam, without much success, by the way, and you sail off into the dark with some lame excuse about a padlock. Tell me again why you had to go break in to the Coast Guard station?"

"I don't know exactly. I think I had an idea there would be something useful stored in there, but it was mostly curiosity. The lock, you see. Why did the side door have a brand-new lock? I felt sure someone else had been in the station fairly recently. I had an idea that I might not be alone in thinking that. And I thought it would be important to know who or why, maybe both."

"So, did you find someone?"

"I did, in a manner of speaking. There's a body in the water under the building. It's been there several days. I think it must be Barstow, the real estate wheeler-dealer who Stone thinks had dealings with Archie and may have been the last to see him alive. I called Stone. He'll have a forensic team in place in the morning, and that will slow our killers down a little, I hope."

"How would that slow them down?"

"With police moving around, asking questions, people gawking, it makes The Bite a very public place. Not the sort of environment the folks who knocked off Archie and undoubtedly killed Barstow as well would want to be found in. Its proximity also makes most of the west coast a dangerous place to land. One entry point blocked, you see?"

"Okay, fine, but you said they might fly a helicopter in. Cops in The Bite won't stop that, will it? I mean, doesn't this make it worse?"

"Actually, flying a chopper in would be better. Look," he unfolded one of the maps he'd collected. "This is the island. I took a pencil and cross-hatched all the areas covered by trees. What do you see?"

"What am I looking for? I don't know. There are little clear spots here and here," she tapped the map with her finger, "and a bigger one here next to the foot path."

"Right. Forget the small ones. They are too small to accommodate a chopper, particularly at night. The large spot is the only place they can land. If they use it, they will have to put it down there. Okay, what else is in the area?"

"We built our first 'lurk' right across the path."

"Exactly, and if they drop in there, we can sit behind the log and take them out as they disembark. Here, where the path divides is a copse of trees and heavy brush, remember? We'd have them in a cross fire. We only have to sit here and wait for them to show up."

"That's good?"

"Better than chasing around the island looking up and down beaches and cliff faces."

"If you say so. But they may not fly in, right?"

"Right, they may not."

"We won't know how they're coming until the minute they actually arrive."

"Yes."

"Oh goody, I feel so much better now."

Ike checked his watch, nine o'clock, time to start moving the pieces across the board. He picked up the sat-phone.

"Are you ready?"

A very frightened Ruth stared at him. "How would I know? How can you tell? This is really going to happen, isn't it?"

"There is still time to leave, you know."

"Forget it. I'm here. If you are going to do this insane thing, I am doing it with you—operative word, insane. Make the call."

Ike dialed Charlie's open phone. "Charlie, how are you?"

"Ike, nice to hear from you at last. Where are you?"

"Can't say. On assignment."

"Assignment? What assignment?"

"Not supposed to say but...do you remember Archie Whitlock?"

"Oh yeah. What about him?"

"He was murdered. I'm up here investigating it."

"Up here? Where would that be?"

"Sorry, can't say. Where are you?"

"Stuck outside of Denver, director's orders. When will you be back?"

"Soon, I think. It depends what happens in the next few days."

"Great. We'll touch base then."

Ike signed off. Ruth looked at him, hollow-eyed. The reality of what was about to happen hit her. "It's really happening," she repeated. A tear rolled down one cheek, from fear or sadness at the possibilities that lay ahead, Ike could not say.

"Game on, kiddo. We'd better grab some rest while we can. We have twenty-four hours, maybe forty-eight before the sky falls."

"Rest. That's a joke, right? You are going to rest?"

"Ruth, I didn't want to put you through this, okay? But since you insist, the first rule of an engagement like this one is to compartmentalize. You have to be able to separate all the elements out. We have at least twenty-four hours. That has to be a separate compartment from the next twenty-four. And that from the one after that. In this block of twenty-four, we rest. The next will require a different set of actions."

"That's easy for you to say."

◇◇◇

The door crashed open. Mark burst into the director's office. No *Trumpet Voluntary* this time either.

"He's in Maine on that island where Whitlock died."

"What the hell is he doing there?"

"He said he was sent to investigate Whitlock's murder."

"Sent? Sent by whom? That's crazy. He could not have had any idea Whitlock was on the island and no reason to investigate his murder even if he had. Never mind. He's there and he wants us to know it. He also wants the hit team to know it. He's drawing them in."

"Yes, sir. What do we do now?"

"Now? We move in. We need to be there to clean up. Who have we got up there?"

"No one, sir."

"Excuse me, no one? Where the bloody…where are the men you put on this operation? Why aren't at least some of them nearby?"

"They're all south."

"South? What do you mean they're all south? Why south?"

"He bought a tent."

"Excuse me? 'He bought a tent.' Who bought a tent and what has that got to do with finding Schwartz?"

"Sir, we tracked Schwartz's movements before he disappeared. He bought camping equipment, cold phones, and a tent. We assumed he decided to camp. Who goes camping in Maine in May? We figured he headed south to the Great Smokies or maybe Florida. Our people are scattered across the Carolinas and Georgia looking for him at the moment."

"Damn! Pull them in. Send them north, chop-chop. Requisition a plane to collect them and a chopper to shuttle over to the island. I hate to be in a race with the bad guys. See to it. What about Garland?"

"We have a trace locked in on his cell phone and he seems to be somewhere in Wyoming. What do you want me to do?"

"As long as he stays put, Garland is not a problem. If he moves, I want to be told immediately. Right now, however, our focus has to be on that island. Get in touch with our babysitter up there and make sure we receive round-the-clock updates. I want to know everything and anything that's goes down from now on."

"Yes, sir. Sir…?"

"You still here? What?"

"Suppose the others get there first?"

"Then we all could be looking for new jobs by Monday."

An almost identical exchange between two other men took place in a room that could have been located anywhere in the world, but, in fact, was in a house set on a hillside in the middle of a three-hundred-acre estate in central Idaho. Its only distinguishing feature was a weather tower that looked like it might have been part of the Idaho Mesonet but wasn't.

◇◇◇

Eden Saint Clare's flight had touched down at Logan as the sun slipped behind the skyline of greater Boston. It took at least forty-five minutes to clear the airport and taxi to her hotel. Now, comfortably wined and dined, and ensconced in a bed with fresh sheets, she should be falling to sleep. She had made a point of ordering decaf coffee, and yet sleep eluded her. She could not erase an image of Ruth, age six, standing on a box set atop a kitchen chair, teetering precariously, one hand in the cookie jar and the other waving frantically trying to reestablish her balance. Eden had caught her before she fell and hurt herself. The cookie jar shattered into a thousand pieces. She had no reason to go to the kitchen at that particular moment, she recalled, but she had gone. So, why remember the incident now? Was she on her way to another kitchen? Was that why she couldn't sleep?

She stared at the ceiling until four in the morning.

Chapter Forty-two

The Great Lakes flight lifted out of Laramie and jounced through a thunderstorm most of the way to Denver. After touchdown, Charlie disembarked and made his way to the Southwest desk where he booked a flight east. He selected a later flight, one that would provide him with a two-hour layover before boarding. It provided the window of time he needed to finish one or two things that would allow him to disappear. He took the first shuttle in line headed to a motel.

At the motel, he checked in for two nights prepaying with the agency's credit card. He went to his room and repeated the process of messing the bed, running water, filling trash cans and dirtying the sink. He made one last call on his store-bought cell phone —two calls actually. As Ike had suggested, he decided to enlist Samantha Ryder into the game. The time zone differential meant he'd be calling her very late, but he knew NSA worked round the clock and the chances of finding her at her desk then were as good as not. She wasn't in. The section chief said she had not been in all day, because she had to take a personal day at home and declared that as near as she could tell Sam had got herself in a family way. Very quaint. Who said "family way" anymore? Charlie fumbled through the scraps of paper in his pockets until he found the one with the home phone number Ike had given him.

She sounded sleepy, and Charlie apologized for calling so late in the evening. He explained Ike's predicament, the need to keep the impending operation compact and contained, and asked her to help.

"Wait. Someone is trying to assassinate Ike? Why?"

"That is the proverbial sixty-four-thousand-dollar question."

"The what-dollar question?"

"I can't believe you don't…how old are you? Never mind. I don't know why they are, but I need you to help me find out. Will you?"

"For Ike, anything. Do you want me and Karl to take off and go to that island? We could, you know."

"No, that is probably not a good idea. You could both lose your jobs. But, there is something you can do that would be much more helpful."

"Really? What do you need me to do?"

"Among your many virtues, Ike claims you are Kryptonite to fire walls and a hacker *nonpareil.* I need those skills."

"Ike has a higher opinion of my abilities, because when it comes to computers he has none, but that's okay. Go on."

"Some years ago when he worked for the CIA, Ike participated in missions in Nigeria, Bosnia, and Libya among others. I need you to find out what happened after they were shut down."

"Afterwards? I don't understand."

"I'm not sure I do either. But here's the thing, as a general rule when an operation shuts down, the file is closed and locked away, figuratively. Any new activity in the area, even the immediate area, starts a new file. Only when something that must relate to the previous one happens does anyone attempt to merge them, you see? Coverage that is linear and continuous is your department over at NSA. We, that is the CIA, are hunter/gatherers, you could say. In these particular operations, once Ike and the men he worked with were pulled out, the file ends. What I need to know is if anything significant happened later in the area or with the local people afterwards and if so, what."

He gave her the years each had occurred.

"Just those three missions, right? You want me to inspect any files that could conceivably be coupled to them? Sure, I would be happy to, but why don't you access that information yourself? After all, you do work there."

"Yes, I do, it says here on my ID badge, but not at the moment." He could almost see the frown forming on her face. "It's a long story, Sam, but the short version is, I am in the doghouse, so to speak, and can't access anything more important than the men's room at the moment."

"That can't be good. So, okay, if I am successful and sneak in and out of the agency's files and am spotted on the way, am I in trouble?"

"Actually, yes. The agency takes a dim view of people reading their files and as you are employed by NSA, a sister agency, but a competitor nonetheless, it could go very hard on you. I wouldn't ask but I don't see any other way."

"I could be fired and maybe do jail time?"

"Possibly, but hey, Ike would always take you back. Assuming you don't go to jail, of course, and even then, I think he'd wait for you to come out."

"Wow, it's wonderful to be so loved and admired. 'Hey kid, where's, where's your mom?' 'In the Big House doing hard time but no probs, she's got a cop job when she gets out.' That about it?"

"Well, I don't think it will go that far but…"

"My worry, not yours. Let me see if I have this straight. You don't want me on the island or wherever because it might cost me my job, but breaking into the CIA's files, which could earn me jail time, is okay?"

"Well, when you put it that way, I—"

"It's okay, I'll do it. Where do I call you when I'm finished? This number or another?"

"This one. It's cold and if you need to download anything, here's an e-mail address."

Charlie spelled out one of his multiple, mostly anonymous e-mail accounts and hung up. Sam would be taking a huge risk. He closed his cold phone and dropped it in his jacket pocket.

Satisfied that he had done what he could in the room, he stepped into the hall and made his way to the rear of the building. He peeked into a room marked HOUSEKEEPING and, seeing no one about, entered and then used the exit it provided to the rear of the building.

He glanced around to make sure no one shared the alley with him. He powered up his traceable phone and sealed it in a plastic zip-lock bag which he tossed up on the roof of the Motel Six. Until the battery went flat as far as anyone who was tracking his phone signal was concerned, he would be located outside Denver. He took the shuttle back to the airport and boarded his flight to Manchester. He could be on the Scone Island by noon the next day.

Charlie's plane had a mechanical problem and sat at the gate for twenty minutes while technicians made sure it had been fixed or did not pose a safety hazard serious enough to delay the flight any longer. Either way, once he landed in Chicago, he had to rush to catch his connecting flight to Manchester and only had enough time to glance at his phone. He had two urgent messages. The first declared his battery needed charging. The second, that he had an urgent text message. He slipped into the plane seconds before front door thumped shut. The flight had not filled so he had two seats in the back to himself. He resisted the temptation to incur the wrath of the flight attendant and turn his phone on again. Besides, he'd noticed the reception bars had effectively disappeared when he'd entered the boarding ramp. He would have to wait until he reached New Hampshire to read his message; that is, if the battery would hold up long enough for him to do so. Either way he could do nothing about them until he landed anyway. He bunched up his jacket to make a pillow and scrunched into the angle between the window and seatback and fell asleep.

In Manchester, he managed to read the message before the phone turned itself off for lack of power. It sent him scurrying to a twenty-four hour coffee shop with free Wi-Fi. He wasted another ten minutes searching for an electrical outlet because when he turned on his laptop, a desktop window opened and announced his computer battery had the same problem as his phone. The phone would have to wait, he needed to get on line and read whatever it was that Sam Ryder had mined from the agency's files that she described only, in text-speak, as; IS WAT U LOOKN 4?, U R GO 2 B SPRZ- CK EMAIL- S. He finally managed to get his laptop plugged in and booted up. When the absence of a rotating hour glass told him the machine was ready to go to work, he opened Sam's e-mail and then several attachments she'd appended to it.

He read them several times. His coffee had turned cold before he made up his mind what he had to do next. He didn't like it, but it had to be done.

He dialed the director of the CIA.

Chapter Forty-three

Tom Stone and the Hancock County forensic team arrived on the island with the dawn. The police launch bobbed in the tide at the end of the floating pier. Evidence technicians and police were in place and working when Ike and Ruth strolled to The Bite. As he'd predicted, nearly all of people on the island had turned out to gossip and watch the police do their job. Henry Potter had an urn of coffee set up on a portable table, and at two dollars a cup, was making an unforeseen but, judging by the happy expression on his face, much appreciated profit. Who said crime doesn't pay? Stone nodded imperceptibly as Ike passed by. Ruth turned to a woman who Ike thought looked familiar. He couldn't say why.

"Ms. Smithwick, What's happening?"

"It's just like the TV show, isn't it? All those men in coveralls and flashlights—so exciting."

Ike conjured up a blurred impression of the woman darting out of the door of Henry Potter's store the day before. So, this was Mary Smithwick. The image of the woman taking a hurried departure had been fleeting at best. So, why did she appear to be someone he knew?

"Yes, I suppose it is."

"Just imagine. That tiresome man who wished to turn the island into some kind of tacky tourist trap has been found dead under the pilings beneath the old Coast Guard Station. Heaven only knows how he managed to do that."

"Really? Do you think he might have fallen out of a boat and washed up there?"

"Could be, but the police pulled him out from inside the station. There must be a hole in the floor in there. Lord knows what with the sea washing under there for eighty years the floor boards could be rotten. But then that begs the question, doesn't it?"

"The question?"

"Well, certainly. What was he doing in there in the first place? That building is government property."

"Government property—the Station?"

"Oh, yes. There's still a great deal of property, bits and pieces, on the island that were taken during the war and are still on their property roles."

"Like Pine Tree Island?"

"Oh, yes. I never understood that one. They never did anything on that island that I know of."

"Well, there's another mystery, for sure. I guess they had a plan and when the war ended, they just took off and dropped everything, like that orange jeep up at the old barracks." Ruth helped herself to one of Henry Potter's coffees. "Put it on my tab, Mr. Potter."

"Yes. Now that is interesting. No one remembers how it came to be on the island and what they used to fuel it. I don't know how true it is, but the story is the troops and Coast Guard people were to be inspected by an important personage from Washington so they brought the thing over from the mainland on a barge with a full tank of gas just for the occasion, you know, to drive her around."

"Her? The important person was a woman…in 1944?"

"Or five. They said it was Eleanor Roosevelt herself who was scheduled to come."

"Did she?"

"Apparently not. The President died in Warm Springs about that time and the visit was called off. The visit was not rescheduled with Bess Truman. She wasn't much for acting the part of First Lady, you know."

"I didn't know that; a bit before my time."

"Before mine, too, but if you spend as many years on the island as I have, you pick up the stories."

Ike had been listening to the two women with half an ear but something in the old lady's voice or mannerisms triggered something buried deep in his memory. He couldn't place it, but it was down in there somewhere.

"I understand you arrived early to the island this year," he said.

"I did. I usually come up after Memorial Day, but the thirty-day weather forecast called for a mild spring and so, here I am. Must have something to do with global warming,"

As Mary Smithwick rambled on Ike realized that whatever it was he wanted to remember about her had submerged back into the depths of his long-term memory and wasn't likely to resurface anytime soon. He excused himself and wandered down to the station. He wanted to check with Stone on the ID of the victim. He'd assumed the body to be that of Frank Barstow. If it wasn't, he had another problem to sort through. He didn't need another problem.

A cop in an olive duty sweater stopped Ike at the door. Stone glanced his way and motioned for him to enter.

"You were right," Stone murmured. "It's Barstow and I need to know why you were fooling around the station and how did you get in?"

"You saw the lock on the side door?"

"Yeah…so?"

"It's new and for sure, not government issue. It's the kind of lock you can buy in any drug store. It didn't belong there. I saw it and wondered. There're too many odd things happening on this island and I had a hunch."

"You had a hunch you'd find a body?"

"No, I had a hunch I'd find something. I didn't know what it would be, just something important."

"So you…What, you broke in? How?"

"Opening a cheap combination lock is a ten minute operation, start to finish. If you have the pick ready, thirty seconds, max."

"Breaking in here would be a federal crime."

"You could call the FBI."

"Would you want me to?"

"That depends on what you found out about helicopters."

"Nothing yet. I have a friend who is a refueler at the Bangor Airport. I think that would be the most likely place for anyone coming this way to jump off, don't you think?"

"Is it? I don't know. The problem is we also don't know who's coming, when, how and from where. A boat could launch from anywhere on the coast."

"Except they would need to know the tides to make effective use of a water approach. If they're not local, they might not want to try."

"They've been here before, deputy. The tides were not a factor then, why would they be now?"

"Right. How long do you need me to muddle around this crime scene?"

"As long as possible. At least post some people to secure it for a day or two."

Stone's radio crackled to life. He stepped to one side to respond. He nodded and glanced at Ike.

"Okay," he said after he signed off. "My buddy in Bangor tells me a chopper has arrived at the airport. He said they had none scheduled for today. That's not all that unusual, but this one he'd never seen before."

"Did he check the tail number?"

"Yeah, he said it belongs to some company called Five One Star. He never heard of them. The owner is registered in Idaho someplace."

"That's it?"

"All he could manage. I told you he's a refueler. He only got that much information because he sweet-talked the dispatcher into peeking into her computer. Oh, he did say one thing. He thought the paint job on the chopper seemed a little odd."

"How, odd?"

"He said it's painted a flat black. Like a night fighter. That's how he described it—night fighter."

"Thanks, Tom. That is very useful."

Ike worked his way through the gawkers back to Ruth.

"Time to go."

"Go? Go where?"

"We have to get ready for an air assault, I think."

"Oh shit. I keep thinking this is a really bad dream and at any moment the alarm clock will go off and all this will go away. Any minute now I will wake up and be twenty-one and going to my first graduate-school class." Ruth squinted at the sun climbing in the east and shook her head. "I'm not going to wake up, am I?"

"Oh, yes you will, tomorrow, the next day—for a long time to come if I have anything to do with it. But not at age twenty-one and not right now. Now we have to stock our 'lurk' on the path and get some rest. I need to contact Charlie or somebody… maybe Sam. I need to know what a company called Five One Star does. I expect the bad guys will arrive after dark."

"When, after dark?"

"No telling."

Chapter Forty-four

The phone call between Charlie and the director ratcheted quickly from conversational, to annoyed, to shouting. In the end, Charlie announced he would meet the director and an extraction team in Bangor. He would wait for one hour and if he had not arrived by then he, Charlie, would go to the island and take care of business himself.

Before he rang off he asked the director what he knew about Martin Pangborn.

"Major contributor to the Presidential campaign, for one, why?"

"I'm waiting for more information about him—information, by the way, which would be easier to get if you hadn't slammed the door on me. But he's tied up in this somehow. In the meantime, you need to load the bus and get up here ASAP."

"You expect me to mount an operation on the scale you suggest on your say-so, Garland?" The director did not seem to be in a generous mood. "You're supposed to be in Denver. We've been tracking you and have you…oh, you SOB. You left your phone in the airport or somewhere, didn't you? So, okay, where are you now?"

"Manchester, New Hampshire, Director, but not much longer, and to answer your question, yes, I do expect an operation, as I said. I would opt for something bigger, but we don't have time. It is not just on my say-so, either. I have information that you need to see."

"Send it to me and then I'll decide."

"Not a chance, Director. If you haven't seen it already or are playing possum, then you have a local problem which will only get worse when the data appears in the logs at Langley. You need to see it, but not on station."

"Garland, listen to me. If you don't want a career ending set-to, you will e-mail that information to me pronto."

"And, with respect, sir, if you do not want a career-ending set-to of your own, you will meet me in Bangor, Maine, in…" Charlie checked his airline ticket and watch, "two and a half hours."

Charlie switched off and headed to the gate. He'd scotched his plans to drive to Mt. Desert Island. He'd thought by doing so he'd avoid any alert his presence at a public transportation facility would trigger at the agency. Now, of course, that would not be necessary. They knew where he was and where he was headed. He needed to get to Scone Island; he hoped with help, but with or without it—either way, get there.

The General Aviation Terminal at Bangor International had a few machines that dispensed snacks and a K-cup coffee dispenser. Charlie helped himself to a cup and munched on some stale potato chips. A tray of catering from a recently landed G4 sat behind the dispatcher's desk. Charlie eyed it hungrily. From his limited experience flying on corporate aircraft he knew the food would be excellent. He hadn't had time to eat before his flight to Maine, and the potato chips were not doing much to ease his hunger. He considered making a new friend with the dispatcher, a thirty-something with suspiciously red hair and a tattoo of Tinker Belle on her wrist. He had an approach line on the tip of his tongue when a Twin Star Helicopter hovered over to the ramp and settled with a whine of decelerating turboprops for refueling. The fuel truck moved into place as the rotors whooped to a stop and a young kid in a smudged uniform jumped out, secured his ground wire, and began pumping Jet A into the chopper's tanks. The odor of kerosene found its way into the lobby in spite of the filtered air provided by the facility's HVAC system. It took a long time to top off the tanks. Charlie wondered about that. He guessed it must have flown non-stop from somewhere pretty far away and burned off all its fuel in the process. Except that it had been painted a flat black and had a civilian tail number, it could have been from an Army facility, or a tour company, or possibly a company in the business of shuttling hunters into the deep woods. The fact of its odd paint scheme and fuel requirements suggested it was none of the above.

Charlie's stomach only allowed him to be diverted from the tray of sandwiches long enough to memorize the tail number—force of habit. Then he turned his attention back to the counter only to discover that while he'd been speculating about the chopper, a lineman slipped in behind the dispatcher and requisitioned the tray, its contents, and had carted them off to his break room. So much for making new friends.

He booted up his laptop and looked up the helicopter's tail number. It belonged to an outfit called Fifty-first Star and was based in Idaho. Idaho? Next, he searched for Sam's latest e-mail. She had posted what appeared to be a confidential file FBI file. Apparently she'd convinced her husband, Karl, to help. The new information explained the Idaho connection but not why it was involved. He had to look up The Fifty-first Star to make that.

The dispatcher smiled at him and turned to peer out the window at the ramp. She keyed her headset and began a conversation with a pilot on approach. The woman at the desk rattled off a series of instructions which seemed to relate to space and fuel and then "rogered" a tail number Charlie did recognize. The director had arrived. He glanced at his watch—ten minutes early. Wow.

The government Citation touched down gracefully on the tarmac—you had to admire those Air Force guys. They knew flying. The plane taxied up to the doors and dropped its steps. Charlie watched as the director descended and pushed into the building.

"This way, Garland," he snapped and led the way into a conference room. His aide started to follow but the director waved him off. "My patience is about gone and my temper near to boiling. This had better be good because I have a list of charges against you that could damn near put you in jail—never mind early retirement."

Charlie sat and waited a second or two until the director did the same. It took him a little over an hour to lay out the general shape of what he'd gleaned from the various hacked and purloined files.

Sometime during the conversation Charlie thought he heard the Fifty-one Star helicopter depart to the opposite side of the ramp. Another fifteen minutes passed with Charlie answering questions fired at him by the director before the latter sat back and nodded.

"You're sure you have this right?"

"Positive."

"So, he knew?"

"Probably."

"And Ike?"

"I don't think so, no."

"The others?"

"Not them either, but no way we could find out now."

"No, I suppose not."

"Do you know what or who the Fifty-first Star is?"

"Some far right survivalist organization in Idaho. FBI's problem, not ours, what about it?"

"Martin Pangborn."

"What about him? Besides being one of the President's supporters and influence peddlers."

"He has already bought three state governors, at least one Senator, and the President's aide, Col. Brattan, is alleged to be in his pocket as well. Pangborn is busy seeding the federal bureaucracy with his people and, more importantly, he's the brains behind Fifty One Star and its chief source of money."

"And?"

"The Fifty-first Star is not just a bunch of middle-aged survivalists who like to talk big and wear camo. It's an armed militia that started back during the California water wars when some in the north thought to separate the state into two. Anyway, Pangborn has a small army at his disposal."

"Again, Charlie, FBI's problem. Why are you telling me this?"

"Daniel Osborn is the man he wants placed in State. Also, Osborn brings new money to Pangborn's cause. For both of them it's a win-win. Pangborn gets money and Osborn gets a governmental post that could, if played right, make him a power broker in a continent that is about to play an important role in international affairs. There is just the small matter of Osborn's past that needed to be put to bed, so to speak. As I said—win-win. But our more immediate concern is that the Fifty-first Star's helicopter took off just now, and unless I miss my guess, it is headed east."

The director waved in his aide, then made a call to the local National Guard. Forty-five minutes later Charlie, the director, his aide, and four very tough young men and one equally tough woman were airborne in a Black Hawk helicopter headed to Scone Island.

Chapter Forty-five

Luckily for Eden, one of the Gotts had his boat moored in Bass Harbor. Had it left for Scone Island on time, she would have had to spend the night in the local Holiday Inn and travel to the island the following afternoon. As it was, she and one other passenger made the trip to the island as the sun started its journey westward.

"Don't you just love the salt air," she said to the man by way of introduction.

He nodded briefly and moved aft without replying.

Eden had known many rude people in her life. As the wife of an academic, she had become inured to the type. Her only thought, one she later deemed unworthy, was that this extremely unprepossessing man could not afford to be rude to anybody.

Her luck held as one of the LeFranc boys had just finished coiling some lines for his father and offered to cart her rather substantial luggage to Aunt Margaret's, now Ruth's, cottage. She remembered that the doors on the island were never locked which turned out to be yet another stroke of luck.

"Hello, anybody home?"

No answer. She wandered through the house and, seeing a fire laid, lit it, mixed herself a small pitcher of martinis, courtesy of the miniatures supplied by the airline, and settled in to wait for Ike and Ruth to return from wherever they'd gone.

After a wait of an hour and the consumption of three martinis, she hiked her chair closer to the fire and fell asleep.

◇◇◇

Mary Smithwick believed it would be a mild spring, but once the sun set somewhere over Bass Harbor, the ambient temperature dropped at least fifteen degrees. Ike and Ruth huddled together in the shallow declivity behind the log he'd dragged to it to create the "lurk."

"It is hard to believe we elected to sit here and wait for imminent death. I have always suspected you were semisuicidal, Schwartz, but I had no idea it was contagious. Whatever possessed me to agree to this?"

"If I am not mistaken, Ms. President *in absentia*, you chose to stay and experience the thrill of my company. It was I, if you remember, who wanted you on a fast boat to the mainland two days ago. As the saying goes, you made this bed. If I failed, it was not on insisting you go."

"Wouldn't have worked. There is no turning back when I get a really stupid spell. Sorry about that."

"Charlie suggested I drug you and lock you up someplace safe until all this was over."

"Why didn't you?"

"Couldn't find the dope."

"Just as well. The thought of returning to a comatose state is absolutely last thing I want right now. Before you do that, just shoot me. Oops, bad figure of speech."

"Better dead than abed? Life is so unfair. Here, have some hot chocolate."

"If this were anywhere, anytime else, playing footsie in the woods with you under a blanket in the middle of night would be fun."

"You're not having fun?"

"Not even close."

"Maybe you could sing some of those snappy camp songs you were so enthusiastic about on Pine Island when we were getting rained on while waiting for the—"

"You needn't rub it in. Oh, and speaking of Pine Tree Island and inasmuch as we have only a fifty-fifty chance of surviving this party, would you mind telling me now why I am buying it?"

"Sure, why not? Do you recall the name of the Coast Guard commander?"

"Gus somebody."

"Gustave Staehle, but I am only interested in the surname."

"So you said."

The name was spelled S,T,A,E,H,L,E but its pronounced, Staley, see?

"See what?"

"I think the late Frank Barstow thought the man he knew as Harmon Staley was a distant relation of Gustav and knew the secret."

"But he wasn't Staley. He was your idiot friend, Archie."

"True, but Barstow wouldn't know that. If he believed the name had been Anglicized to the simpler spelling, or if he hadn't seen it spelled out, he might reasonably have assumed this Staley was connected to the other one."

"What's reasonable about that? There must be a zillion Staleys loping around this part of the world."

"Probably not millions, but enough. How about one who bought a dilapidated house on a remote island in the ocean off the coast of Maine? What are the chances?"

"Okay, I'll bite, what secret? What do you think Barstow thought Staley, that is Whitlock, knew? Or was it the other way round? Who knew what?"

"Neither of them knew but thought they were on to it. They both had detailed maps of the island. They both seemed to have a notion that there could be some major money made here if they could find it."

"I give up. Find what?"

"Electricity."

"Electricity? Sorry, either the thought of dying in the next hour or so has slowed my cortical functions to dead stop or you are being obtuse. I'm voting for the latter."

"What is missing from this island that if it were in place would skyrocket the value of the real estate here?"

"Okay, it has no phone service, no electricity, and no ready supply of water."

"Exactly, and both men had maps, including hydrological studies and topographical. I am no expert, but after inspecting the first there seems to be a decent aquifer under this rock. Phone service is only a tower, or a satellite away, and that leaves electricity."

"They thought they could bring it to the island?"

"They thought it was already here."

"No."

"Yep, Archie assumed he'd find it and so did Barstow. Only they got it wrong. Barstow first thought it would be in the Coast Guard Station and then when he couldn't find it there, believed that Archie bought Cliffside because he knew where it was. Archie thought he'd find it in the biggest house on the island."

"And?"

"As I said, they were both mistaken. It's on Pine Tree Island. The government, the Coast Guard, some World War II agency, laid a cable from the mainland to the island. It was never connected at either end, probably because the war ended and it, like the jeep and the artillery pieces now resting in the ocean, were abandoned and then forgotten. Do you remember the concrete box I told you about—the one with the *Property of the U.S.C.G* painted on it? Well, that cable terminates in it. I saw it. There is a stump of a utility pole next to it and evidence a small building was planned for the site. If we own the island, we own the power cable. All we would have to do is connect it at the front end and figure out how distribute it at this end. Got it?"

"Wow, I could become a capitalist. We're playing Monopoly and I landed on the electric company. Wait, what about the water works?"

"A community well and pumping station would do it, I think. That was the reason to look for the hydrological survey. Remember I said I wanted to check out Cliffside and—"

"And you found all that stuff, and now we are sitting in the dark inviting the Grim Reaper to our party."

"That wasn't the original idea, but yeah, that's the way it turned out."

"So, the sland could move into this century."

"Or the last one which would be near enough. The question is do we want it to?"

"I'll need to think about that. In any case, if we survive, we buy the island. Whether it makes the forward leap to modernity will be our decision, not some opportunists, like the late Frank Barstow."

"Spoken like a true ivory-tower liberal. Good for you."

"Knock it off, smart-ass. You agree with me and you know it."

"Shhh…"

"Don't shush me. I'm right and you are not the political Neanderthal you pretend to be and—"

"Be quiet. Listen."

Ruth stopped speaking. In the distance they heard the faint growl of a turboprop engine approaching from the west.

"That's them?"

"It must be. You remember what to do?"

"Night-vision goggles down unless there is light. Up, if there is. Don't aim at anything or anyone in particular, just shoot straight at them as fast as I can. Use a fresh piece rather than reload—do you really call them pieces? It sounds naughty, and—"

"You got it. Okay, sit tight."

"You didn't answer my question. Do you really call your guns pieces, and isn't that a Freudian thing? Guns that shoot bullets and—"

"Hush."

"It's getting nearer. How come I can't see anything?"

"They won't have their running lights on. We'll only know they're here when they drop down over the houses or the trees. They may turn on their landing lights for a moment to check their spot. If they do—"

"Night vision goggles up. I know."

The bulk of the aircraft, nearly invisible in the moonless sky, loomed over the housetops, its motor snarling like a very large and angry wasp.

"That's one hell of a helicopter. Jesus, these guys are equipped."

"I have to tell you something, Ike."

The thwip-thwip of the helicopter's rotor blades hacking the air and the deafening rumble of its twin motors drowned out any possible communication.

"I love you," she yelled.

"What?"

"I said I wanted you to know—"

"Goggles up, they've switched on the landing lights."

"Ike!"

"Heads down. Here they come."

Chapter Forty-six

The helicopter wobbled, steadied, and then settled with a barely discernible thump a dozen yards in front of them. Instinctively, Ike put his hand on the top of Ruth's head, forcing it well below the edge of the log which provided their only protection from a rain of bullets which he assumed would come the instant the new arrivals piled out of the chopper and discovered them. And that must come sooner or later.

"Ow, Ike, have you forgotten, I broke my neck once already?" Ruth howled and twisted away.

Ike did not hear her both because of the engine noise and because his focus had shifted to his next move. He picked the Very flare gun from the ground, opened the breech, grabbed a cartridge from the bag of supplies and aimed in the direction of the helicopter. The rotors were still whirling but the engines were disengaged and idling, that is, they were idling to the extent turbo jets could be said to idle. He pointed the muzzle upward and squeezed the trigger just as the chopper's door slid open. The gun popped as the powder used to propel the missile went off.

Instead of sailing skyward, the projectile was drawn by the rotor's wash into a low arc and leaving a trail of bright orange sparks straight toward the chopper. Rather than lighting up the area and the machine as he hoped, it sailed straight into the passenger compartment. A split second later, the interior of the helicopter was engulfed in flames. Men poised to dismount were silhouetted against the fire. They scrambled to the door and leapt up and away like puffy stick figures, some with their clothing alight. Ike dropped the flare gun and raised his pistol.

"Oh shit!" he said.

"What just happened?" Ruth yelped.

"Tell you later."

He began firing at the men scrambling on the ground in front of him. Ruth crouched next to him, holding her pistol two handed and calmly squeezed off rounds spaced a half second apart. Like a metronome, she swung her weapon right and left. Fifteen shots each from the heavy clips. When the clips were empty, they dropped their weapons and picked up another. Before resuming fire, they paused to take in what they'd done.

"What do you think?" Ruth said.

Before Ike could answer her question, the blast of a louder explosion created a shock wave that nearly knocked them off their feet. A ball of fire that might have been seen in Bass Harbor, had anyone been looking, mushroomed skyward.

"Holy cow, Ike, what the hell is going on?"

"Short answer—I wanted to light a flare to cancel their night vision goggles and give us a clear view. I didn't look to see what I grabbed from Archie's bag and I must have loaded one of his incendiaries."

"You lit up the chopper."

"Yep, and the flames reached the fuel tanks and kablam. Judging by the size of that fire-ball I'd guess they were carrying a full load of gas."

These last words were drowned out by a second roar as the port side tank blew, which sent the rotors pin-wheeling off into the trees. The hull lurched forward on it nose, folded in half, and collapsed on its side. If the pilot had not joined the others at the door he could not have survived. Except for moaning, cursing, and the crackling of the flames as the hull of the chopper slowly crumpled from the heat, all was quiet.

"Wowzer, you really know how to show a girl a good time, Schwartz. That looked like the old movie of the Hindenburg blowing. So, what do we do now?"

"We secure these birds before they recover and get organized. Then all we do is wait for the cops or whoever answers my call first." He opened the sat-phone and called Stone and Charlie.

Neither one answered.

Eden's fellow passenger had already disengaged Tom Stone from any possible support he might have provided. One round from a silenced automatic had dropped him on the beach. Stone did not receive the *coup de grâce* from his assailant. The exploding helicopter spun his assailant around and directed his attention elsewhere. The man hesitated, guessed that the tide would soon take the policeman out to sea, and raced away toward the flames. No one, he thought, could possibly have missed that blast, and only a fool would not expect it to trigger at least a call from the storekeeper to the police on the mainland. And if the fire meant the chopper had blown, he'd need to use his alternate exit from the island. The boat should be pulling up to the cliff steps about now. That is, it would if the blast hadn't sent its crew packing. That was the trouble with hired goons—no loyalty. He would have to take care of that later. Right now he needed to eliminate Schwartz if he was still alive and any other witnesses, including any from the helicopter who weren't already dead. There must be no way anyone could trace this back to him. He dashed up the road to the path and then slowed. He had no idea what had happened or who had survived, and until he did, he thought it best to stay well out of sight.

Just outside of the ring of flickering light he stopped and surveyed the area. More importantly, he saw a man and a woman moving back and forth, bending over, shoving inert figures around, and then dragging them to a central spot. It took him a few seconds to realize what they were doing. The man had to be Schwartz and the woman, his fiancée. How had they managed to destroy a fully functional helicopter and truss up the surviving crew like that? If the authorities arrived before he acted, the whole operation was in the toilet.

He moved up behind the two who stood, arms akimbo, watching over the men lying at their feet.

"Do you think we have them all?" Ruth strained to look past the fire and into the trees.

"Oh, yeah. Four on the ground and what's left of two more of them in the chopper. I only saw one door open which means they all had to jump from the one facing us. So, that's the lot."

Ruth looked at the four men they'd zip-tied and laid side by side like cordwood on the ground. "This is horrible, Ike. My God, what have we done?" Ruth gulped for some air. The realization of what had just taken place hit her like a punch to the solar plexus. "I think I might be sick."

"We did what we had to do. It's not a pretty sight, but consider the alternatives. You saw the weapons they were packing. A single burst from any one of those imported pieces and the two of us would be hard to identify except by our DNA. Where the hell is Stone? He had to have heard the blast at least."

Ruth gasped and choked.

"So, go right ahead and be sick. It's the usual reaction to stuff like this. Hell, I might even join you."

Ruth staggered to one side away from the light. She bent forward and took a deep breath. An arm snaked around her throat and jerked her upright. Whoever had her in his grip shoved and pushed her back toward the light and Ike.

"Schwartz," the owner of the arm said. "Drop your weapon."

Ike spun toward the voice. A man he did not recognize had his arm around Ruth's neck and, more importantly, a pistol at her temple. Ike hesitated and then let his pistol fall to the ground.

"You are an embarrassment to me, you know," the man said.

"How's that?" Ike had no idea who the man was or how he had managed to come up on them, but he hoped he could make him talk long enough, or at least until he'd maneuvered him away from Ruth.

"You really don't know?"

"Sorry, I can't even guess who you are or why these idiots flew in to make a mess of the island. Maybe you would like to enlighten me."

The man snorted and dragged Ruth, his gun still planted against her head, next to the recumbent figures on the ground.

"Hey," one of them rasped. "Cut us loose, Doc."

"Sure, no problem."

In quick succession he put a bullet in the head of each of the trussed figures on the ground.

Ruth threw up on his sleeve. He shoved her away with a curse. She staggered over to stand next to Ike.

The man shook his sleeve and cursed some more. "You're telling me you don't recognize me at all?" the man said.

"No clue." Ike's eyes swept the perimeter for help.

"If you are looking for the policeman who was watching the shoreline, forget it. I shot him. He won't be coming. In fact, no one is coming. Your pal Garland is still in Denver and his boss is in Washington with his hands tied in red tape and protocol. It will just be the three of us."

Ike moved to put himself in front of Ruth.

"That won't do you any good, Schwartz. You're both toast, either way."

Ruth crouched behind him. "Ike?"

"It's okay, Ruth." He tried to be taller, wider to keep her out of the man's sights. "As long as we're going to be toast, would you tell me who you are and why?"

"Daniel Osborn."

"Doesn't ring any bells."

"Too bad for you. Everyone should know why they die. You're going to because I can't take the chance that you won't eventually remember me. Now, I'll say goodbye. I have a boat to meet."

Ruth stepped out from behind Ike and stuck out her chin. "You know what, buster? I'm damned well sick and tired of this crap. First a damned helicopter comes in with these jerks on a mission to kill us, and now you. All I wanted is a little peace and quiet and to mind my own business, but oh no, do I get it?

No! What I get is idiots trying to run me down with a truck, or shoot me from a helicopter, and now you. Well, I am done here. If you're going to shoot, do it and get it over with. Otherwise, I'm going to kick you in the—" Ike shoved Ruth to the ground as the shooter leveled the pistol at her.

Chapter Forty-seven

The shot, when it came, was not the pop Ike expected from a gun with a noise suppressor still attached, but an honest to God bang from a Colt .45 automatic. Osborn's head jerked sideways. He staggered forward and fell to the ground at their feet. Ike stared first at Osborn and then at an elderly woman who stepped out of the shadows and into the light, a large pistol in her hand.

"This place stinks," she said. "I hate the smell of burning kerosene. Sorry it took me so long to get here, Ike." She looked around at the wreckage, the bodies and then leaned forward to help Ruth to her feet. "Maybe just as well I did. Any earlier he'd have done me, too."

"My God is that you, Alex? Jesus! I thought you were dead."

Ruth grabbed at Ike's arm and heaved herself upright. "Ike, how do you know this woman?"

"She and I sometimes worked together back in my previous life. Alex Barr was a senior agent and a legend."

The woman grinned. "No, no, you have to be dead to be a legend, and, as you must have noticed, I am still on the right side of the sod, so I don't qualify. Ike, I guess we have some catching up to do."

"You were sent to keep an eye on Archie Whitlock?"

"Is that who it was? Didn't do such a hot job, did I?"

"You never worked with Archie?"

"No. That's why the director sent me I guess. That and the fact that little old ladies tend to be discounted in serious situations and make good cover. Also, he knew that retirement did not sit well with me, so he asked if I would make myself useful. I said I would, for old time's sake, you understand. It turned out I was not such a good babysitter, though."

"How come I never saw you? It might have helped earlier."

"After the baby went down, I stayed in the shadows. If they got curious and started interviewing people, it wouldn't do to have the local cops sniffing around. I planned to leave but the boss said stay in place in case a clean-up crew other than our people dropped in."

"If you had ventured out and spotted me, maybe none of this would have happened."

"Maybe. Are you sure about that? I don't know what the hell was going on here, but the director sent me out the door to look for you only a little over an hour ago."

"He probably would have let me swing even if you'd spotted me."

"Your call. I wouldn't know. So, am I correct in thinking you are married?"

"Engaged, soon to be, more like."

Ruth turned away "Ike I…never mind. Excuse me, but this has been a really bad day." She threw up a second time.

Because she was otherwise engaged, she missed the whine of another set of twin engines belonging to a second helicopter that now drifted toward them over the treetops. This one had all of its lights on all the way in.

"I don't believe this," Ike muttered.

Eden Saint Clare did not wake up when the first helicopter flew low over the cottage rooftop, nor the second one. She did not wake up when an explosion rattled the windows nor when gun fire, like hail hitting a tin roof, sent the indigenous wildlife stampeding to the other end of the island. When the front door slammed open and a man crashed in and fell face down in the foyer, she woke and went on high alert. She snatched up her cell phone and punched in 9-1-1. Her adrenaline rush nearly brought on a cardiac accident. At any rate, that's how she would remember it later.

"Come on, come on," she muttered through chattering teeth. "What's the hold-up?" She looked at the phone and then remembered that there was no service on the island. "Damn, of all the times to be rustic and uncomplicated."

She had two choices: retreat out the back door or make a dash over the man and out the front. The body had not moved since its dramatic entrance. She took a cautious step closer. She could see he wore a uniform with what appeared to be insignia that might belong to a police officer. She chanced it, stepped over the recumbent man, and out onto the porch.

The second helicopter was clearly marked as belonging to the Maine National Guard. Ike, who had started to retrieve his pistol, stepped over to Ruth and lifted her upright instead. He pulled out a nearly clean handkerchief and guided her shaking hand to wipe her face. The chopper hovered a foot or two off the ground. The wash from its rotor fanned the flames which by now had spread to several bushes and a small pine tree. Figures, some in black, jumped free from the copter's doors and then it veered off, gained altitude, and disappeared over the treetops.

Ruth dropped her head on Ike's shoulder. "Are these more people we have to shoot?"

"No, it's the cavalry, a little late, but finally here and in force. Hello, Charlie, what kept you?"

"If that's Charlie Garland, I want my gun. I'm going to shoot the bastard."

"I'm happy to see you too, Ruth. Have you met the director of the CIA?"

"Shoot him first," she mumbled and leaned heavily on Ike.

Ike scooped Ruth up in his arms and headed toward the cottage. "I hope someone will eventually tell me what the hell happened here, but right now, this lady has had a very busy day and it is way past her bed time. Oh, yeah, whoever this guy was—Osborn—he said he had a boat to meet. You might want to look at the bottom of the steps over on the east side near Archie's place. Also, he said he shot a policeman. That would be Deputy Stone. While you're at it, you should try to find him. That is, as long as you are here on clean-up duty. I'd love to stay and hear how you plan to explain all this, but it will have to wait. Ruth and I are going home." He started down the path.

The director's aide began barking orders to the chopper crew. It reappeared and headed northeast. A few moments later the braaat of .50 caliber machine gun bullets pumped from the helo's Gatling could be heard coming from vicinity of Cliffside. So much for Osborn's alternate escape.

"Okay," the director yelled, "You four, put out the fire and then pack these stiffs up and load them in the chopper when it comes back."

"What about Osborn?" Charlie asked.

"Toss him in the downed bird and let him toast for a while. I want it to look a little like an accident."

"Sir?"

"Forget that. Toss him in with the others. Then take a magnet to what's left of the bird's avionics. When the FTSB investigators arrive I want them to be able to corroborate with a straight face that this happened to a chopper which had strayed off course."

"An accident? You really think they will buy that?" Ike asked.

"They will have to buy what we're selling. As of this minute Daniel Osborn chartered a flight from the Five One Star Corporation to fly him into the woods for a weekend of moose hunting. Somehow the guidance equipment failed and the crew flew northeast instead of north-northeast. I will have to report this to the President, of course, and his aide. Very tragic; the country has lost a great man."

Ike had heard enough. He continued his walk away from the voices and toward the cottage.

Fifteen yards further on Ruth lifted her head. "Is it just me or do you hear someone calling my name?"

"Sounds like it."

Ike made out a figure standing on the front porch. "I don't believe this."

"You don't believe what?"

"I don't believe that's your mother standing on your porch yelling for help."

"This has to be really a bad dream. Please, please wake me up right now, Ike. I don't think I can take anymore."

Chapter Forty-eight

Eden raced forward and met them on the path. She gasped something that could have been either "denim" or "dead man."

"Mother, what ? Denim? What the hell are you doing here?"

"There's a dead man in the hallway. Come inside and see."

At the front door, Eden pointed to Tom Stone lying flat on his face in the foyer. "He is dead, isn't he?"

Ike dropped to one knee and felt for Stone's carotid pulse. "He's alive and his pulse is reasonably strong. He'll live. We can assume Osborn didn't have time to finish him off. But now he becomes another problem for the director to solve." He rolled Stone over and made a crude pressure dressing for the deputy's chest wound.

"Who?" Eden's expression kaleidoscoped from fearful to baffled and back again as she peered at the wounded policeman, then Ike, and Ruth.

"Which who? This is Deputy Stone from the Hancock County Sheriff's Office. The director is from the CIA."

Ruth sagged in Ike's arms. "Ike, I need to sit."

"Right. Sit and drink something. Eden, if you haven't already done so, you will find the fixings for drinks in the kitchen. I need to sort out the deputy and light some lamps. When you're done, you might want to see if there is anything worth eating in the fridge. I'll fire up the generator and we can at least have some toast and peanut butter."

"You have a generator and electricity?"

"We do."

'Wish I'd known that when I got here. Is anyone going to tell me what's going on?"

"Later. Take care of your daughter. She's had a bad night and then you can tell us what you're doing here as well."

"Since you ask, I—"

"Not now. Drinks and food."

Ike built up the fire in the parlor and had Ruth swaddled in blankets and a drink in hand when the director and Charlie stomped across the porch and into the house. Eden paused in her clucking over Ruth long enough to shoot Charlie a dirty look. She seemed singularly unimpressed to be in the presence of the director of the CIA.

"Another spook," she snorted and sat next to Ruth who, Ike believed, was showing the first signs of post-traumatic shock disorder. What they'd gone through would shake up a seasoned combat veteran. The effects of adrenaline after-burn were evident in her pallor and clammy skin. He substituted cups of cocoa for the bourbon and water. It seemed to help. She sat a little straighter and some of the color returned to her cheeks. After a moment she glared at the director.

"Someone in this room owes me and Ike an explanation."A bandaged and very sore, but recovering, Deputy Stone sat upright in his chair and groaned. "And I think that goes for Tom Stone too. How are you, Deputy?"

"I'm hurt and I am embarrassed and I would very much like to know what the hell happened here tonight." Stone leaned back against the wall and fainted.

"You'll need to do something about him, you know."

The director opened his sat-phone and called the helicopter back. "I gather he is bright and willing, perhaps even recruitable. We'll call it a matter of national security and that should handle both the young man and his boss. Where were we?"

"An explanation why we were in this mess in the first place seems to be the question hanging in the air. We'd all like to hear you tap dance through this one, Mr. Director," Ike said.

"It's complicated."

"And the sun rises in the east. Director, you can do better than that. Tell me something I don't already know. Ruth and I were very nearly killed out there tonight. If Archie Whitlock hadn't mixed an incendiary device in with his flares and Alex Barr not made an amazingly well-timed appearance, we might not be here now. How soon did you know someone was after me and why did you sit on your hands and let this happen? Oh, and who the hell is Daniel Osborn?"

"That's more than one question. Okay, not necessarily in order, here's how it played out. Since you insist, Osborn is a problem solved…Wait, don't interrupt. Osborn was about to be nominated for an important post at State—the African Desk, in fact. He had the backing of a very high roller whose campaign contributions to the President over the years represented an obscenely big number. You know how that game is played. Ordinarily there wouldn't be a problem putting some hack in where a permanent staff could keep him straight and seemingly competent, but in Osborn's case the President received some unspecified but very strong negative feedback from several of the sub-Saharan nations."

"Negative feedback? What sort of negative feedback?"

"As far as I know, nonspecific is all I have."

"You're the director of the goddam CIA," Ruth rasped. "'As far as I know' doesn't cut it. Sir, you run the agency that is supposed to know all kinds of sh…stuff about everybody. So, why didn't you know this time?"

"That is a good question and one for which I have no immediate answer. Charlie will verify I have been tracking everything in and out of the agency since the appointment was announced. Our people in southern Africa were unsuccessful in digging out anything we could prove with any certainty. The countries that objected made it clear that the appointment would not sit well with most of southern and eastern Africa. I should say they made it *very* clear they were not happy."

"But wouldn't say why?"

"No. The President found himself between a rock and a hard place and asked me to check Osborn out. We were in the process of doing that when Archie turned up dead."

"I don't see how they connect."

"Neither did I, but at the same time that news came in, the President's aide began to press hard to close the files and stamp Osborn 'ready for prime time.' I tasked Charlie to find out how the people who got to Archie managed to find him in the first place. I hoped that would lead us to the reason for Osborn's African problem. And, secondarily, if it was a leak within the agency, I wanted to be the first to know, so I had Mark, my aide, overlay Charlie's search."

"Sorry, boss, but that doesn't make any sense," Charlie said.

"Not to you, maybe, but you didn't have the President's pit-bull, Brattan, yapping at your heels. He, by the way, is a protégé of another influence peddler, and this may spell the end of his career in government. Anyway, that's when Al Jackson went down. So, we had another piece of data, but no place to file it."

"I still don't understand why you left Ike swinging in the breeze," Ruth said. "He doesn't have anything to do with you people, at least not anymore."

"In the first place, we didn't know where Ike was, because the two of you decided to play hide-and-seek and Ike is very good at the hiding part. If we'd known where you were sooner this might have played out differently."

"Really? The way I see it, it's a good thing Ike was successful at being invisible." More color had returned to Ruth's cheeks, whether as result of her rising anger, the cocoa, or the earlier shot of bourbon wasn't clear.

"You will have to trust me on this."

"Yeah, yeah. People sell ponzi schemes with that line, Mr. Director."

Chapter Forty-nine

The director of the CIA did not ordinarily feel a need to explain himself to anyone, except the President and occasionally the Senate committee charged with the oversight of his budget and therefore his operation. He took a breath and gathered what little patience he had remaining.

"Ms. Harris, please, just listen for a minute and then you can raise hell with me. Charlie can tell you the connection. I'd like to think we would have eventually found it in-house ourselves but Charlie or Charlie's hacker turned it up first."

"And found it in spite of his being sent off to the middle of nowhere like a naughty school boy, I gather." Ruth was not ready to be mollified. "So, Charlie, what did you find?"

"While I twiddled my thumbs and brought down a corrupt police department in Colorado—that's another story for another day—I had time to think. We'd agreed it had to have something to do with one of the missions Ike and Archie did with Bernstein and Jackson. There were three of them, as you know—four, if you count the training thing. Nothing was forthcoming from the director and—"

"The pressure was on me to wrap the due diligence on Osborn," the director interrupted. "Then, Ike and Garland have a relationship that I believed would compromise anything we might try to do if Charlie got involved, particularly when he refused to tell us where you were, so I sent him away. And Ike decided to play lone wolf up here which meant I had limited choices. Lucky for all of us that Charlie came through in the end anyway."

"The operative word is luck, Mr. Director. Really!" Eden finally joined the conversation. Ike was convinced she had no idea what had happened and probably never would, but the lack of information was not the sort of thing to stop her from voicing an opinion.

"As you know," Charlie said, "Ike and I have a mutual acquaintance who's conveniently connected to the FBI and a special way but, more importantly, is skillful at rooting around in other people's hard drives and servers and electronic whatnot. I asked this person to look at all the intel in the three areas subsequent to the three operations we spoke about. She did as I asked and sent me some critical data. Data that, had the director known, would have obviated all of this including, I am forced to say, Archie's killing. But the agency, though in possession of the reports, had not extracted the information and made the connection on their own. Thus, four dead on our side and however many on theirs."

"Once Charlie sent it back to us, we only had to confirm and get up here."

"A day late and a dollar short, I'm thinking. If it hadn't been for Mrs. Barr and her sharp-shooting you would have had nothing but corpses and funerals to show for all your efforts." Ruth muttered.

"We'd have had enough to stop the confirmation and enough to put Osborn away forever."

"Fat lot of good that would have been for me and Ike."

The director slammed his fist on the arm of his chair. "Ms. Harris, I am sorry you were caught up in this. Why you stuck around and suffered this, I will never understand, but I have to say what happened here and in the previous week was never about you and Ike."

Ruth made a rude noise.

"Easy there, Harris," said Ike. "Hear the man out. So what was the connection that Sam…I assume it was Sam who tip-toed around the agency's firewall…what did she find?"

"Ostrofsky."

"Who?"

"The doctor in Nigeria. Do you remember?"

"I thought you said he was dead."

"Nope, not dead—well not until tonight when Mrs. Barr dispatched him with a clean shot to the head."

"You've lost me. Osborn was Ostrofsky?"

"Yes, and it's about what Archie knew. Archie had ways of finding things out and using the information to his advantage, if you remember."

"I do, and I recall he said he found out something about the operation, but he always said things like that, so I let it slide. You're saying Archie knew that Ostrofsky was up to something in that hospital?"

"He did and incidentally used that knowledge to extort a sizable number of Krugerrand from the doctor until, that is, the doctor was reported dead. Shortly afterwards we sent Archie to oblivion, or so we thought."

"Archie was on the take? No surprise there. So, let me guess, they thought, whoever *they* are, that Archie might have shared that information with the rest of us. Therefore, if Archie had to be rubbed out—"

"The safest thing to do would be to eliminate all possibilities. I don't know if they believed the three of you knew anything, but they figured they couldn't take the chance that you didn't."

"Wait a minute. You put Archie away with a false ID and the whole disappearing package. How did they find him?"

"Do you remember Archie's third wife—or was it number four—whatever, Cora?"

"Vaguely. Why"

"The Las Vegas police have her on a slab in their morgue. Someone strangled her last week and left her in the street. We're assuming they couldn't find Archie, but they did find his ex-wives—at least one of them. Somehow she knew where he'd gone to ground. Archie must have hooked up with her."

Ruth started to fade. She sat forward and asked, her voice hoarse, "Okay, enough already, just cut to the chase, what did

Archie Whitlock know that was such a big deal that it justified murdering four people and your lot sitting on your hands and doing nothing while Ike and I took on the bad guys alone… with Ms. Barr included, of course?"

"Trafficking in human organs."

"Excuse me?"

"He wasn't swapping arms for blood diamonds. He was swapping them for people."

It took several seconds for the idea of someone running a human abattoir in the heart of a moderately civilized nation to sink in.

"That would explain the razor wire and the guards around the hospital. It wasn't to keep people out. It was to keep people in. But who were his buyers?" Ike asked.

"Two sets of buyers, some local and some international."

"Local? I can hardly believe that." Ruth was back in form.

"Body parts, particularly those connected with sex, have always comprised an important part of the African and Asian folk pharmacopeia. Traditional medicine and witch doctors used to harvest them illegally. With the growing modernization of most countries, particularly as regards police and humanitarian laws, their sources have dried up. Ostrofsky stepped in and filled that niche with the bits and pieces left over from his organ donors. I guess donor is not what they were, actually. They were certainly not willing donors, anyway."

"That's awful! But how did he do it?"

"He had a sophisticated tissue typing laboratory on site, several surgical suites, and buyers around the world—Europe mostly. If someone needed a kidney, heart, you name it, all they needed to do was talk to someone who would check with someone else and for the right price Ostrofsky would slice and dice. Do you recall a helipad on the premises, Ike?"

"I wondered about it, but assumed it had been built for med-evac work. He helioed the parts out to…where? South Africa, Botswana? No, Abuja or Lagos. From there he'd be only hours away by private jet to anywhere in Europe, Africa, or the east. Am I right? And you're telling me that Dr. Ostrofsky and Osborn are one and the same?"

"As it happens, yes."

"And no one figured that out until Sam hacked into your files?"

"Not exactly, well, no...but you must understand—"

"What's to understand? Our friends in Africa hint there is something really rotten about this guy. They may even have believed he was the butcher they had to deal with a decade or more before, but as he was under the wing of the privileged and political elite in this country and what, a major contributor to several politicians' campaigns? So, they were diplomatically cautious. And all you could do is wonder why? Please, say it isn't so."

"Ike—"

"Mr. Director, with respect, you know how I feel about you personally and the agency generally and that in spite of the mess it made of my life at one time. Having said that, clearly this latest fiasco has to go down as one of the agency's biggest screw-ups ever. How in the world? Even for someone like me, who has seen the darker side of your game...I'm appalled."

"But the mess was caught in time."

"Caught in time! Jesus, at what cost and to whom?"

Ruth heaved herself up out of her chair, staggered slightly, and surveyed the room with a scowl.

"I've heard enough. I'm going to bed. Mother, the guest room has a fire laid and it's yours. The rest of you are on your own. I expect the bunch of you to be off the premises and gone in the morning. Goodnight. And tomorrow, Schwartz, we move to Plan B."